N.P. MARTIN

BLOOD
SUMMONED

ETHAN DRAKE SERIES: BOOK TWO

N.P. Martin

Blood Summoned

Ethan Drake Series Book 2

Copyright © 2019 by N. P. MARTIN

info@npmarin.com

Cover design by Original Book Cover Designs

FREE BOOK

The darkness in the forest was absolute. Dense, dark clouds covered the moon, allowing not a chink of light to penetrate. The wind rustling through the tall trees and the ever-present chorus of crickets and owls had been a constant for the last two days now.

That and the sound of Haedemus' voice, which hardly ceased, despite how many times I'd told him to put a fucking sock in it.

Didn't he ever go hunting in Hell? I asked him, to which he replied, of course he did, but added that it didn't matter about staying quiet because there was usually nowhere for the victim to run, and most prey in Hell didn't bother running anyway out of pure apathy.

"Though I must say, Ethan," Haedemus said as I rode him through the forest, weaving in and out of trees, his step assured on the sometimes steep and rocky slopes. "This little trip has been enjoyable so far. It's been a nice change of scenery from that dreary city you call home. Although, this place does remind me of the Suicide Forest in Hell, only without all the self-harmers everywhere and their sad faces. Fuck, how I hated those suicidal bastards and their pathetic attempts at killing themselves, feeble attempts that were always doomed to complete failure. I mean, as soon as they died they just came right back again, always with the same look of despair on their stupid human baby-faces."

"Like the look on my face," I said. "From having to listen to you this whole fucking time."

"Admit it," he said. "You enjoy my company, don't you? Why else would you take me along?"

"As I already told you, you're just a means of transportation. I thought it would be easier than walking."

Haedemus snorted. "Whatever, big guy. You can't hide your feelings from me. I can feel us getting closer with every step."

"Yeah, we're a real walking, talking buddy movie you and I."

"Your sarcasm is not lost on me, Ethan," he said. "And neither is your ironic use of the term 'buddy movie'. I know what a buddy movie is, you know."

"Do they have a cineplex in Hell? I never knew."

"No, but thanks to many, *many* damned souls and their continued obsession with pop culture, I was able to glean the finer plot points of many movies. They sound fun, I have to say. Maybe we could watch one when we get back from finding this person you're after out here."

"Sure," I said, keeping my focus on my surroundings. "I'll bring the popcorn."

"Fuck off, Ethan," he said, a sour tone to his voice. "You don't have to ridicule *everything* I say, you know."

"Why not?"

Haedemus snorted. "Your mother must be so proud of you, Ethan."

"My mother's dead."

"Lucky for her then she doesn't have to see what a bitter cunt her son has become."

Giving his mane a sharp tug, I said, "Watch it."

"Oh, hit a nerve have I? I enjoy hitting your nerves, Ethan. I get a special pleasure from—"

"Quiet," I hissed, pulling him to a stop.

"Don't try to silence me into submission. It won't—"

"I heard something, asshole. Shut it a minute."

Off to the left, I'd heard a cracking sound like a branch breaking underfoot. Blinking rapidly three times, I activated the infrared vision chip implanted in my cornea and began to scan the forest for signs of life. Small animals glowed bright red and orange in the distance, but nothing larger.

"It's those damn Faeries again," Haedemus said, his voice quieter. "They're just being nosey little bastards, as they are wont to do. I remember them from my mortal life. Most of them are harmless, if highly annoying. Thankfully, Hell's gates are barred to them."

I had to admit, I had little experience with Fae. Out of all the MURKs, the Fae kept to themselves the most, the more powerful of them choosing to remain in Faerie most of the time, where they had their own way of life and political system in the form of the Courts.

The Wyldefae—the little fuckers who'd been following us since entering the forest—spent most of their time here in the mortal world. As Haedemus said, most of them are harmless, but some of them grow to be large and powerful beasts who use their size and strength to feed their appetite for human prey.

It was these fuckers I was concerned about here in the depths of the forest, but as I continued to scan the area in infrared, I saw nothing larger than a deer in the far distance.

"Ride on," I told Haedemus after I'd finished scanning the area.

"Ride on, he says." Haedemus craned his neck to look at me. "Where to exactly? This woody nightmare is fucking never-ending."

"You said you were enjoying it a minute ago."

"I was until I realized I was hungry and horny. Now I'm miserable."

"Can't you munch on a squirrel for now? Maybe fuck a deer?"

"Fuck a deer, Ethan? Is that supposed to be funny? I don't fuck deer."

"I forgot you only fucked dying men."

"I'll fuck you in a minute, Ethan, if your cheek continues, you with your backpack full of provisions. You didn't even think to bring me a nice liver or kidney to snack on out here, did you?" He shook his head and whinnied. "No, you didn't, because Ethan is a selfish bastard who only cares about himself."

"You want a Snickers bar?"

"No, I don't want a fucking Snickers bar, Ethan. Shove your Snicker's bar up your—" He stopped talking as he raised his head, his jagged ears pricking.

"What is it?" I asked him.

"Magic, I think."

"Faerie magic?"

"No. Magic cast by a human."

I stared off into the dark woods as I considered the significance of Haedemus' discovery. If someone was casting magic this far in the forest, it had to be someone who lived here.

Someone like Scarlet Hood.

"Where's the magic centered?" I asked Haedemus.

"It's faint at this distance," he said. "Maybe a mile or two away."

"Any idea what kind of magic? Is it defensive?"

"Hard to tell at this distance. I'll know better when we get closer."

We rode farther into the dark forest, what little light there now was from the waning moon seeming to diminish as the trees grew closer together and the undergrowth got thicker.

"Take it slow," I said to Haedemus, my voice hushed. "We don't know what we're walking into."

"Maybe you should summon your Hellbastards to scout ahead, though I'd prefer it if you didn't." He veered right to get past a dense thicket of trees, taking us onto a slight slope that was dotted with large boulders. "I never told you this, but the smallest one—"

"Cracka."

"Yes, him, he kept asking me to show him my penis while I waited outside your building. He was vulgar. I don't know how you put up with them."

"You get used to them."

"I always hated Hellbastards. They're Hell's equivalent of annoying children, only worse. They try to fuck everything, and if they can't fuck it, they eat it instead."

"Sounds like someone else I know."

"Piss off, Ethan. You humans think you're so superior, when you are all just as bad as—"

"Wait."

"What?" He came to a stop at the brow of the slope. "Ah, I see."

At the bottom of the slope was a large clearing, and in the clearing was a small cottage with a thatched roof. The ground around the whitewashed cottage was flat and well-tended, covered with short grass and all kinds of wildflowers. Around the side of the dwelling, I could make out that the tilled ground and the shadowy outlines of the herbs and vegetables growing in it.

I got down off Haedemus and crouched on top of the hill, taking the high-powered rifle from around me and sighting through the infrared scope so I could get a better look at the cottage. There were no lights on, and no smoke coming from the chimney either. "Doesn't look like anyone's home."

"The whole place is warded with magic," Haedemus said. "I'm not sure I can go near it."

"I can."

"You're going down there?"

"What do you think we're doing here? I didn't just come to sightsee."

"She might be waiting for you. I'd be surprised if she didn't know you were here."

"If she's here at all."

I sighted through the scope again, checking out the small windows at the front of the cottage. Nothing moved behind the glass. "Can you sense anyone?"

"No," Haedemus said. "But that doesn't mean Miss Hood isn't here somewhere. She's probably watching us now from a distance. If she's as good as you say, she probably knew we were coming miles back."

"Then why aren't we dead?"

"I'm already dead."

"Why aren't I dead then?"

"Maybe she's just watching, waiting for you to enter her kill zone. Honestly, Ethan, if this woman is as dangerous as you say, I don't know why you're even here."

"I didn't know you cared," I said, still staring down at the cottage.

"I don't. I'm just saying. Anyone would think you had a death wish."

Placing the rifle on the ground, I stood and took out the SIG Sauer P226 pistol I had with me. "She's not here."

"How do you know?" Haedemus said.

"I'd probably be dead now if she was."

"Like I said, a death wish."

"Stay here. I'm going down for a look around."

"What for? You said she isn't here?"

"Just wait here. I'll be back."

"Don't expect me to follow you to Hell if you die," he called after me in a hushed voice. "Because I won't."

Ignoring him, I made my way down the slope to the clearing, staying low and keeping to cover as much as possible, finally crouching by a juniper bush as I stared over at the cottage.

There was a chance Scarlet Hood was inside, but I doubted it. Living in the forest as she did, I'd be surprised if she didn't have a deal going with the Faeries. They would've let her know about Haedemus and me long before now. That being the case, Hood probably would've ambushed us by now, if not killed us outright from a distance.

If I was right about her, though, she wouldn't kill without talking first. I didn't think she was the monster people made her out to be. She may have been a professional assassin, but she would want to know why I was here before she squeezed any trigger. She would want to know who sent me first. That's why I wasn't too worried about getting killed out here.

Besides, despite the deal I had with Carlito, I wasn't here to kill Scarlet Hood.

I was here to talk.

Making my way around the back of the cottage, I stopped to point my gun at one of half a dozen shadowy figures standing by the edge of the trees, realizing a second later that the figures were dummies carved from wood, put there for target practice I was sure.

There was a rope swing attached to an overhanging branch, which prompted a memory to flash through my mind. A memory of Callie on the tree-swing I made for her only last year, out the back of the house in Crown Point. For a moment, her smiling face was clear as day in my mind as she squealed her delight when I pushed her high into the air, Angela standing by the back door warning me not to push too high.

Sighing, I turned away from the rope-swing just as my Infernal Itch flared up without warning. "What the hell?" I muttered as the tattoos on my arms and back began to swirl madly under my skin, their extreme agitation signaling that danger was imminent.

Looking around, I thought perhaps that one of the bigger Faeries had followed me here and was preparing to ambush me, but after switching to infrared vision, I saw nothing in the surrounding forest.

It was only when I turned around again did I see the grassy earth a few feet away break up and get pushed out as if something was about to emerge from the ground.

"What the fuck is this?" I said, stepping back, my gun pointing at the broken earth, just as a massive hand burst out of the ground, clawed fingers stretching until most of an arm appeared. An arm covered in coarse hair by the looks of it.

"Uh, Ethan?" Haedemus called from the top of the slope. "You might want to come back up here."

Moving quickly around to the front of the cottage again, I got there just in time to see an enormous head burst from the earth, yellow eyes glaring at me as the monster peeled back its rotten lips to reveal a pair of huge incisors.

All around, monsters were bursting free from the earth, climbing out of their underground tombs with the express purpose of ripping me asunder.

The few that were free stood on thick hind legs and howled into the night, making me realize I was looking at werewolves.

Undead fucking werewolves.

My presence here had activated Hood's magical wards, the zombie werewolves a part of her elaborate security system.

Clever, but also ruthless.

"Ethan!" Haedemus shouted. "Behind you!"

I turned just in time to see one of the newly freed werewolves come racing toward me from around the side of the cottage, barreling forward on all fours, saliva dripping from its mouth, half its face missing like someone had shot it with a heavy gauge weapon.

Wishing I had heavier firepower myself, I pointed my pistol at the zombie werewolf and got off four shots that didn't slow the monster down in the slightest.

When it jumped at me, I rolled to the side, coming up to fire once more at the creature, hitting it in the head this time with another two shots, which did fuck all to stop it.

I hardly had time to lament my weapon's lack of efficacy, for werewolves were coming from all directions now.

Dropping my gun to the ground, I reached across myself and unsheathed the heavy-bladed weapon strapped to my belt. It was one of Cal Grimes' blades, made from folded steel, slightly bigger than a machete, curved with a jagged outside edge.

As one of the undead werewolves reached me and took a swipe at my head, I ducked under its arm and swung the blade as hard as I could at the creature's torso. The blade was so razor-sharp it easily cut through the werewolf's rotting flesh. A fine testament to Cal's skills as a forger.

When another beast came at me straight after, I took advantage of the monster-tendons in my legs, and used their power to spring high off the ground before bringing my blade down on the werewolf's shoulder, slicing right through it until the creature's arm fell to the ground with a wet thud.

But that didn't stop my hirsute foe, who kept on coming at me regardless of the damage done to it. I soon realized that nothing would stop these bastards, for they were all dead anyway.

But as the snarling fuckers now surrounded me, I had no choice but to keep fighting until I could escape back up the slope again to Haedemus, assuming he was still there and hadn't run off in a panic.

In a situation like this one where you have multiple foes coming at you from all directions, you want to be glad you still have a Combat Offense Booster fitted. It heightens your reaction time, meaning you can move about three times faster than normal for short periods, as long as the system doesn't short out, which it had a habit of doing sometimes.

Just don't fucking fail me now, I thought as I started to swing my blade at whichever monster was nearest to me, slicing through rotten flesh and decaying bone as easily as a dick slidin' into yo' mama...should your mama be that way inclined, of course...which I'm sure she isn't...being your mama and all.

Anyway, gotta hand it to Cal, his blades were sharp as fuck.

Swinging the blade with one hand, I used my other hand to land punches with my reinforced knuckles as I kept on the move, ducking under arms as thick as tree trunks as I sliced open ribcages on the way past; firing low kicks at crumbling knees to try to slow the bastards down some, avoiding getting clawed or bitten for the most part.

Although my luck soon ran out when the number of monsters increased until it seemed like they were everywhere, some still not even out of the ground yet.

Jesus, how many of these fucking things are there? And where the fuck is Haedemus?

The surrounding air was thick with the stench of fetid breath and rotting flesh as I continued to try to fend against the attacks coming at me, but there were so many, it was inevitable one of the fuckers would get me.

A loud cry of pain escaped me as one of the bastards sunk its teeth into my shoulder from behind, shaking its head like crazy as it did its best to rip my arm from its socket. It probably would've succeeded if something hadn't knocked it off me, that something being Haedemus, who had now joined the fray.

The Hellicorn was even taller than the werewolves, and he reared up on his back legs, bringing his massive front hooves down on the heads of the werewolves, knocking them to the ground.

As another werewolf went to run toward me, Haedemus speared the beast with his long, jagged horn, jerking his head upward so his horn split the werewolf partially in two.

The second I got a chance, I ran toward Haedemus with the gored blade between my teeth, grabbed his mane, and swung myself up onto him.

"Let's get the fuck outta here!" I shouted as I swung my blade at the werewolves surrounding us, chopping down on them from above.

With a hellish neighing sound, Haedemus reared up for a second and then bolted toward the slope, crying out as a werewolf clawed his side on the way past. "Ow! You hairy fuckwits!" he shouted.

Switching to infrared vision, I took control of the Hellicorn and steered one-handed through the trees as we galloped back through the forest again. Behind us, the werewolves stayed in pursuit, howling as they sprinted after us on all fours.

"Motherfuckers are following us," I said.

"No shit," Haedemus said. "What did you expect the mutts to do, take a nap in the fucking yard?"

Undead or not, the werewolves were fast, not to mention relentless. As I focused on not crashing into any trees while trying not to pass out from blood loss, I couldn't help but wonder how long the beasts would keep up the chase.

Very fucking long as it turned out.

Several hours later, just as dawn began to break, the undead werewolves finally stopped their pursuit of us. Though I still kept riding hard, even though my vision had blurred by this stage and I was having trouble staying balanced on top of the Hellicorn.

"I think we should stop now," Haedemus said, his

breathing as labored as I'd ever heard it. "I can't go on any longer."

"Don't...stop," I said, my eyes beginning to close as my head dropped.

"Oh sure...keep fucking going...he says. Never mind that I'm...completely fucked here...and—"

His voice faded out, and blackness closed in around me as I began to slip off his back.

By the time I hit the ground, I was out of it.

2

"Ethan. Wake up, Ethan. I hope you haven't died on me. Have you? Oh for fuck's sake, you have, haven't you, you inconsiderate—Ethan, you're alive! Hallelujah! Praise the Lord and all that jazz..."

"Fuck you."

"And still the same charmer as before, I'm glad to see."

Sunlight hurt my eyes as I opened them, having to cover them with my hand until they adjusted. "How long was I out?" I asked as I sat up, stifling a cry as pain shot through my wounded shoulder, spreading down my back and arm.

"Long enough for me to think you were dead, you selfish asshole," Haedemus said.

"Next time a werewolf takes a chunk outta me, I'll try not to pass out so I don't upset you."

"Who said anything about being upset? I just don't want to incur the wrath of Xaglath—I mean *Hannah*—if you die on me."

When my vision cleared, I looked around to see that we were still in the forest, and probably a full day's ride to civilization. It made me wonder why Scarlet Hood lived so far out. How did people contact her to arrange a hit if she lived out here? And how did she get back and forth? Surely not on foot? Maybe there was some shortcut out of the forest that I didn't know about. Or perhaps she could teleport. These days, you never know.

Another wave of pain took me out of my thoughts, and I craned my neck to look at my shoulder. Reaching across, I peeled back my ruined and bloody trench coat, then the shirt underneath to see several deep holes in my flesh. I still had some movement in my arm, meaning nothing was broken or dislocated, which was a fucking miracle considering how violent the werewolf had been when it bit down on me.

Blood still seeped from the jagged holes in my shoulder and the top of my arm. Not as much as earlier, but enough that I had to stop the flow. Doing so would've been easier if I still had my backpack with the few medical supplies inside, but that was still lying around Scarlet Hood's place somewhere, probably ripped to shreds by now by the undead beasts who came after us.

"What are you going to do about that?" Haedemus asked, licking his lips as he stared at my bloody wound.

"Getting hungry there, Haedemus?"

He turned his head away. "Don't worry, Ethan, I'm not going to eat you if that's what you're thinking. While you were out of it, I hunted down a Faerie and ate it. The flesh tasted disgusting, but it filled a hole."

"So now we're going to have Faeries out for revenge after us? Great."

"They wouldn't dare. The little bastards fear me too much. I'm like a demon to them."

"Fuck it, I don't care." I took off my trench and used my blade to cut a long strip from it, which I then wrapped around my wounded shoulder. "I just want out of this fucking forest."

"So we came out here for naught then?"

I said nothing as I gave him a look and stood up. He wasn't wrong. I'd just wasted two days in the wilderness when

I could've been working a mass suicide case with Walker. I didn't doubt her ever-increasing competence, but she could get a little lost in herself with so many personalities competing within her, with a demon on one shoulder and an angel on the other, not to mention Hannah Walker's personality and Walker's own combination of all three. And if that sounds confusing, imagine how she feels. Jeez, look at me, having sympathy for the devil. I must be getting soft in my old age.

Haedemus had to crouch down so I could climb up on to him, and even then it hurt like hell as I mounted him. But once I was up, I held his mane with my right hand and let him do the navigating while I listened to him drone on about being thirsty and how hungry he was.

Unsurprisingly, he drank blood in Hell to sustain himself, as many demons and beasts did, apparently. A lack of water in Hell forced the inhabitants to improvise, even though they didn't need water to survive since they were already dead. What they fed was an urge, not a need; an urge Haedemus carried with him into this world. I told him if we found water he could stop and get a drink, but we never did. It was just trees and brush until we finally made it to the small mining town of Little Rock about half a day later.

By the time we got there, I was struggling to stay conscious I'd lost so much blood. Not only that, the fucking werewolf that bit me must've transferred some kind of infection into my bloodstream, for I had developed a fever and my breathing made me sound like I was asthmatic.

When we emerged from the forest, the first building we came across was a small church perched upon a hill that overlooked the rest of the town. With sweat oozing from every inch of my body and the blood boiling in my veins, I ordered Haedemus to stop outside the church. "I need to rest a minute," I said.

"Here?" Haedemus said. "It's a church."

"I don't—" I fell off him then, hitting the ground with a

heavy thud, landing on my injured shoulder, hardly having the energy to cry out with the pain.

"Ethan, are you alright?"

As I struggled up off the ground, I said, "What...the fuck...do you think?"

"I'm guessing no," he said. "I think you need a doctor or something, not a priest."

"Don't need...either."

"Oh right, because you're so tough and everything." He gave his massive head a shake. "Honestly, Ethan, you look about ready to die. You're not going die on me, are you?"

"Will you...miss me?"

"Well, apart from Mistress Xaglath you're the only one I know in this cursed place, so don't be a selfish asshole and die on me, okay? If you do, I'll eat your remains and shit you out again. Is that what you want, Ethan? Hmm?"

"God...just shut up." I started staggering toward the church doors. "I'm going inside to rest...for a while."

"What about me?"

"Do...what you want."

"As usual. Thanks, Ethan. I—"

I never heard the rest of what he said as I staggered inside the church, which smelled of old wood and leather and...piss, strangely enough, though that could've just been my senses going haywire. Either that or I'd pissed myself, but I was so drenched in sweat it would've been hard to tell.

The church was empty, with no sign of a preacher or anyone else. I walked up the center aisle a bit and then slid myself onto a pew before lying down across it.

I wasn't sure if I was dying, but it felt like I was. The virus from the werewolf's saliva was attacking my system, and I needed something to counter it. Which I had back at my apartment, but that was over fifty miles away.

I just needed a little rest, and then I could make the final leg of the journey back to the city.

But as I closed my eyes, a voice roused me from my semi-consciousness.

"Are you okay, my son?"

Raising my head a bit, I saw a nun in a black habit standing there in the aisle, looking down at me. For a nun, her face was a vision of beauty, with large green eyes and a serene smile on her flawless face.

"Not...really...Sister," I said as my eyelids dropped, delivering me into blackness for an indeterminate amount of time.

When I next opened my eyes, the nun with her beautiful face was leaning over me with a gun pointed at my head.

For a minute, I thought I must've been hallucinating from the fever, but then the nun said, "You tripped the alarms at my cottage. Cop or not, normally I would put a bullet in you right now and be done with it, but this is your lucky day, Detective."

"My...lucky day?" I whispered, smiling, only seeing her bright green eyes as darkness closed in around me for what felt like the final time.

"I will save your life," she said. "Then we're going to talk."

My eyes closed, still smiling, I said, "Sounds...lovely."

Then I blacked out.

WHEN I CAME TO SOMETIME LATER, MY FEVER HAD GONE, AND my breathing was back to normal. Sitting beside me on the pew was the green-eyed nun from earlier.

No, not a nun.

As I sat up, the realization of her real identity sunk in. "You're Scarlet Hood."

"Finally," she said. "You're awake. Don't try anything stupid." She held up her gun for me to see, then placed it back down by her side.

"What did you do to me?" I asked her.

"Gave you a shot."

"Of what?"

"Just something to counteract the virus in your system. You should be back to normal soon. I'd get that bite wound looked at, though."

I stared at the blood-soaked piece of trench coat wrapped around my arm and shoulder. "I intend to. What do you want?"

"I could ask you the same thing…Detective Drake."

"How do you know my name?"

"You first," she said, her porcelain face still framed by the nun's habit. "Who sent you to kill me?"

Swinging my legs off the pew and onto the floor, I sat up straight and found a crumpled pack of cigarettes in my trouser pocket, along with my zippo lighter. When I lit the cigarette, I coughed on the first drag, and Scarlet started waving her hand to keep the smoke away from her. "Hope you don't mind," I said.

"You're going to smoke in a church?"

"So? You brought a gun in here."

"Just blow it away from me."

I did as she asked, blowing the smoke to the side of me. "Did you kill a nun to get that habit?"

"What do you take me for?"

"A ruthless assassin," I said without hesitation.

"I kill only those who deserve it," she said. "And the nun is taking a nap in the confession box."

"And the preacher? I don't see any sign of him either."

"Also sleeping. I didn't want any interruptions."

"You're very thorough," I said, impressed.

"I just don't believe in taking chances."

"And yet you're talking to me now."

She pointed the gun at me again, which I saw was a SIG Sauer. "I can just kill you if I don't like what I hear."

"So what do you want to hear?"

"Who sent you to kill me?"

"I didn't come here to kill you," I said, before taking a drag on my cigarette.

"Don't lie to me."

"I'm not. I *was* sent to kill you, but decided against it when I got a feeling there was something else going on." I turned my head to look at her as she stared straight ahead. "You've taken down a few traffickers lately, including the cousin of the man who wants me to kill you. The man is Carlito Martinez. You know him?"

Her face tightened with anger as she looked at me. "I know him. He's next on my list."

"What list? What did all these guys do? Are you killing them for someone else? Are they all contract hits?"

"Do you work for Martinez?" she asked, ignoring all of my questions.

I shook my head. "I just owe him a debt."

"What debt?"

"Doesn't matter."

"Yes, it does. Tell me." She pointed the gun at me again, her finger on the trigger this time.

"I owe him money. Eighty grand."

"What for? Are you a gambler?"

"No, but my ex-wife was," I said. "She ran up the debt playing online poker. She was going to lose her house, which meant my daughter wouldn't have a roof over her head, and I couldn't have that. So I went to Carlito for a loan."

She stared at me a moment as if trying to figure me out. "Your wife and daughter were killed."

"Yes. How would you know that?"

"Your pet unicorn—or whatever it is—likes to talk." She gestured behind her with her head, and I turned around to see Haedemus standing by the church doors, busy lapping holy water from the font.

"Oh, hey," Haedemus said when he noticed me looking at

him. "Don't mind me or anything. I'm just a hell beast drinking holy water in a church."

"You told her about me?" I said, glaring at him.

"What can I say? She's very persuasive."

"More like you just have a big fucking mouth."

"Ethan," he said in mock shock. "Watch your language. We're in God's house here."

"Fuck you." I turned my head back to look at Scarlet again. "So what else did he tell you?"

"That you're a detective with the FPD and that you work occult investigations." She paused to glance at me. "He also said you were mean-spirited and selfish, not to mention supremely arrogant."

I looked back at Haedemus, who pulled his rubbery, decaying lips back into something that I guessed was supposed to be a smile that showed his rotten teeth. "She's twisting my words. I didn't say any of that. I told her how kind and considerate you were, what a great friend you—oh fuck it, I told her you were an asshole, because you are, Ethan. It's something you need to work on if you want us to keep being friends."

"We're not friends, you stinking Hellicorn."

He almost choked on his holy water. "Ethan—now I'm just offended. Was there any need for that kind of hurtful remark? My undead heart is in bits here. What if I called you a stinking human?"

"You have, more than once."

"Well, there you go then. You know how hurtful it can be when—"

"Shut up!" Scarlet said, snapping her head around to look at him, causing me to smile. "Or I'll shoot you."

"Great, another asshole," Haedemus said. "I will wait outside while you two finish your meeting of assholes." Turning, he pushed the doors open with his horn and walked outside without saying another word.

"Don't ask," I said as she stared at me as if waiting for some explanation.

For the first time, a slight smile appeared on her face. "It's a strange world when a police detective is riding around on a...what did you call it? A Hellicorn?"

"Even stranger now that a top assassin dressed in a nun's habit is sitting pointing a gun at me," I said, taking the last drag of my cigarette before crushing it underfoot. "Are you going to tell me why you're choosing not to kill me?"

Scarlet stared straight ahead for a moment, then said, "This Carlito guy. How well do you know him?"

"Well enough. Why?"

"Did you know he's in the sex trafficking business?"

"No, not exactly. I mean, I had an inkling he was. Carlito keeps his business interests closely guarded. Why are you so interested, anyway?"

Removing the nuns' habit from her head, she revealed her short, dark brown hair. As assassins go, she was stunningly beautiful. No makeup except a little around her eyes and a light shade of lipstick. "My younger sister was taken about a week ago."

"You have a sister? I didn't know that."

"Why would you?" she said, throwing me a sharp look. "We've never even met before now."

"I know, but your reputation precedes you. I've never heard a sister being mentioned."

"I didn't think anyone knew about Charlotte. I was wrong."

"How old is she?"

"Seventeen, soon to be eighteen."

"Do you know who took her? I'm guessing not if you're going through a list."

"I'm an assassin, Detective, not an investigator. I kill people."

"So you're just gonna keep killing until you find your sister?"

"That was the plan."

"Was?"

She turned to look at me. "Until you wandered across my path."

"You want me to help you find her?"

There was a trace of vulnerability in her eyes as she nodded. "I'm letting you live. In return, I want your help."

I considered what she said for a minute as I lit up another cigarette, wishing I had the Mud bottle with me, but I left it in the remains of my trench back in the forest, remembering only to take my phone and Callie's locket before I discarded the coat.

I could see that Scarlet was doing her best to hold her feelings in. Underneath she was probably distraught as hell, living with the dread that her sister was dead in a ditch somewhere. I knew that feeling well from driving to Crown Point that night, not knowing if I would find my daughter dead or alive. I wouldn't wish a feeling like that on anyone. I couldn't help Callie, but I could help Scarlet now.

Besides which, Carlito would be gunning for me, especially since I hadn't checked in with him in two days. He'd think I'd gone back on our deal and he'd have his men out looking for me. If he ever got a hold of me, Carlito would probably kill me, if only to make an example of me. Take me out to the alley outside the club and beat me to death with the blood-stained baseball bat he kept behind the dumpster for just such occasions. He would try to anyway, but I wasn't invincible, and I certainly wasn't fucking bulletproof. Having the great Scarlet Hood on my side would help matters no end, I was sure.

"Okay," I said. "I'll help you get your sister back, assuming she's still alive. How long has it been now?"

"Eight days," she said.

"Eight days, and you have heard nothing?"

"No, but I have to believe my sister is alive somewhere." She turned to fix her green eyes on me. "You don't know Charlotte. She may be naïve to the ways of the world, and to people, but she's also strong and highly capable. I trained her myself. So did my grandmother, before she——"

"What?"

"Nothing, it doesn't matter." She turned away and looked around to the other side of the church for a second, toward the confession boxes, as if she heard a noise, then turned back to me. "We should leave now. I think the priest and the nun are waking up."

"I'd like to stay to see the nun's face when she realizes she's been stripped of her modesty," I said. "Then I'd like to see the priest's face when he sees sweet Sister Mary half-naked. Do you think he'd get hard?"

She stared at me a moment before shaking her head. "I think maybe the drugs I gave you have gone to your head, Detective."

"Believe me, they haven't gone to my head enough."

"I'm not sure anymore if I want to work with you," she said, not entirely joking. "Maybe I should kill you now."

"Do that, and you'll never find your sister."

"Fine," she said, standing up and walking to the center aisle before stripping off the nun's outfit to reveal a pair of red leather pants and a black top. She was supermodel tall with a body to match, apart from the long scars on her arms, and on her lower back, making me wonder how she got them. Despite her natural beauty, she had the look of someone who'd been through the wars. Putting the gun into the back of her leather pants, she stood and stared over at me. "Something wrong?"

"No," I said, getting up. "Just admiring what a top assassin looks like."

"Perving you mean."

"Yeah. Don't shoot me."

We exited the church before the priest and nun woke up

and saw us. It was dark outside, the night mild and filled with the sound of crickets chirping.

Haedemus stood at the bottom of the steps, staring down at the town below. "Oh," he said, turning around. "The meeting of assholes must be over. Thank fuck. This buttfuck town is depressing me. I've also concluded that all crickets should be wiped out. What was God thinking when he gave them the ability to make that infernal noise? No doubt he thought it would be funny, just to annoy everyone. He's such a fucking dick, I tell you."

"What was he thinking when he created you then?" Scarlet asked.

"Please, sister," Haedemus said. "God didn't create this majesty before you, Hell did."

"Majesty?" Scarlet said. "You look like you just crawled out of the grave. Does your dick even still work?"

I sniggered at that. Haedemus just stared in mock shock with his bulging red eyes. "I beg your pardon? Did you just ask if my dick was still working? Hold on a second."

As Haedemus closed his eyes and stood still, Scarlet turned to me and said, "Is he doing what I think he's doing?"

"I don't know," I said. "Haedemus, what the fuck are you doing?"

"I'm getting hard for Countess Bathory here," he said, just as the tip of his penis emerged from his foreskin. "I won't have anyone saying *this* beast is impotent."

"Jesus Christ," Scarlet said. "I was kidding."

"Quiet," Haedemus said. "I'm trying to fantasize here. It's working. I can feel myself getting hard. Get ready to pick your jaw up from the floor, sister."

"I'm going now," Scarlet said, walking away.

"But I'm almost there," Haedemus shouted after her. "Ethan, tell her."

I shook my head at him as I started after Scarlet. "Put that sausage meat away, for fuck's sake."

"Well, I can't now, can I?" he said. "I must wait until it goes down. Bloody waste of a good erection this is."

"Scarlet," I said as she neared the edge of the forest. "Where are you going?"

She stopped and turned around. "I'm going back to my cottage to get a few things. I'll meet you in the city."

"You're gonna walk back?"

"I have an ATV parked nearby. With the shortcuts I know, it doesn't take me long getting back."

"Okay," I said, then gave her the address of my apartment in the city, along with a crumpled card with my phone number on that I fished out of my back pocket. "Do me a favor and call me first."

"Why?" she asked.

"My pets don't like unannounced visitors, and you seem the type to let yourself into places."

She shook her head slightly. "You have pets? You don't seem the type. What kind?"

"The hellish kind," I said as I walked away. "I'll see you soon."

"Detective," she called, making me stop and turn around. "I'm trusting you here. If you make me regret it, I'll kill you."

There was no emotion in her voice. She was just stating a fact. "I know you will." Something occurred to me then. "Hey, you're a werewolf hunter, aren't you?"

She cocked her head to one side. "And what makes you think that?"

"I've heard things. Plus the undead werewolves buried in your garden were a dead giveaway."

"I have a special hatred for werewolves."

"Why?"

"It doesn't matter."

"Well anyway, I figured since I'm helping you with your sister that you could help me with something."

"You're pushing your luck. You're still breathing. Isn't that enough?"

I stared at her a moment, then said, "A werewolf killed my wife and daughter. I'd like to find the cunt."

"I'm sure you would." She thought for a moment. "If you find my sister, I'll help you find the wolf that killed your wife and daughter. *If* you find my sister."

I nodded my thanks, and Scarlet disappeared into the dark forest. Turning, I walked back to Haedemus but slowed when I noticed he was moving his hips back and forth in a strange way. It was only when I came up alongside him did I realize what he was doing— slapping his thick, meaty todger against his belly. "Oh Jesus Christ, Haedemus," I said. "Fucking really?"

"Shush, Ethan," he said, sounding out of breath. "I'm trying to concentrate here."

"I can't believe your standing outside a church fucking masturbating."

"I—I—oooooooawwwwfuuuuuuuck—"

"Jesus Christ." I turned away just as he spilled his hot semen onto the ground with a long, drawn-out moan.

"Oh fuck," he said after he was done, his massive penis still hanging out. "I didn't realize how much I needed that."

"Well, I'm glad you're satisfied," I said. "I'm not sure I even want to get on you now."

"Don't be a prude, Ethan. Get on up here and bask with me in my post-orgasm glow."

"Just kneel so I can get on, you fucking cretin. My shoulder is still fucked in case you forgot."

Haedemus knelt, but he did so a little too fast and cried out when he trapped his penis between his stomach and the hard ground. "Shit, that hurt."

"Serves you right." I climbed up onto him, and he squealed as my weight pushed down further on his trapped penis.

"Ethan, you heavy bastard you," he shouted, quickly pushing himself up straight again.

Smiling, I tapped my boots against his side. "Giddy up gee-gee."

"Now I have dirt stuck to my penis. Thanks a lot, Ethan."

3

B ecause of the damage done to my shoulder, I couldn't ride Haedemus as hard as I would've liked, so it took us several hours to get back to the city. When we got there, I rode the Hellicorn into Bricktown, ignoring the stares of those who could see us—the Awares and the MURKs—and the shocked, often fearful looks on their faces. Sometimes Haedemus would taunt them, shouting over, "What? You've never seen a grown man ride a Hellicorn before?" or, "I know, right? Magnificent, aren't I?", or once even, "The devil rides out, baby," to some MURK crossing the street. Most seemed horrified, even the MURKs. I was thankful we were invisible to the rest of the Unaware population, who doubtless would've fled in a mass panic if they'd seen us riding down the street like we fucking owned the place.

Before we went to my apartment, I stopped off at The Tattoomb, a ratty tattoo parlor on Gristle Lane. "Wait here," I told Haedemus. "And try not to eat anybody while I'm gone."

"That never gets old, Ethan, hearing you say that. What do you take me for?"

"Someone who ate the homeless guy outside my apartment building."

"Fair point. Just don't keep me waiting."

When I walked into the cramped tattoo parlor, the proprietor, Larry Swinger—a man in his late fifties with longish gray hair and a goatee, bare arms inked all the way to his fingertips—was bent over some teenage girl's naked ass, a cigarette dangling from his mouth as he inked the girl's dimpled left cheek with a design I couldn't make out. "With you in a second," he half-growled as he kept his eyes on what he was doing.

"Watch you don't slip there, old man," I said.

Larry stopped inking to turn his head and look at the cheeky bastard who'd said that. When he realized it was me, he broke into a smile. "Well, fuck me," he said, straightening up. "Ethan fucking Drake, as I live and breathe."

"What's up, Larry?" I walked farther into the parlor, smiling at the blond girl as she looked up at me, her face dropping when she saw my bloody shirt.

"What's up with *me*?" Larry said, putting the machine down as he stared at the state of me. "What the fuck is up with *you* more like? What happened?"

"I need your services," I said.

"No shit." He turned and addressed the girl. "Sit tight, honey. I'll be back soon."

The young girl tutted but settled down on the stretched out leather chair again, which was probably the most expensive thing in the whole parlor, everything else still as it was in the eighties when the place opened. I followed Larry into the back, through a door into a smaller room just big enough to hold a hospital gurney, a few cupboards, and a sink. The room smelled even worse than the last time I was in it, which was nearly ten years ago. It smelled like someone had shat themselves moments before I arrived. "What the fuck, Larry? You ever disinfect this place?"

"What for?" he said as he rifled through cupboards and

drawers, gathering up his tools. "People just keep bringing their germs in, regardless."

I sat up on the edge of the gurney and took off my tattered shirt, wincing when I had to remove the bandage from around my shoulder. "I need stitching up."

Larry approached after washing his hands and putting on surgical gloves. Before he became a tattooist, Larry was an ER doctor at Wilshire General, where he became a morphine addict and got so fucked up one time that he killed a patient. He lost his license after that, but once he got out of jail, he found his skills in demand by those who couldn't go near a hospital, either for financial reasons or to avoid any awkward questions and possible criminal charges.

Peering at my bloody wound now, he said, "Yep, you'll need stitching up. Did something bite you?"

"An undead werewolf."

"No shit? There's something I don't hear every day."

Larry had me to thank for opening his eyes to the MURK activity in this town. Before that, he was blind to it like every other Unaware, until I stumbled in here one day after having had my chest clawed to bits by a feral vampire. Larry knew it was no animal attack, so I just told him the truth, which he accepted without protest, saying, "I always knew there was weird shit in this town."

"So are you busy these days?" I asked him as he began stitching me up.

"Always busy," he said as he pierced the flesh on my shoulder with the surgical needle and pulled the thread through. "I get hunters in here all the time. I swear some of them must think I'm fucking Jesus himself, the shit they expect me to fix. One guy came in here last week with his left eyeball in his hand and asked if I could put it back in the socket for him. You believe that?"

"What did you say?"

"What do you think? I told him to get a fucking eye

patch." He started laughing, as did I. "So what have you been doing all this time, Ethan? You still a cop?"

"Yeah, I'm still hanging in there," I said.

"Did this happen on the job?"

"No. Not that it matters. I don't think my insurance would cover me for werewolf bites anyway."

"You gonna turn into one of those fuckers now?"

I snorted. "That's a myth, thank fuck. Mutts are born, not made."

"Lucky for you then."

"Yeah."

He worked on in silence for another few minutes, occasionally tutting as he did his best to repair the damage while I sat and smoked a cigarette, occasionally wincing at the sharp pain of the curved needle going through my skin. Then he said, "Can I give you some advice, Ethan?"

"Sure thing, Larry. Not sure I'll listen, though."

"I'll give it to you anyway." He came around to look at me. "Stop this shit before you get killed. Your body looks like a fucking patchwork quilt. A man can only take so much."

"You know I can't do that, Larry."

"I heard about your wife and daughter," he said. "You want it to be you next? I'm only saying this because I like you, Ethan, even though I haven't seen you in years. You're one of the more genuine ones. I'd hate to see you end up in the morgue. Or worse, torn apart by some fucking monster."

"Something has to get us eventually," I said as he finished stitching me up, applying a bandage over the sutures.

"I'd rather it be old age than some grisly, violent death." He took off his surgical gloves and tossed them into a steel bin in the corner of the room. "You know what you should do?"

"What?" I asked as I put my bloody shirt back on.

"Write a book on your experiences. Let others learn from you."

I couldn't help but smile and then chuckle at the idea.

"I'm not sure it would be a book anyone would want to read. Besides, I still got work to do."

"Yeah, I know you do."

"Thanks for the stitches, Larry. Can I sort you out next time?"

"Don't worry about it," he said. "It's on the house. Just come by again when you're fully healed. I'll fix your tattoos for you, as long as there isn't too much scar tissue."

"Thanks," I said again. "I owe you, Larry. I'll let you get back to tattooing that teenager's ass."

He smiled. "Yep, it's a hard life I got."

Outside, Haedemus was standing on the side of the road between two parked cars. "Finally," he said, turning to face me. "It seems like all I do is wait around on you, Ethan. We will have to discuss the terms of this partnership in more detail at some point, so we can make things more equal between us."

I shook my head at him as I grabbed his mane and climbed up onto him, grimacing at the pain in my shoulder. "What the fuck are you talking about? There is no partnership here."

"Oh, well excuse me. I thought since I saved your damn life in that vamp club that you looked at me as more than just your mode of transportation."

"What do you want, a fucking badge? Get going."

"A badge?" he said, seeming to like the sound of that as he started moving down the street. "Why, Ethan, that's a great idea. We could be a *real* buddy movie then, like Crocket and Tubbs, or Riggs and Murtaugh, or even Starsky and Hutch, though I'd have to be Hutch obviously since I'm much more handsome than you are."

"Where do you even get these names from?"

"I told you before, the minutiae of human culture is endlessly discussed in Hell. Damned souls have great trouble in letting go of their past lives, so talking about what once was is their way of trying to hold on to their identities. Not that it works, mind you. They all end up losing themselves, eventually."

"You didn't."

"You can't keep a good horse down, Ethan. You'd do well to remember that. Speaking of which, my hunger is approaching dangerous levels."

"What the hell does that mean?" I said as I steered him toward my apartment building.

"It means, at a certain point, I won't be able to control myself," he said. "I may even try to take a bite out of you, Ethan."

"You fucking better not."

"Get me dinner then."

"Fine. I'll see what I can do."

Leaving Haedemus outside to eye up the drug dealers standing at the top of the dark street, I went inside my apartment building and came across Daisy Donovan sitting on the landing, a cushion under her as she sat reading a book which I could see was *The Dark Half* by Stephen King. "Reading a classic, I see," I said as I stopped to talk to her. "King's last great book."

"It's the first book I've read by him," she said, wearing the same shorts and T-shirt she always seemed to have on, making me wonder if her mother ever bought her any clothes. "I'm enjoying it."

"Try *Pet Cemetery* next," I said. "You'll like it."

"I will." She frowned when she noticed my bloody shirt. "What happened to you?"

"Animal attack," I said, taking out a cigarette and lighting it as I leaned against the railings.

"What kind of animal?"

"You don't want to know."

"Did you kill it?"

I shook my head. "I just ran."

"Not fast enough."

"Yeah," I said laughing. "You know, you should move your bed out here. You spend more time out here than you do in your apartment."

"My mom has the TV up loud. It makes it hard for me to concentrate on my book."

"How is she?" I asked. "Any strange men coming around?"

"No," she said. "That whole thing with Jarvis shook her up good. She hasn't even drunk since."

I raised my eyebrows. "Really? That's good, I suppose."

"I'm sure it won't last. She has these dry spells once in a while."

"Well," I said, moving away. "You know where to come if you need anything."

"Thanks, Ethan."

"No problem, sweetheart."

"Ethan?" she called out, stopping me in the hallway.

"Yeah?" I said, turning around.

"Do you have a daughter?"

The question took me aback slightly, but I didn't show it. "Why?"

"I just saw a picture of a girl in your apartment that night I was in. She looks like you. Where is she?"

"She died," I said after a pause.

"Oh," Daisy said, dropping her gaze. "I'm sorry."

"Yeah, so am I," I said. "I'll see you later, Daisy."

"Ethan?"

I turned around again. "Yeah?"

"What was her name?"

Swallowing, I said, "Her name was Callie."

"That's a nice name," she said smiling, before going back to her book.

~

I ENTERED THE APARTMENT FOR THE FIRST TIME IN NEARLY three days to a chorus of singing. I say singing; it was more like a bunch of strangled cats trying to remember the lyrics to their favorite song...while drunk.

The Hellbastards were crowded onto the couch in front of the TV, crowing along to the theme music of *Fraggle Rock*, an eighties puppet show similar to *The Muppets*, though a bit more moralistic. "*Dance your cares away,*" the five diminutive demons all sang together. "*Worries for another day, Let the music play, Down in Fraggle Rock, Work your cares away, Dancing is for another day, Let the fraggles play, We're—*"

"*Gobo,*" Scroteface sang.

"*Mokey,*" Toast sang next.

"*Weembly,*" Snot Skull shouted.

"*Momo,*" sang Reggie.

And finally, Cracka jumped up and screeched, "*Red!*"

Then they all jumped up and shouted, "*Weeee! Wowie!*"

I just stood shaking my head at them for a minute, wondering what the hell I had brought into this world. Then Scroteface finally noticed me and shouted, "Boss! You're home!"

"The boss is back! Yay!" Cracka screeched, jumping up and down with his usual uncontained excitement.

"Calm down, boys," I said. "Before you give me a damn headache. Cracka, what the fuck is that on your head?"

"You like, boss?"

"Is that a fucking...*Chihuahua* on your head?"

"He's trying to copy me, boss," Scroteface said, who still wore the skin of a dead tabby cat on his head. Between the two of them, they had the place smelling like a fucking abattoir.

"Screw you, asshole," Cracka said to Scroteface as he tried to head-butt him with the Chihuahua's head, making little yelping sounds like he was pretending the dog was attacking the cat.

Adding to the stench in the place was Reggie, who sat puffing on a fat cigar that he had got from somewhere, the cigar poking through his dreadlocks as it hung from his mouth. Next to him was Toast, who seemed to have acquired a pair of bright green budgie-smugglers in my absence, along with a red string vest and a yellow skull cap that contrasted brightly against his blackened skin. "Toast, what the actual fuck?" I said as I took in his outlandish outfit.

"You like boss?" he said, standing up to show me his new getup.

"You look like asshole," Cracka said to him, and then punched the budgie smugglers, laughing as Toast doubled over, bits of blackened skin falling off him onto the couch.

"May I remind you I sleep on that fucking couch," I said. "Stop messing it up."

The only one who still looked normal—for a Hellbastard anyway—was the four-armed Snot Skull, though his greenish skin was splattered with blood. "Snot Skull," I said. "Why do you have blood on you? It looks suspiciously fresh." Snot Skull sank into the sofa as they all fell quiet and stared at the TV. "Alright, out with it. Who did you kill this time? Another homeless bum?"

"No, actually," Scroteface said. "We're trying to do good now boss like you said. No more innocents."

"So who'd you kill?" I asked again.

"Man in park," Cracka said.

"He was talking to little kiddies," said Reggie, blowing out a thick plume of smoke.

"He bad man," Cracka added.

"So you killed him?" I said. "What did you do with the body?"

"We left it in the bushes in the park," Scroteface said.

"After we had our way with him," said Snot Skull with an evil smile, his bulbous nose glistening with mucus.

"Alright," I said nodding. "There's a hungry Hellicorn downstairs. Go and take him to where the body is. He'll eat it."

"Eat it?" Scroteface said.

"Disgusting," Cracka said.

"Really?" I said. "And the shit that you guys do isn't?"

"We don't like that Hellicorn," Reggie said. "He talk too much."

"I don't give a fuck," I said, switching off the TV to a chorus of moans. "Get going before I send you all back to Hell."

"Fine, boss," Scroteface said. "We go now."

"And get rid of those fucking animal skins," I said. "You're stinking the place up something terrible. And when you get back, you're cleaning this shit hole up."

When the Hellbastards had all left, I put Howlin' Wolf on the stereo before grabbing a bottle of Jack Daniels and a glass from the kitchen and sitting down on the couch, wrinkling my nose at the stench left behind by the Hellbastards. I swear, I'm gonna have to get them a fucking cage or something. Little bastards are wrecking my apartment, not that my place is a fucking palace or anything anyway, but you have to have some pride, right?

Sitting back in the couch, I drank half a glass of whiskey and closed my eyes as I listened to Howlin' Wolf perform *Spoonful*, my thoughts melting away for a few precious moments as I got lost in the music.

When the song was over, I reluctantly opened my eyes, took my phone out of my trouser pocket and switched it on for the first time in two days, surprised that the battery still had a charge. Within moments, several text messages came through, most of them from Carlito Martinez, but also two from Walker.

I looked at the messages from Carlito first, not surprised to see that they were angry messages asking where the fuck I was. The last one, sent just this afternoon, read:

AS YOU HAVEN'T BEEN ANSWERING MY CALLS OR TEXTS WE ARE NOW DONE ETHAN. YOU'VE MADE AN ENEMY OF ME. I'M COMING FOR YOU.

Shaking my head after reading the message, I sighed as I refilled my glass. I knew it was coming, this angry retribution from Carlito, but reading the message now made it real. He was out to get me. Meaning: He would try to set me up for something and land me in jail, whereupon he would have me killed. That, or he would skip the setting up part and just try to have me killed. Meaning: He wanted to kill me himself.

I think he thought we were friends, so he'd feel my perceived betrayal even more. Fuck him. Let him come for me. If he thinks I'll be an easy target, he's in for a grave shock. And now that I knew he was into sex trafficking, I'd have no problem taking him down, along with his whole organization.

I read the texts from Walker next. She was updating me on the mass suicide case. The last text said she had closed the case, which was good to hear. She seemed to have enough of a handle on her existential issues these days that she could be a competent detective, which meant I didn't have to worry all that much about her slipping back into demon mode.

After lighting a cigarette, I gave her a call. "Hey," I said when she answered. "How's it going?"

"Good," she said. "I'm glad to hear from you."

"Did you miss me?"

"Yes, actually," she said, somewhat sheepishly.

"Well, I'm back now. You wanna update me?"

"Sure," she said. "Did you get my text? I closed the suicide cult case. The hellot leader is in custody, though it remains to be seen for how long. You know what these hellots are like, they always seem to find a way out."

"What'd you charge him with?"

"Well, the cult members all killed themselves of their own accord," she said. "The leader didn't force anyone to drink the Kool-Aid, so to speak."

"Nice reference. You sound more human every day."

"Gee, thanks," she responded.

"And sarcasm too. I'm impressed."

"Anyway, we got the guy on fraud, kidnapping, money laundering, and bribery. We just have to see if the charges stick."

"It's out of your hands now. You did your job. Time to move on. What else has come in?"

"I'm glad you asked that," she said. "A pregnant girl landed into the precinct about an hour ago saying she'd been abducted into a cult some months ago."

"Jesus, another cult? These fucking things are becoming a scourge."

"Well," Walker said, "from what I could glean from the girl, this particular cult sounds bad. She's pretty messed up at the moment as if she was on drugs or something. She's in with a doctor now. You want to come in for the interview?"

"Of course. Just let me get cleaned up. I'll be there as soon as I can."

With Howlin' Wolf still jammin' in the background, I got up off the couch to take a shower. Almost the second I did, there was a loud bang as the front door came crashed in, causing me to freeze for a split-second by the kitchen entrance just as a heavyset Cuban guy in a blue tracksuit and dripping with gold chains came walking in, a silver-plated pistol in his hand.

"Carlito sends his regards," the heavy-accented Cuban gangster said, before opening fire on me.

With nowhere else to go, I dived through the kitchen doorway, crying out when my injured shoulder slammed against the wall.

"There's no point in hiding," the intruder called out, who I doubted was alone. He had to have had at least two or three other men with him. No way Carlito would send just one guy to take me out. "You're coming with us, dead or alive, asshole. It makes no difference to us, though the boss said he wanted you alive so he can kill you himself."

With no weapon on me, I grabbed the first thing to hand, which was a large kitchen knife. The knife was in my hand for all of two seconds before a different gangster barged into the kitchen to confront me, his gun outstretched as he fired a shot that whizzed past my head, missing me by mere inches.

Without a second thought, I threw the knife in his direction, satisfied to see the blade penetrate his throat. The shaven-headed gangster gagged and choked as blood burst from his mouth, but he must've been full of coke or something, for he could still keep his gun held out and pointed at me as he squeezed off another round. The bullet missed, lodging in the wall behind me, so I dropped down low and dived at the guy, my shoulder slamming into his lower abdomen as I forced him up against the door.

His gun arm had dropped, but he was still squeezing off shots as I grabbed his wrist and slammed his hand against the wall, finally forcing him to drop the gun.

The fight wasn't out of him yet, however, and even though he had a knife sticking in his throat, he used his other hand to punch me in the face.

Covering with one arm, I used my other hand to grab hold of the knife and pull. A burst of warm blood hit me in the face, but I didn't care as I immediately stabbed the knife into the side of my assailant's neck, which finally put the fight out of him.

With blood jetting from his neck, covering the walls and

me along with it, the guy slid down the door onto the floor as he finally died.

Grabbing the dead guy's pistol from off the floor, I ejected the magazine to see there was still some rounds left in it. Slamming the mag back in, I started dragging the dead guy across the floor so he was no longer barricading the kitchen door. I didn't know how many guys were left outside, but I was about to find out.

With my hand on the door handle, I took a breath and got ready to fling the door open and face the music, but as I did, I heard a shot being fired in the living room, a shot that sounded like it had been suppressed.

The sound of something heavy hitting the floor quickly followed. A split second later, another suppressed shot, and then another heavy thud.

What the fuck? Was someone else out there?

Only one way to find out.

I flung open the door, the gun in my hand pointing into the living room.

The first thing I saw was the guy who'd kicked open my front door. He was lying slumped against the couch with a hole in the center of his forehead. Then to my left, there was another guy lying on his back on the floor, also with a hole in the dead center of his forehead.

As I inched my way out of the kitchen, I soon saw the cause of these two deaths standing by the front door.

"Looks like I was just in time," Scarlet Hood said with a smile.

4

Scarlet Hood stood by the busted front door wearing a black leather outfit with a red poncho over the top. In her hand, she held a pistol with a suppressor attached to it. "Detective," she said, smiling. "What big eyes you have. Almost like someone just tried to kill you."

"I thought I told you to call first," I said, the dead guy's blood dripping off me as I moved past her and out into the hallway. "Did you see a little girl out there?"

"No," she said frowning. "And you're welcome, by the way."

Daisy must've gone into her apartment when Carlito's men came into the building. Or at least, I hoped she did. "I had it handled," I said as I came back into the apartment, closing the door behind me, even though the frame was now busted.

"Didn't look like you did. These two guys would've shot you before you got anywhere near them."

"You don't know me very well if that's what you think." I shook my head at the mess in the living room, and then at the blood seeping from the kitchen. Fuck it. How was I gonna explain this to my fellow officers if they showed up? Assuming someone in the building had called the cops upon hearing the gunshots.

"If you're trying to think of an explanation to give the cops," she said as she walked farther into the room, putting her gun away beneath her poncho, "just say you don't know them and that they were probably gangbangers out for revenge."

"As ridiculous as that sounds, it'll probably have to do."

"Ethan?"

I turned at the sound of the voice by the front door. Daisy stood there staring at the two dead bodies on the floor with a look of mild disgust on her face. "Jesus, Daisy," I said. "You shouldn't be here."

"I knew they were bad guys as soon as I saw them," she said. "Where's the other one?"

"Doesn't matter," I said. "Go back to your apartment. You don't need to see any of this."

Daisy switched her gaze to Scarlet then. "Who are you?" she asked.

Scarlet seemed amused by Daisy as she smiled over at her. "Scarlet," she said. "Scarlet Hood."

A smile spread across Daisy's innocent face as she seemed to realize something. "You remind me of someone."

"Oh yeah?" Scarlet said. "Who?"

"It doesn't matter who," I said, ushering Daisy out to the hallway. "If the cops come, you saw nothing, okay?"

She nodded. "Sure. Are you okay? You have a lot of blood on you."

"It's not mine."

"I'm glad," she said as she walked back down the hallway. "I wouldn't like it if you died."

"I'm not going to die. Don't worry about it."

"My mom says you'll get what's coming to you someday. I told her to shut up."

A slight smile appeared on my face. "I'll see you later, Daisy."

"Later, Ethan."

I watched her go as she turned around and went back into her apartment.

"Cute kid," Scarlet said when I went back inside. "Seems old for her age."

"She's been through a lot."

"Haven't we all?"

Looking into her green eyes, I glimpsed pain in them; pain that wasn't anything to do with her missing sister, but a more profound pain. That pain we all carry around with us; the pain of past traumatic experiences, causing me to wonder what hers were. You didn't just wake up one day and decide to become an assassin. Something had pushed her into it. I was sure I would find out what at some point, but for now my only concern was the three bodies in my apartment.

Taking out my phone, I called Walker, who answered straight away. "You on your way?" she asked.

"No, not yet," I told her. "I've hit a complication."

"What happened?"

"I'll explain later. Just do me a favor, will you? Check with dispatch if there have been any reports of gunshots in my building."

"Gunshots? Are you okay, Ethan? Do you need me to come over?"

I looked over at Scarlet, who was busy checking out the few framed photos I had sitting on shelves that also held my vinyl record collection. "I'm fine. Just check for me."

"Gimme a minute."

While I waited on Walker, I stared at Scarlet as she stood with a photo in her hand, the only photo I had of me, Callie and Angela together as a family. She appeared to spend a long time staring at it. Was she judging me? Blaming me for what I'd lost? If so, she could—

"Ethan?" Walker said.

"Yeah?"

"Nothing's come in. No one has reported any gunshots."

"You're sure?"

"I just spoke with dispatch. I'm positive."

Relief washed over me as I realized I wouldn't have to try to explain what happened here. Nor would I have to waste a large amount of time that I didn't have filling out endless paperwork. "Okay, thanks, Walker," I said. "I'm going to be a little while longer getting to the precinct. Start without me if you want."

"It's fine. The girl is still with the doctor, anyway."

"Alright, see you in a while then."

Before she hung up, she said, "Ethan?"

"Yeah?"

"Can you do me a favor?"

"Sure. What is it?"

"Can you stop calling me Walker and use my first name from now on?"

"Eh, sure, okay. Hannah."

"Thank you, Ethan. I'll see you soon."

After shaking my head at the phone, I put it in my pocket and looked over at Scarlet, who had finished looking through my stuff it seemed. "We're in the clear," I said.

"You mean *you* are," she said, raising her eyebrows at me. "What are you going to do with the bodies?"

"I have an idea," I said as I telepathically contacted Scroteface.

Yeah, boss?

I need you back here. There's cleaning up to do.

I don't think the mouthy Hellicorn has finished eating yet.

Tell him there's more food here if he wants it.

More food, boss?

Just get back here.

~

WHILE I WAITED ON THE HELLBASTARDS GETTING BACK, I HIT the shower and stayed there under the hot water for a good twenty minutes, rinsing all the blood off me, staring at the crimson water as it spiraled down the drain like so much wasted life.

I emerged from the shower refreshed, glad to have washed the accumulated filth from my body. When I dried off, I walked into the living room naked, forgetting for a second that Scarlet was still there. She froze when she saw me, her green eyes looking me over, no doubt taking in the dozens of scars on my body, and the dark tattoos on my arms, shoulders and back. It was hard to tell what she was thinking as she openly stared for a further moment before turning around. "You don't have towels?" she asked with her back to me now.

"I forgot you were here," I said, heading to the bedroom where most of my clothes were.

"I'm sure."

"Don't flatter yourself. I got better things to think about."

"Like being a dick?" She turned around, her eyes on mine this time as I paused by the bedroom door and shook my head at her before going inside.

Prior to getting dressed, I went to the shelves where I kept all my medicinal ingredients and selected a jar that contained a dirty yellowish ointment—my go-to healing oint-ment, made from mostly natural ingredients, but enhanced with demon and vampire blood for added healing abilities that also helped to speed up the healing process by a significant degree. Dipping my fingers into the gooey ointment, I applied some to the sutures on my shoulder and arm before wrapping gauze over the top. Thanks to the ointment, another day or so and I could remove the stitches.

Once done, I got dressed in fresh clothes, putting on dark pants, a shirt, and a black tie. I also had a spare trench coat hanging up, which I put on, transferring my phone into one pocket. Next, I attached a holster with my service pistol in it onto my belt, followed by my badge.

When I'd finished, I went back to the shelves and located the large Mud jar, before finding a dropper bottle and filling it with the murky liquid. I was tempted to take some now, but as I was so fatigued from lack of sleep, I didn't think it would be a good idea. So instead, I selected a smaller jar from the shelves, this one containing a red powder that I had named Snake Bite. After tapping out a small amount onto the back of my hand, I snorted the stuff up my nose, gasping as it immediately entered my system. The drug was stronger than any amphetamine out there and would be enough to keep me going for the next several hours at least. I swear, if I marketed any of this stuff, I'd make a fucking fortune.

Suited and booted, I went back into the living room and then into the bathroom to retrieve Callie's locket, which I kissed before putting it into my trench pocket.

When I came back out again, the Hellbastards burst through the front door, squabbling among themselves as usual, although they all stopped when they firstly saw the two dead bodies on the living room floor, and secondly when they noticed Scarlet standing by the window, who didn't appear at all put out because five vertically challenged demons had just entered the apartment.

All the Hellbastards stood there gazing at Scarlet like she was the most beautiful thing they had ever seen. It was actually funny, although you can never tell what's going through the Hellbastard's minds. Were they admiring her beauty, or just thinking of all the depraved things they could do to her?

"Well, hello there," Scarlet said, coming to stand in front of the diminutive demons, their usual belligerence piped down in the face of such a vision standing before them.

"Hello," said Cracka in the quietest, gentlest voice I'd ever heard him use.

"And what's your name?" Scarlet asked, hunkering down to get nearer his level.

"My name Cracka," he said, all doe-eyed and coy. "What yours?"

"You can call me Scarlet."

"Scarlet," Cracka repeated as he looked back at the others, a smug smile on his face as if he was now Scarlet's favorite in all the world. The others all came forward and introduced themselves one by one, as polite as I'd ever seen them be with anyone.

"What are you, a fucking demon whisperer?" I said to her, my body now buzzing with energy from the Snake Bite I'd snorted.

Scarlet smiled. "I have a way with creatures."

"Can we go home with her, boss?" Scroteface asked, the tabby cat still stuck to his skull.

"Please?" Cracka said, giving me doe-eyes, still with a dead Chihuahua on his head, despite me telling him to get rid of it.

"No, you can't fucking go home with her," I said. "Jesus, what's next, you gonna ask her to the fucking prom or something?"

"What's a prom?" Reggie asked, a fresh cigar in his mouth.

"Never mind," I said. "In case you haven't noticed, there are three dead bodies in here that need getting rid off."

"I only see two," Snot Skull said, barely looking at me as he too gazed upon the Scarlet Wonder before him.

"There's one in the kitchen," I said. "Where's Haedemus? We're going to need him."

"Outside," Toast said, standing with his hands on his hips, still looking ridiculous in his green budgie-smugglers and red vest. "He's saying he's got indigestion from eating the kiddie fiddler. He needs to lie down a while."

"Oh, does he?" I said. "Well, go out and tell him to go

around the back of the building. He can rest up later." When none of the Hellbastards made to move, I shouted, "Now please! Scroteface, you do it."

"Why me, boss?" he moaned.

"Because I'm telling you to. Now move before I throw you out the fucking window."

"Don't be so hard on the little darlings," Scarlet said, tickling Cracka under his chin, who promptly got a massive erection.

"See what you did?" I said to her.

"Oh," she said, backing away.

"Tickle me again," Cracka said, wrapping his small hand around his oversized member. "Please."

"Alright, enough," I said stepping in front of them all. "We have bodies to move. Let's go."

When the Hellbastards finally got their act together, they helped me drag the three bodies downstairs to the back of the building while I tried not to get blood on me. Haedemus was waiting in the back alley, no doubt wondering why until he saw us emerge with the bodies. "Ethan," he said. "I appreciate the gesture, but I'm seriously stuffed here. I don't think I can eat anymore."

"Shut up," I said as I dumped a body on the rubbish-strewn ground. "I need you to take three bodies to the scrap yard. You can stash them there somewhere and munch on them at your convenience. Just don't let Cal see you bring them in."

Haedemus blinked his red eyes at me. "You did this just for me? Ethan, I don't know what—"

"Get a grip, Haedemus," I said. "I didn't kill these punks for you. I killed them because they tried to kill *me*."

"Oh, I see," he said. "So you weren't thinking of me. And here was me thinking we'd finally made a breakthrough in our relationship."

"What's he talking about, boss?" Scroteface said as he

stood over one of the bodies.

"That's a question I ask myself all the time, Scroteface," I said.

"Oh, ha! ha!" Haedemus said. "Hilarious, Ethan. How about you carry these bodies to the scrap yard yourself?" He turned away then, throwing his head up in a huff.

"Oh, for fuck's sake," I said. "I don't have time for your tantrums, Haedemus."

"You don't have time for me at all, Ethan."

Scroteface sniggered. "Drama queen."

"Fuck off you little demon bastard," Haedemus said. "Before I spear you with my horn."

"I'd like to see you try," Scroteface said squaring up to the Hellicorn, who towered over him by many feet.

"Alright, enough of this shit," I said. "Haedemus, I need your help here. I promise I'll be forever grateful if you take the bodies to the scrap yard."

"Words, Ethan, words."

Fuck me. And I thought humans were hard to deal with. "Okay, you know that trip to the beach you're always on about?"

"Yes," he said, narrowing his eyes at me. "What about it?"

"As soon as I get time, I'll take you there. We can watch the sunset. It'll be great."

Haedemus continued to stare at me. "Do you mean it?"

"Jesus, yes. I mean it."

"Look at me," he said as he grotesquely peeled back his lips to reveal his rotten teeth. "I'm smiling here, Ethan. You've made me happy."

"That's great," I said. "I'm glad."

"What about us, boss?" Scroteface said as I lifted the first body and draped it over Haedemus' back.

"What about you, Scroteface?" I said, lifting the second body and placing it alongside the first.

"When do we get to go to the beach?"

"Are you fucking kidding me? You have freedom of movement, you little shit. You can go anywhere you want, including the damn beach."

"I mean with you," he said, and the other Hellbastards all nodded as they agreed.

"Oh," I said after I'd placed the last body on Haedemus' back. "You mean like a big family fun day out?"

"Yeah," they all said together.

"Not gonna happen," I said and walked back inside the building.

∾

Leaving the Hellbastards to clean up the apartment and all the blood in the kitchen, I left with Scarlet to go to the precinct. As she had turned up to the city on a street-lethal, bright red Kawasaki motorbike, I offered to take her in my old Dodge so we could talk on the way to the precinct.

"It's good that we're going to the police station," she said as I put Motorhead on the car stereo, blasting out *Ace of Spades* as I gunned the Dodge down the street.

"Why?" I asked her. "You gonna turn yourself in?"

"Hardly," she said. "Just don't mention my name when we get there."

"What should I call you then?"

"Whatever you want."

"Daisy Duke it is then."

She shook her head at me. "Jane Smith will be fine."

"Okay, Jane," I said. "I'm thinking you know more about the circumstances of your sister's kidnapping than you're letting on, so why don't you fill me in."

"Are you on something?" she asked. "You seem very hyped up."

"I haven't slept in three days. I may have taken a little something to keep me going. Don't worry about it," I said,

51

taking the next corner at speed, sending her flying into the door.

"I'll worry if you get us killed before we even get there."

"Please. I could drive this thing in my sleep. Just tell me what you haven't told me yet."

"It's two things," she said, grabbing the handle above the door as I sped into another corner, almost hitting another car that pulled out as I was driving by, causing Scarlet to shake her head, probably wishing she had driven herself on the motorbike. "First, it was one person who took Charlotte. I tracked their path the whole way through the forest until the trail ended at a back road. Going by the tracks, it seemed as if Charlotte had gone willingly with whoever took her. There were no drag marks, no signs of any struggle. It's like she just went for a walk with this person. And let me tell you, Charlotte is gifted physically. If she wanted to kick someone's ass, she could, easily."

"Could it have been someone she knew?"

"No, that's impossible."

"Impossible? Why?"

"Charlotte has had no other human contact since we came to the forest when she was just five years old, apart from with our grandmother and me, and our grandmother is in a coma in a private medical institute in Bedford at the moment. Has been for the last six years."

"Six years? I'm sorry," I said. "What happened to her?"

"It doesn't matter," she said, turning to stare out the window at the dark street. "It's not relevant right now."

"How do you know it isn't relevant?"

"Because it isn't," she said. "Just listen to me. Charlotte has had no contact with the outside world for the last twelve years."

"That's a long time."

"It is what it is," she said, opening her window when I lit a cigarette. "You see how odd it is, though, that she would go willingly with a stranger, despite everything I've taught her about security over the years?

"I guess so," I said, blowing smoke into the car. "Could be she was mind-controlled somehow. Vampires can control minds. So can mentalists, witches, warlocks, magicians with the right magic, and anyone who has a mind-control chip implanted. It's not as rare an ability as you might think."

She went silent for a moment as she considered all of this. "So it could be anyone."

"Yes and no," I said. "It still has to be someone with a good reason to take her. Maybe someone out for revenge against you."

"Wouldn't they have contacted me by now, though? If only to gloat, and to let me know they have her?"

I nodded. "I guess so. What's the other thing you haven't told me?"

"I followed the tracks to the road as I said, which is where I noticed the tire tracks."

"You think Charlotte was loaded into a vehicle?"

"Most definitely," she said. "I even found a witness."

"Who?"

"Just an old lady who lives along the road. When I asked if she saw anything, she said she saw a Volkswagen camper van driving along the road, which is significant because the road is private. It doesn't get any traffic normally."

"Okay. That could be helpful."

"I was thinking you could check the traffic cam footage at the station, see if the van shows up anywhere."

"It's a good idea," I said, slowing down for a light up ahead. "But too much time has passed. Any footage would've been deleted by now."

"Fuck," she said, slamming her fist against the door.

"Don't panic," I said, swinging the car around in the street before heading in a different direction. "I know two guys who can help."

5

Pan Demic smiled as he opened the door of the penthouse, parting his long black hair from his face with thin fingers as loud death metal played in the background. "Drakester, my man," he said before looking at Scarlet. "And—"

"This is—" I started to say.

"Scarlet fucking Hood," Pan Demic said before I could even finish.

"I was going to say, Jane Smith," I said glancing at Scarlet, who was staring hard at Pan Demic as if he would jump her bones any second.

Another voice piped up from inside, that of Artemis. "Did I just hear the name Scarlet Hood mentioned?" he said. "Tell me it isn't—" He froze with a wondrous look on his pale, bespectacled face as he came to stand by Pan Demic.

"Dude," Pan Demic said, hardly able to contain himself. "It so fucking is."

"Jesus Christ," Artemis said, clamping his hands to his head like his mind had just been blown. "I can't believe it."

Shaking my head, I barged past the two of them as I walked into the penthouse. It was like walking into the Batcave it was so dark, thanks to the black-painted walls and the covered windows. Scarlet stepped inside as well a few seconds later, still unsure of what to make of the two Technomancers ogling her like smitten schoolboys. I should've known they would know who she was, though how they knew, I wasn't sure. The reason Scarlet had such a fearsome reputation was that she came and went like a ghost, with no one knowing exactly what she looked like. Most people who saw her face ended up dead straight after.

"Miss Hood," Artemis said as he did a ridiculous bow in front of Scarlet. "It is a true honor that you grace us with your presence on this monumental night."

"This isn't a D&D session, Artemis," I said. "We're here because we need your help."

"The gods have indeed smiled down on us tonight," Pan Demic added, completely ignoring me as he continued to gaze at Scarlet, who was pretty weirded out at this point, and looked like she wanted to draw her gun on these two head-melters. "We never dreamed that such a legend as this would ever walk through our doors."

"I walk through your doors all the time," I said. "You never say shit like that to me."

"Silence, Drakester," Artemis said, showing me his hand. "Your legend status pales in comparison to Miss Hood's here."

"Gee thanks," I said, eliciting a smile from Scarlet.

"I have to ask," she said, finally addressing the two of them. "How did you recognize me?"

"From the video," Pan Demic said like it was obvious, then turned to Artemis. "Show her."

As excited as I've ever seen him, Artemis—grinning like a kid at Christmas—ran to the bank of computer monitors in the center of the living room and dropped into his customized leather chair, which had bat wings stitched into the back of it, along with a pointed devil's tail. He tapped the keyboard at blinding speed, and a few seconds later, the video in question appeared on the screen in front of him.

Pan Demic ushered Scarlet over as he sat down next to Artemis, in a chair that had The Devil tarot card painted on the back. Scarlet seemed interested in what was on the video, if a little annoyed that it existed at all. As if to assuage her concerns, Artemis told her not to worry, and that they were the only ones who had a copy. I couldn't help but smile as I looked at Scarlet, who shook her head at me before focusing on the video.

The video was taken from security cam footage it looked like, so there was no sound, and as far as the terrible twosome were concerned, there was also no need to lower the volume on the death metal, so the harsh music continued to blast unabated in the background.

The date on the video footage said it was recorded in December three years ago. It appeared to have been shot in a restaurant filled with about a dozen men all dressed in suits— mafia guys if I didn't know any better.

Going by Scarlet's face, she recognized the scene straight away as she mashed her bright red lips together and nodded to herself.

Looking back to the screen, I saw a commotion begin in the restaurant as some of the men pulled out their guns, at least two of them getting blown away by Scarlet, who was still off camera at this point.

"And here she comes," Artemis said in an awed whisper.

As if on cue, Scarlet's form appeared on the screen, wearing a black one-piece leather outfit with a hood covering her head. She advanced on the men in the restaurant with some kind of automatic weapon; her shooting platform near perfect, the result of years of practice and experience in the field.

She took out about half the guys in the room with the automatic before the magazine ran out. When it did, she dropped the gun and took out a pistol from a holster strapped to her leg and continued her slaughter with that, blowing guys away left and right, expertly diving across tables to avoid getting shot herself, using her close-quarters skills on anyone who got within a few feet of her, always finishing them with her pistol.

In what seemed like no time at all, she had taken out every guy in the room.

All except one.

A hugely overweight man who was cowering in the room's corner behind an overturned table. As Scarlet approached, he tried to shoot her with what looked like a .22, causing Scarlet to roll to one side. When she came up, she kicked a chair in the fat man's direction; the chair crashing against the table he was hiding behind, knocking the table back onto him so he ended up on his back like a beached whale.

Scarlet stood over the man for a moment, and then shot him—twice in the chest and once in the head, before turning and heading back out the way she came. On her way out, she stopped and looked up at the camera, her face now plainly visible despite the hood. She raised her gun, and a second later, the screen went black.

"Well?" Pan Demic said as the two of them turned in their chairs to face us. "Was that fucking awesome or what?"

"I've totally lost count of how many times we've watched that video," Artemis said. "Like a thousand fucking times or something."

"More," Pan Demic said, leaning down for a snort of coke.

"I'm feeling a little creeped out now," Scarlet said.

"Don't be," Artemis said as he accepted the coke mirror and rolled-up twenty-dollar bill from Pan Demic. "I mean, we're just in awe of your skills, that's all. You're like a female John Wick, only better. I mean—" He stopped to snort a huge line. "You're fucking for *real*."

"Fucking A," Pan Demic said, now staring at Scarlet's form, no doubt filling up the wank bank for later.

"That was impressive. I don't think I've seen anyone with that level of skill," I said, leaning over to get the coke mirror from Artemis, and then added, "Maybe one."

"Let me guess," she said. "You?"

I winked at her. "You got it."

Scarlet rolled her eyes. "Whatever you say."

"Fuck," Artemis said as if he just remembered something. "We have footage of the Drakester as well."

"Shit, that's right," Pan Demic said. "We could totally do a side-by-side comparison."

"You fucks have a video of me?" I said after snorting a large line of coke, a drug I don't usually touch, but I didn't know when I was going have time to sleep next, so I needed all the help I could get to keep me going. "Where from?"

"From that time you took out that thrill kill cult a few years ago," Pan Demic said. "About ten or more of those crazy murdering fucks all attacked you when you found them about to kill everyone in the Jones Theater in Peterborough. You remember that?"

I nodded. "I remember. One of them shot me."

"But you got back up," Pan Demic said. "Like it never even happened. Fuck it, Artemis, Ctrl+Alt+Run VT."

"Don't bother," I said. "I haven't got time for this. I got a case to get to."

"What's the matter, Drakester?" Artemis said in a wheedling voice. "Afraid Scarlet here has you beat on style points?"

As Scarlet laughed, I said to Artemis, "Fuck off."

"Alright, Drakester," Artemis said, snatching back the coke mirror. "We'll not embarrass you in front of the great Scarlet Hood. What is it you need, anyway?"

"Traffic cam footage," I said. "Probably deleted, but I'm sure you guys can work your magic and get it back again."

"Just to be clear," Pan Demic said looking at Scarlet. "This is for you, right?"

"Yes," she said.

"Then consider it done."

I smiled over at Scarlet. "I'll leave you in the boys' capable hands then."

"You're going?" she asked, seeming almost afraid to be left alone with Artemis and Pan Demic.

"You're Jane Wick," I said as I started walking toward the door. "What do you have to worry about? Call me when you're done. I'll come pick you up."

"Gee thanks," she called out over the music, making me smile.

As I reached the door, I overheard Pan Demic say, "Hey, Scarlet, did you know that *They Live* was not a satirical low-budget sci-fi movie romp? It was actually a historical documentary from an alternate Earth fifty years ahead of us. Ditto for *Prince of Darkness*. John Carpenter's best movies were the ones he channeled from parallel universes. Sadly, this ability of his has faded over time, which explains why he doesn't pump out classics anymore…"

Good luck, Scarlet, I thought on the way out the door.

WHEN I GOT TO THE PRECINCT, I FOUND HANNAH DOWN IN the subbasement, which served as a base of operations for Unit X, even though we hardly ever used the place. The area once functioned as the primary 911 call center for the whole city until they moved to swankier premises across the river. The gloomy subbasement held thirty desks left over from the call center days, most of which were now pushed against the walls, leaving a large open space in the middle of the room with just two desks in the center, one each for Hannah and me.

Both desks held a phone and a computer, along with a stack of manila folders containing reports on the half dozen cases we had worked so far, redacted versions of which ended up in the central file system.

Hannah was at her desk typing on her computer when I walked in, a lit cigarette burning away in a glass ashtray beside her. She also had earphones in, which she removed as I walked through the door, smiling like she was pleased to see me, her demon Visage hovering behind her as usual, almost blending with the shadows in the room.

"You finally made it," she said as I came and sat down at my desk, opening the top drawer to take out a bottle of Jack Daniels and two glasses, filling both glasses before handing one across to Hannah.

Dressed in tight-fitting black pants and a black leather jacket, she wore her dark, lustrous hair down. Looking at her, I couldn't help but picture her naked body and the Yakuza tattoos that covered her skin.

She must've sensed what I was thinking, for she looked away coyly for a second as she took a drag of her cigarette. My heart thudded against my chest as I considered the possibility of fucking her right there on her desk. No one would catch us, for no one else ever came down here to this dungeon.

"It's good to see you," I said, staring into her dark eyes. "You doing okay?"

She nodded. "I'm doing good."

I continued to stare at her as the drugs in my system exacerbated my wanton desire to lay her across her desk and fuck her. Drinking her Jack, she gazed over the top of the glass at me, her eyes filled with unmistakable desire now. Even her Visage seemed to glow a little brighter as it shifted in anticipation, almost.

A mutual need arose, hanging in the air between us until I couldn't take it anymore and I downed the rest of my drink before going to her, standing over her as she gazed up at me, her mouth hanging open, her eyes widening as she waited on me to take her.

I pulled her up out of her chair by her wrists, then slid my hands under her armpits and lifted her straight up before setting her back down on the edge of the desk, her legs spreading wide as she smiled up at me.

Leaning over, I grabbed a handful of her hair and pulled her head back, eliciting a gasp of pleasure from her. Her Visage, eyes faintly lit, swayed back and forth behind her, as if daring me to continue.

My breathing heavy now, I dropped my face down next to hers, pulling her head back so I could kiss her long neck, running my lips up over her chin until my mouth met hers and we started to kiss, both of us breathless now as she reached up and grabbed the back of my neck to pull me tighter against her.

Taking my trench off, I let it fall to the floor and then undid her pants, sliding them along with her underwear down to her ankles as she spread her legs wide to reveal her glistening cunt. With an eagerness I hadn't felt in a long time, I spent the next several minutes with my head between her legs as she moaned loudly, gripping my hair with both hands, pushing into me with her hips, her hot juices running into my mouth, spilling down my chin.

"Fuck me," she demanded, pulling my head back so she could look at me, an amber glow in her eyes. "Fuck me now."

Standing up, I roughly pulled her forward, turning her around before pushing her back down onto the desk, running my hands over the perfect curves of her ass for a moment before sliding inside her. She cried out so loud, I was sure someone on one of the floors above would hear her, but I didn't care as I started fucking her, my cock rock hard from the coke and the Snake Bite in my system.

As I fucked her, I grabbed her long hair and pulled her head back sharply, causing her some pain that she didn't seem to mind, and which only seemed to increase her pleasure.

"Harder..." she moaned. "Fuck me harder."

And I did, slamming into her as her demon Visage looked on from above, seeming to will me on until I finally came inside her, crying out as my body stiffened and shuddered with a pleasure so intense it was almost unbearable.

As the waves of my orgasm began to subside, I leaned over and lay on top of her, both of us breathing hard, our bodies still quivering as I inhaled her sweet scent.

When we were both dressed again, she came and put her arms around me, leaning her head against my chest. "I'm so glad you're here," she whispered. "I don't know what I'd be without you."

"Yeah," I said, stroking her hair as I stared at the desk. "Me neither."

She pulled away, looked up at me, and smiled. "I guess we should see if the girl is ready for an interview. You know, like do our jobs."

I smiled back. "Our jobs, yeah. That would be good."

"You think anyone heard us? You were loud."

"*I* was loud?"

She laughed. "I don't care if they heard or not. We're outcasts here, anyway."

"Didn't take you long to get with the program."

"It's just you and me," she said, putting on her jacket. "That's how I like it. That's how I hope it stays."

"Well," I said, putting away the Jack bottle. "I don't think anyone else will be joining us down here anytime soon if that's what you mean." I looked over at her. "By the way, I never thought to ask, typical male that I am—are you on any contraception?"

Hannah cocked her head to one side. "What do you think?"

"Yes?"

"Yes, Ethan. You don't have to worry about getting me pregnant."

"Assuming it's possible, given your celestial origins."

"I'm not sure. The former Hannah was on the pill, so I continue to take it."

I nodded. "Glad we got that straight."

"You can fuck me till your heart's content. No need to worry."

I laughed and shook my head at her. "Let's go."

As we headed for the door, she asked me what happened at my apartment earlier, and I told her Carlito sent men after me.

"Fuck," she said. "That's bad."

"Yeah."

"What are you going do?"

I opened the door for her, and she stepped out into the dark hallway, heading for the stairs that would take us up to the basement and then the first floor of the precinct. "I don't know yet," I said.

"I don't think you have many options, do you?" she said as we made our way through the basement now.

"Carlito isn't exactly leaving me one. Even if I did as he asked, he'd still try to kill me. I've crossed the line as far as he's concerned, and there's no going back."

"Did you find Scarlet Hood?" she asked as she opened the door of the basement which led to another set of stairs.

"Yeah, I did. I'm helping her find her sister."

"Okay," Hannah said. "That's different to putting her head on a silver platter."

I laughed. "Yeah."

"Will you need my help?"

"We'll see," I said. "Keep your focus on this new case. Take the lead."

"Really?" A wide smile crossed her face.

"Really."

Before we got to the door that would take us out to the first floor of the precinct, Hannah stopped and pushed me against the wall, standing on a higher step so she could kiss me, taking me aback slightly. "You've no idea what this means to me. Thank you."

"You're welcome," I said. "As long as you know, all the paperwork is on you."

She smiled. "I can handle that."

As we both emerged from the basement exit into the main reception area, I told Hannah to go on ahead and prep the girl for the interview while I headed to the men's restroom.

As I stood in front of the urinal about to relieve myself, I heard the door open behind me, and a second later I looked across to see Detective Jim Routman standing next to me, wearing his usual brown suit and jaded demeanor as he flicked his eyes in my direction.

"Ethan," he said, scratching his heavy jowls with one hand while he held his cock in the other.

"Jim," I said, barely looking at him, the fact that he framed an innocent woman for murder—Barbara Keane— still fresh in my mind. Not that the old codger gave a shit as he stood with a smug look on his lined face.

"Saw your partner bring that pregnant girl into the interrogation room. What's that about?"

"Not sure yet."

"Well, she looks crazy. Should be right up your street." He smiled like this was funny.

"Don't think I've forgotten what you did, Jim," I said, staring straight ahead. "Makes me wonder how many of the people you put away actually deserved it."

"Fuck you, Ethan. They all deserved it."

"Maybe in your mind. Why'd Barbara Keane deserve it?"

"Because she killed her fucking husband and kids, that's why."

"She didn't. You know she didn't."

"Fourteen years ago I put that bitch away," he said. "How would you know I framed her? Her ghost tell you or something?" He chuckled to himself again.

I said nothing as I shook myself off and zipped up, then headed over to the grimy sink to wash my hands. Routman came to the next sink a second later, and I looked at him in the mirror. "I can't believe I used to look up to you," I said.

Routman shook his hands off in the sink and snapped a paper towel from the dispenser, glaring at me as he used it to wipe his hands dry. "You of all people have no right to judge me, Ethan."

"What's that supposed to mean? I don't recall framing any innocent people."

"No," he said, tossing the used towel in the waste bin. "You just run around like you're Dirty fucking Harry, wasting anyone who gets in your way." He stepped toward me. "You gonna waste me next, huh, Ethan? Like that kid, Troy? What happened to him? How'd he end up in pieces? Did you do that to him, Ethan? I mean, I'd read the report, if there was one."

"There's a report," I said. "It's just above your pay grade. And I didn't kill the kid."

"I wouldn't care if you did. He killed three good cops. He deserved what he got."

"So you're saying it's okay for us to be judge, jury, and executioner now, is that it, Jim?"

"Open your fucking eyes, Ethan. We already are. Someone always has to pay."

I could destroy him right now. It would be as easy as showing him my hand and the swirling tattoo ink that would appear there at my behest. Hypnotized by the ink, I could tell him to forget himself, to forget who he is, who his family is. By the time I was done, he wouldn't even know what planet he was living on, and he would drift in a gray mind-fog for the rest of his life.

But I did nothing, maybe because I knew deep down, he was right. Someone always *did* have to pay, even if that person was innocent. It was the way of the world and the way of the justice system. The scales always have to be balanced. Routman knew this on some intuitive level, as most cops do.

He stared at me for another moment before walking to the door. When he got there, he turned to look at me again. "You stink of sex. You fucking that Jap partner of yours down in the basement now or something?"

I didn't respond, staring at him until he smiled and walked out the door. When he was gone, I looked at myself in the mirror for a moment, and then walked out the door behind him.

6

H annah was already in the interview room with the pregnant girl when I walked in. The room was windowless and cramped; the walls painted a dull gray color. In the center of the room was a Formica table, with the girl sitting in a plastic chair on one side and Hannah sitting on the other, an empty chair beside her. In a recess in the sound-proofed wall, a DC recorder was taping everything that was being said.

"Detective Ethan Drake has entered the room at…3:16 a.m.," Hannah said for the tape after checking her watch.

I remained silent as I sat down next to her and stared across at the girl, who was younger than I expected, only seventeen or eighteen. She had long, golden-brown hair and large, dark blue eyes that expressed her fear and confusion. Though going by her dilated pupils, the drugs given to her by the doc were helping her to remain calm and quell the tide of emotions that would otherwise have reduced her to a total mess. Her pretty face was pale and drawn, and she had dark circles under her eyes like she hadn't had any proper sleep in months. The look in her eyes was haunted like she had suffered deep trauma recently. She also looked to be at least seven or eight months pregnant.

Occasionally, she would stare down at her swollen belly like there was some parasite or alien life form growing inside her—something she didn't understand, had little to no connection with and only wanted rid of. She had my sympathy, though it remained to be seen if it was fully deserved. As always, I would reserve judgment until I heard her whole story. I was happy to sit in silence while Hannah led the interview.

"Could you state your full name for the record?" Hannah asked the girl in a gentle but professional tone.

"My name is Clare Jenkins," the girl replied, her eyes staring emptily at the table.

"Can you also state your age?"

"I'm …eighteen."

"Do you have an address, Clare?"

The girl frowned as if she was trying to remember, then gave an address somewhere in Brockton, a wealthy suburb in north Bedford. When asked if her parents knew she was here, she replied no. "I haven't seen my parents in nearly a year."

She'd probably been on the system this whole time. Just another statistic; another person unable to be found. Until now, that is.

"Would you like us to contact your parents?" Hannah asked.

Clare didn't answer right away, staring down at her swollen belly for a long moment before looking up. "I don't want them to see me like this."

"That's okay," Hannah said, her Visage blending in with the wall behind her. "We don't have to contact them yet, but I'm sure they'd like to know you're alive. You've been missing for nearly a year."

Tears flooded the girl's eyes and spilled down her cheeks as she turned her head away, and Hannah and I exchanged glances.

"I need to tell you everything first," Clare said. "You have to stop them before they—"

"Before they what, Clare?" Hannah said. "Stop who?"

"*Her*," she said. "Gretchen...and her monsters."

Hannah looked at me briefly before asking Clare, "Who is Gretchen? Does she have a surname?"

"Carmichael. Gretchen Carmichael. And she's the Devil."

Hannah wrote the name down in her notebook, then looked back up at Clare. "Earlier when you came in, you mentioned you were part of a cult. Is this Gretchen woman the cult leader?"

Clare nodded. "Yes."

"Did this woman abduct you, Clare?"

"Her demons did."

"Her demons?"

"Her devil spawn."

"What do you mean by that, Clare?"

Clare fixed her large blue eyes on Hannah, almost looking through her. "It's what's in me," she said, her face twisting up in disgust and dismay. "I'm carrying the Devil's child."

There was a pregnant pause in the room before I broke my silence. "I think we need to go back to the beginning here," I said. "You need to tell us everything, Clare. What happened when you were taken?"

Sighing, Clare shifted in her seat as if the extra load she was carrying was causing her great discomfort. "This chair is killing me," she said. "God, I just want this thing out of me, I want it out—" She looked on the verge of a panic attack until Hannah said she would get her a different chair, at which point Clare started breathing deeply in through her nose and out through her mouth.

"How far along are you?" I asked her.

"Three months," she said, laughing slightly; laughter

which soon turned to tears. "Three fucking months."

"But you look—"

"Ready to drop? That's cause I am. I told you, I have the Devil's child in me."

"A demon did this to you?"

She stared at me, maybe surprised that I would even suggest such a thing. "You could say that."

Hannah came back in with a cushioned leather chair, positioning it next to Clare and helping her into it, before sliding the other chair back against the wall. When she sat back down again, she said, "Better?"

Clare nodded. "Thank you."

Hannah smiled. "No problem."

"So tell me, Clare," I said. "Why has it taken you a year to escape the clutches of this cult? What was stopping you before?"

Clare looked at me like she didn't like my tone, as if I doubted her credibility. "Are you saying I'm lying about all this?" she asked, her eyes wide with indignation.

"I'm just trying to establish the facts, Clare, that's all."

"We want to help you, Clare," Hannah said. "But to do that, we need to know everything. Do you understand?"

Clare stared at us both for another moment before nodding. "I understand."

"Good," Hannah said. "Tell us why you didn't escape before now."

"Because," she said. "When the cult takes you, they pump you full of drugs to make you compliant, and so they can prepare you for the ritual. They indoctrinate you every day with their beliefs, and there's nothing you can do about it. You have to do as they say. It's only after the ritual that they take you off the drugs because they want nothing harming the baby. But then they lock you up until the baby is born."

"So how did you escape?" I asked her. "It couldn't have been easy, especially in your current condition."

"It wasn't," Clare said. "It was blind luck I got out at all. There was a power failure, and the electronic locks on the room doors opened because of it. I wasn't the only one who tried to escape that night. It was chaos, pregnant girls running everywhere, security all over the place. Somehow, I made it through and got outside. I stole a car and made my escape. Drove right through the security gates in an SUV." She smiled slightly at the madness of it.

"I'm impressed," I said. "You did well."

"Thanks."

"Did any of the other girls make it out at the same time?" Hannah asked.

"I don't know. I wasn't thinking of anyone else." She turned her head to the side, as if in shame.

"It's okay," Hannah said. "You've nothing to be ashamed of. You're helping those other girls by being here now."

Clare nodded, smiled slightly. "I hope so."

"How many other girls are there?" I asked.

"Maybe a dozen with…child," she said. "More than that again who are being groomed for the ritual. Some boys as well. There has to be at least one boy for the ritual."

"You keep mentioning this ritual," I said. "What's it entail?"

Clare took a deep breath before continuing, looking down at her swollen belly for a second. "It's called the Drencher Host Ritual, and they spend months preparing us for it," she said.

"In what way?" Hannah asked. "Do they make you do things? What things exactly?"

I glanced over at Hannah then, something in her voice making me do so, only to see her demon Visage move closer to the table, a sure sign her demonic side had been awakened by the dark turn in the conversation. She seemed too interested in this ritual for her own good. I was also worried that Clare would see the Visage in the room, now that her eyes had been opened to the dark side, so to speak. But perhaps because of the drugs in her system, she didn't seem to notice the dark, winged specter hovering behind Hannah, casting its shadow over her psyche. Hannah still seemed in control for now, but I made a mental note to keep a close eye on her.

"They make us do bloody sacrificial rites over and over," Clare said as if she was still there in her mind. "We use the blood of innocents, smearing it over a statue of the demon as we howl our praises to it over and over and over…calling the demon's name."

"What's the demon's name, Clare?" Hannah asked, leaning forward on the table.

"I—I can't say it—"

"Who is it, Clare?" Hannah's voice rose in pitch as she leaned farther forward. "Say the name."

"Hannah," I said, giving her a look, noticing a faint amber glow in her eyes. She stared at me for a second and then sat back in her seat.

"It's okay, Clare," I said. "You're safe here."

"Safe?" she said as if I was joking. "How can I be safe when they're everywhere?"

"Who?" I asked. "Who's everywhere, Clare? The cult?"

"The demon spawn," she said. "The same demon spawn I have inside me right now."

"What happened at the ritual, Clare? Is that when you got pregnant?"

She nodded. "Yes."

"Were you raped?"

She nodded again. "In a way. But I let it happen. I *wanted* it to happen."

"That's how the cult wanted you to feel," I said. "That's why they drugged you and brainwashed you. Whatever happened, it wasn't your fault. None of this is your fault."

Wiping tears from her eyes, Clare stared at the table for a second, then said, "I remember everything. There was fourteen of us at the ritual—thirteen girls and one boy. Gretchen was there, telling us what to do. She stood behind an altar while we all formed a circle around her. Then the boy—I don't know his name—he gets up onto the altar when Gretchen tells him to, and he lies down, naked. We're all naked." She stopped and swallowed as if she was trying to keep the bile down, then continued a moment later. "When Gretchen told us to, we all began to—to—" She stopped again, on the verge of breaking down completely. "I can't—I can't say it—"

"Say what, Clare," Hannah said in a quiet voice, her Visage still hanging over her. "What can't you say?"

"I—I—"

"Tell us, Clare. What did you do? What did—"

"We ate him!" Clare screamed. "We fucking ate him!"

She clamped both her hands over her mouth as if she would be sick, but this wasn't enough to stop herself, and she pulled her hands away from her mouth again as she vomited onto the floor between her legs, retching and crying at the same time.

As Hannah cocked her head to one side and looked on almost dispassionately, I got up and went to Clare, holding her long hair back as she continued retching. When she was done, she slapped my hands away and told me to get the fuck off her, which I did, stepping back, my hands in the air. "It's okay," I said.

"It's fucking not okay," she shouted. "It's not! It's not okay! It's—" She halted and grimaced, grabbing her belly as if she was in great pain.

That's when Hannah got up, going to Clare and taking hold of her hand, telling her to breathe, that it would be alright. "Good girl," Hannah said. "Just breathe, that's it."

"I'll get her some water," I said, leaving the room at that point to go outside, pausing in the hallway for a second to take a breath myself.

I'd seen and heard a lot of bad shit in my time, but Clare's testimony horrified me in a way that nothing else ever had. I was disgusted and angry that a formerly pure soul like Clare had to go through such a sickening ordeal. What if it was Callie? What if she had grown up only to have something terrible like that happen to her? At this, I had to remind myself that something terrible *did* happen to Callie.

Jesus, sometimes it gets too much to bear. The ceaseless horror. The depressing darkness. *When will it ever end?* I thought as I moved down the hallway toward the water dispenser, knowing that for me, it would never end. Not until I was dead, and even then, there was always Hell, wasn't there?

I went back inside the interview room to find that Clare had calmed down, though she still appeared to be in some pain. "She's having contractions," Hannah said.

"Maybe we should end the interview and take you to a hospital," I said as I handed her the cup of water.

"No," Clare said. "Not yet. I want to finish telling you everything. I want you to stop these people, even though I'm not even sure they can be stopped."

"We'll see about that," I said looking down at the vomit on the floor. "I'll get a mop."

"Leave it," Clare said. "It's fine. Let's just get this over with."

"If you're sure," Hannah said, sitting back down in her chair again, her demonic urges in check once more it seemed.

Clare nodded after drinking some water I gave her. "I am."

"Okay," I said, sitting back down. "Before we broke off, you said you...ate this boy on the altar. Can you explain that?"

She took another moment to compose herself, as though preparing herself for the horror that was about to come spilling out of her mouth.

"The boy willingly offers himself up for sacrifice," she

began. "He is to be the host for the demon's agent. For that to happen, the girls have to feast on his flesh, as Gretchen put it. We all had to eat the lower half of his body while he was still alive and conscious. And we did. We used our teeth and fingernails to pull off bits of him. The boy didn't scream as one of the girl's bit off his big toe with her buck teeth. He didn't scream when another girl pulled the tendons from his legs like gummy worms. And he didn't scream when I bit the head of his penis off and swallowed it down. He bit his own tongue off so he couldn't make any sounds as we all calmly and methodically ate every piece of him below his ribcage, pinching off his arteries so he didn't bleed to death."

When she stopped talking, she looked across at us, looking for the horror and disgust in our faces, looking for the judgment, the condemnation that came from the fact that she could do something so vile to another human being. But she saw none of those things. What she saw instead was two cops staring back at her with non-judgmental, passive expressions on their faces, which perhaps horrified her further, that we could sit there and listen to such things being said without wanting to hit her or be violently sick.

"I'm sorry you had to go through that," Hannah said after a long pause. "What happened next?"

Clare snorted and shook her head a little at our apparent lack of shock, but continued anyway. "I don't know how, but the boy survived the first part of the ritual. He was there on the altar, half his body gone, digesting in our bellies as Gretchen looked on with a satisfied smile on her face. A few of the girls vomited up most of what they'd eaten, but the rest of us somehow kept it all down. Understand, we were all still drugged up, and after so many months of relentless preparation, our minds weren't our own. We took pleasure in what we did, for fuck's sake——" She paused to shake her head. "It all seemed so…*normal*, as sickening as that sounds."

"We get it," Hannah said.

"Anyway, the demon's agent was waiting in the wings, so to speak," she said. "Once we'd eaten the boy, and it was clear he was still alive and conscious, the demon's agent possessed what was left of the boy, taking over his body, turning his eyes as black as coal. The boy had become a drencher."

"A drencher?" I said.

"That's what Gretchen called it, that thing."

"Then what happened?" Hannah asked.

"Then we lay on the floor and waited our turn."

"For what?"

"For the drencher to come and drench us with its seed," she said, staring at the table as if she was remembering every gruesome detail in her mind. "It would walk around on its two arms, blood dripping from its exposed ribcage, trailing entrails behind it. Then it would hold itself up over the top of us, dripping blood onto us as it leaned its head down and—and put its mouth over ours and then—" She paused. We waited. "Then it vomited its vile seed into our mouths, and we swallowed it all down so it could somehow make its way into our wombs."

"Christ," I said, looking at Hannah. Even she seemed disgusted.

"And the result of all that," Clare said, "is this evil growing inside me, supposedly half-human, half-demon. That's what the whole thing is about, building an army that Gretchen will command. That she *does* command." She looked up at us. "You believe me, don't you?"

"Yes," Hannah said. "We believe you, Clare."

"How long has this been going on?" I asked her. "Do you know?"

She shook her head. "I don't know. What I know is that this thing inside me, once it's born, it will age five years for every year it's alive, stopping when it gets to twenty."

"So in four years," Hannah said, "that baby inside you will be twenty years old?"

"That's what I heard anyway," Clare said. "I heard a lot of stuff. I'm not sure how much of it is true. Either way, once this thing is out of me, I never want to see it. They can fucking burn it for all I care."

"These…hybrids," I said. "They look human?"

"Yes," Clare said. "They're all over the school."

"The school?"

"The old boarding school. That's where all this happened. That's where Gretchen lives."

"You know the school's location?" I said.

"I have a rough idea," Clare said. "I was in a state when I drove away from the place, so I wasn't exactly paying attention."

"Just give us a rough idea," I said, just as my phone vibrated in my pocket. "We'll soon find it."

Taking out my phone, I saw I had a text from an unknown number, a text which read:

COME PICK ME UP. JANE WICK.

Shaking my head and smiling slightly at the phone, I put it back in my pocket and looked at Hannah. "I have to go," I told her as I stood up. "Get a location for the boarding school from Clare here and then drive her to the hospital. And run Gretchen Carmichael's name through the system, see what comes up."

"Okay," Hannah said. "I'll call you when I'm done."

I looked at Clare before I left the room. "Thank you for coming in," I said to her. "What you did took guts." I stopped when I realized my choice of words might have been a little inappropriate, and going by Clare's face, so did she. "Anyway. We'll take this Gretchen woman down, along with her whole cult. You have my word on that."

Clare nodded but said, "I think it might be too late, Detective." She looked down at her pregnant belly. "Too late for some, anyway."

7

"Those two are hard work," Scarlet said as she got into the Dodge and sat in the passenger seat. "They never shut up. Did you know hummingbirds are insects? Apparently, this has been covered up for years." She puffed her cheeks out and shook her head at me. "I mean, Jesus. I'm exhausted from just being with them."

"Did you at least get what you needed?" I asked her as I pulled off, my arms heavy as I turned the steering wheel. I would have to sleep soon, I realized. I would fall off my feet if I didn't.

"Yes and no."

"Meaning?"

"Pan Demic and Artemis got a bead on the camper van," she said, pulling on her seat belt, even though I was driving at a slow pace compared to earlier. "But they could only track it to about ten miles from the city limits. After that, it disappeared, probably onto the back roads where there were no cameras."

"Were you able to see your sister in any of the footage?"

She reached behind her and pulled out a picture from her back pocket, handing it to me. It was a still from the camera footage. It showed two people in a Volkswagen camper van. The driver, of slim build, wore dark glasses and a baseball cap, so it was impossible to make out who it was, especially since the image was so grainy. Next to the man in the passenger seat was a girl with short blond hair, wearing a plaid shirt. "Is this your sister?" I asked.

"Yes," she said. "That's Charlotte."

I glanced at the photo again as I went to turn a corner. "She doesn't seem to be restrained or in any kind of distress. She seems...relaxed."

"I know. I don't understand it."

"Do you recognize the driver?"

She shook her head. "No."

"Okay," I said. "I'm going to take you someplace where we can talk. When we get there, you will tell me everything. That's the only way we'll figure out what's going on here."

"Where are we going?"

"The scrap yard."

AFTER OPENING THE GATES TO CAL'S PLACE, I DROVE INSIDE and made my way slowly through the mountains of scrap until I reached my trailer. As I parked the car, I wasn't surprised to see Haedemus hanging around outside.

"Well," he said, standing tall outside the trailer. "Look who decided to show up."

"I wasn't aware I was supposed to," I said, suppressing a yawn, even the coke not doing much to keep the tiredness at bay now.

"You weren't," Haedemus said. "I just thought I'd say that. I'm bored hanging around this place."

"What did you do with the bodies?" I asked him.

"I stashed them as far back in the yard as I could," he said. "Hopefully those two mutts won't find them."

"Did Cal see you?"

"No."

"Good."

Scarlet approached Haedemus then and put her hand on his snout and started stroking him. "You're a fearsome beast, aren't you?" she said. "When you're not masturbating outside churches."

"That was your fault," Haedemus said, enjoying the gentle stroking motion of Scarlet's hand. "You forced me to prove myself."

"I'm not sure that I did," Scarlet said. "But anyway."

"Come on," I said to her. "Let's go inside. I don't know how much longer I can stay awake."

"Not yet," Haedemus blurted. "Keep stroking. It's nice." Scarlet seemed unsure but kept stroking his head, anyway. "I'm starved of attention in this place. My Mistress brings me here and then ignores me, leaves me to fend for myself. And Ethan over there isn't exactly the world's greatest BFF either, are you, Ethan?"

I was about to reply when I noticed his penis had dropped. "Oh, for fuck's sake," I said.

"What?" Scarlet said, following my gaze. "Oh, right." She stopped stroking Haedemus' head and stepped back away from him.

"I can't help it," Haedemus said. "I get so easily aroused here, and I don't know why. I think it must be the fresh air or—"

"Or because you're a fucking pervert," I said. "Shall I tell Scarlet how you ended up in Hell?"

"Don't you dare, Ethan Drake," he said. "Don't embarrass me."

"You've already embarrassed yourself," I said. "Let's go, Scarlet."

"Going inside to have filthy human sex, are we?"

Haedemus asked, following along behind Scarlet as if he was going inside. "Can I join in?"

Scarlet threw him a disgusted look. "No one is having sex."

"Tell me about it," Haedemus said, then looked at me. "I've decided I want a pony, Ethan. I'd like you to get me one."

"Sure," I said. "I'll run out now and get one from the store."

"Isn't a pony a little small for you?" Scarlet asked.

"Oh, I don't want it for sex. Just to cuddle. Like a human child cuddles a teddy bear. Though perhaps it could lick my member the odd time too."

"Eww, stop it," Scarlet said.

"He doesn't know how," I said, holding the trailer door open for Scarlet as she stepped inside.

"Fine then, leave me," Haedemus said.

"I will," I said.

As I was closing the door, he shouted, "If I hear sex noises I'm coming in. You've been warned!"

Once inside, Scarlet and I just looked at each other and laughed. It was the only reasonable response to the Hellicorn's randy behavior. "He's hard work," she said.

"Tell me about it," I said as I planked myself down on the couch and sighed, glad to take the weight off.

"Though oddly endearing at the same time." She sat down on the couch next to me.

"I don't know about that."

"Admit it. You like him. You wouldn't keep him around otherwise."

"He's come in useful. He helped save my life."

"There you go then. Who's his Mistress?"

"My partner, Hannah. She's a fallen angel."

Scarlet raised her eyebrows. "For real?"

"You've never met a demon?"

"Not personally, no."

"Most of them are cunts. I'd stay clear."

"Your partner isn't."

"She's different."

"How?"

I felt my eyes close as oblivion reached out to grab me. "She…just is. I…"

"Ethan? Ethan?" She reached out and punched me on the arm. "Don't you fall asleep on me."

I snapped my eyes open and shook my head as if to clear it. "Fuck," I said. "I need coffee. You want one?"

"Sure," she said. "Though I doubt there are any clean cups in here. What is this place, your secret hideout?"

"Something like that." I managed to find a jar of instant coffee, which I proceeded to spoon into the cups after I'd put the electric kettle on to boil. A few minutes later, I brought the cups over to the couch and handed one to Scarlet, who regarded the tarry substance inside with suspicion.

"You sure this is coffee and not tar?" she said.

"I like it strong." I took a sip and tried not to wince, for it tasted disgusting. It would have to do, though. "So tell me about your sister while I'm still awake enough to listen."

"Charlotte is not my sister by blood," she said, placing her cup on the floor as she sat back on the couch and crossed her legs. "My parents adopted her when I was fifteen. They'd been trying for years to have another baby ever since I came along, but there were complications I won't go into. Anyway, they adopted, since that was the only way they could have another child. They got Charlotte when she was just a few months old."

"Interesting," I said.

"What?"

"Nothing. Carry on."

"Well, everything was great for a while," she went on. "My parents had good jobs. We lived in a big house. I went to an expensive school where I did well, had lots of friends, excelled at sports. We had a good life."

"So what happened?"

"My parents were killed in a car crash."

"I'm sorry."

"Yeah, so was I." She went silent for a moment before continuing. "Anyway, Charlotte and I, we had no other family except my grandmother on my father's side. I'd only met her a few times and didn't like her. I thought she was harsh and weird in her ways. But since I couldn't exactly raise Charlotte alone, we were forced to go live with Doris, our grandmother. That's her cottage you were at in the forest. She——"

That's as much as I heard before oblivion reached out and pulled me into its sweet embrace.

～

"ETHAN! WAKE UP!"

I awoke with a start, unsure of where I was for a moment until I saw Scarlet standing by the window. "Fuck," I said, shielding my eyes. "Why's it so bright in here?"

"It's coming from outside," Scarlet said, a sense of urgency in her voice, though I didn't know why.

"What the fuck's going on?"

"I think your friends have turned up again." She was standing by the side of the window, pistol already in hand.

"What?" I hauled myself off the couch and went to the window, squinting out at the blinding lights beaming through the glass. Outside, there appeared to be three vehicles about ten yards from the trailer, beaming their headlights on full power. "Shit."

"You think it's Martinez?" Scarlet asked.

"I know it is. Motherfucker must've had me followed."

Scarlet pulled the slide back on her gun. "What do you want to do? Is there another way out of this trailer?"

"Just the front door," I said, taking out my gun as I stepped to the side of the window.

"Do you have a shotgun here?"

"No."

"What do you have?"

"The gun in my hand."

"That's it? I thought you'd be more prepared than this."

"Gimme a break. I hardly even stay here anymore. Plus, you can't just go out there with guns blazing. They'll cut you down before you even get a shot off. I don't care how good you are."

"So what do you suggest? I'm not waiting here for those guys out there to open fire on this trailer. You could spit through these damn walls they're so thin."

"Just let me think," I said, but a second later there was a voice from outside.

"I know you're in there, Ethan." It was Carlito. "Why don't you come out so we can talk?"

"What do you want, Carlito?" I shouted back.

"You know what I want, Ethan. I know that bitch Scarlet Hood is in there with you. Send her out, and I might let you live."

"Fuck you, Carlito."

"That's how you want to play this?" he shouted back. "Okay."

I squinted through the window to try to make out the Cuban gangster, but the headlights were so bright it was impossible to see.

Then I heard another voice that made me feel sick to my stomach, a voice that was young and afraid. "Ethan?"

"Fuck me," I said, looking at Scarlet. "He has Daisy."

"Who's Daisy?" she asked.

"The girl from my apartment building."

"Great," Scarlet said. "You had to be friends with her, didn't you?"

I threw her an angry look. "Hey, we wouldn't be in this position if you hadn't killed Carlito's fucking cousin. Couldn't you have just talked to him? You had to kill him?"

"He left me no choice."

"I'm sure he didn't."

"You hear that, Ethan?" Carlito shouted. "I have your little friend here. You didn't think I knew about her, did you? I know everything, Ethan. I also know that if you don't send Hood out here, I'm gonna blow this girl's brains out. You know I'll do it. You gotta ask yourself, Ethan: Whose life is worth more? Hood's or the girl's? You got five seconds."

Scarlet and I stared at each other as Carlito started to count down from five. When he got to three, I said, "Fuck," and rushed to the door, pulling it open and then raising both hands as I squinted against the brightness of the headlights. "Don't shoot."

"Where's Hood?" Carlito asked. "I said to send her out."

He was standing by the front of a black SUV, dressed in a white suit. Two other identical vehicles flanked the middle one. Men with automatic weapons stood around the cars, most of whom had their guns trained on me.

"God damn it, Carlito," I said, looking over at him as he stood behind a terrified Daisy, one hand on her shoulder, the other hand holding a gold-plated pistol to her head. Motherfucker had no morals, holding a fucking gun to a kid's head like that. "Let the girl go."

"After you get Hood out here," he said. "Otherwise, I'm just gonna kill all of you. You hear that, Hood? You better get out here now!"

I was about to say to Carlito that we could talk about this, when some of his men suddenly swung their weapons to the right. A second later, Cal came into view, shouldering a mag-fed Mossberg shotgun. "What the fuck's going on here?" he demanded, stopping by the side of the trailer.

"Stand down, Cal," I said.

"Like fuck, I will," he said, topless, wearing only jeans, his feet bare. "This is my yard, and these Latino motherfuckers ain't got no right to be here."

"Go back inside, old man," Carlito said. "Before you end up dead."

"Listen to him, Cal," I said. "I got this handled. Go back to your trailer."

"Doesn't look to me like you got anything handled," he said. "What the fuck is that little girl doing here?"

"Jesus Christ, Cal, just listen to me for once," I shouted. "I said I got this!"

Cal glanced at me, his hard gray eyes boring into me. "I ain't going nowhere."

Stubborn bastard, I thought as I looked back at Carlito, dropping my gaze down to Daisy for a second, hardly able to look at her fear-stricken face, though despite her terror, she appeared to be holding it together, for which I had to give her credit. Plenty of grown adults would've crumbled by now. "Carlito—"

"No more talking, Ethan," Carlito barked, pressing the gun harder against Daisy's temple, causing her to squeal in fear. "Get that fucking bitch out here, or I swear to—"

"Let the girl go," Scarlet shouted from behind me. "I'm coming out."

"Are you crazy?" I said, stopping her. "You know what they'll do to you?"

A look of resignation entered her green eyes. "I know what they'll do if I *don't* go out there." Despite the torture and certain death she was facing, she showed no fear. "Find my sister, Ethan. And when you do...tell her I love her."

She pushed past me and stepped out of the trailer. The second she did, someone shot her in the neck, not with a bullet, but with a tranquilizer dart. Scarlet's hand went instinctively to her neck where the dart had hit, and two seconds later, she toppled to the ground unconscious.

Carlito looked at me and smiled. "I'm not taking any chances with that bitch," he said, then shouted for his men to get her into one of the vehicles. Two guys ran over and lifted Scarlet, dragging her across the dirt before dumping her into the back of one of the SUVs.

"Let the girl go, Carlito," I said.

Carlito smiled and held Daisy for another few seconds as if he would shoot her anyway, but then turned her loose. Daisy was hesitant at first, too afraid to move until I beckoned her over to the trailer and told her to go inside.

"You're lucky Hood is the honorable type," Carlito said. "She just saved your fucking life. For now."

"Meaning?"

"Meaning I haven't decided what I'm gonna do with you yet," he said, pointing his gun at me now. "I thought we were friends, Ethan. You disappointed me."

"What are you going to do with her?" I asked.

"What the fuck do you care? You hardly know the bitch. But for the record, I'm gonna torture her for three whole days, and if she's still alive after that, I'm gonna blow her brains out. Then I'm gonna feed her to my pigs." He laughed when he saw the look on my face. "You didn't know I had pigs, did you, Ethan? I can throw those hungry motherfuckers a body, and there'll be nothing left of it the next day except what they shit out afterward. Who knows, maybe I'll feed you to them too, Ethan. A pig for the pigs." He laughed at his stupid joke before turning and walking to the vehicle closest to him. "This isn't over, Ethan. You'll be hearing from me again."

When he was inside the vehicle, all three turned around and drove off, leaving nothing but a cloud of dust behind them.

In the ensuing silence left behind, Haedemus came walking out from between two mounds of scrap just up ahead.

"Well," he said. "That was tense, wasn't it?"

Inside the trailer, I sat next to Daisy on the couch as I did my best to comfort her, knowing she would probably have nightmares for the rest of her life about this. Her face was white as a sheet as she sat shaking with fear and adrenaline, wearing only shorts and a T-shirt. Finding a blanket, I draped it around her as she stared at the floor. "Daisy," I said, knowing whatever words I said to her would be inadequate. "I'm sorry you had to go through that. I didn't know—"

"They asked me if I knew you," she said in a small, anxious voice.

"What?"

"I didn't know who they were," she went on. "I was too busy reading my stupid book."

"It's okay, Daisy. This wasn't your fault."

"I should've said I didn't know you, then they wouldn't have taken me, and your friend would be okay." She started crying then, and I put my arm around her and held her, wondering at the same time why everyone who found their way into my orbit ended up getting hurt.

Cal came walking into the trailer just as Daisy finished crying. He was still carrying the Mossberg shotgun, which he rested against the wall. "Is she alright?" he asked, sounding like he hardly cared, though I knew he cared deep down somewhere in that calloused heart of his.

"What do you think?" I said.

"I'm okay," Daisy said. "I just want to go home to my momma."

"Does your momma know?" Cal asked her.

"Know what?" Daisy said, wiping her eyes.

"That you were taken."

She shook her head. "I don't think so. She was sleeping off a bottle of vodka."

"What's a little thing like you doing out of your apartment at this hour, anyway?" Cal said.

"I don't sleep much," Daisy said. "I sit outside and read."

"You're a reader, huh?" Cal nodded approvingly. "Good for you."

I stood up. "Come on, Daisy," I said. "Let's get you home before your mother realizes you're missing."

"She won't," Daisy said. "She never does."

I glanced at Cal, who shook his head before saying to Daisy, "So, eh, maybe you'd like to come by sometime. I can show you my library. I guarantee you'll be impressed."

Daisy managed a smile. "You have a lot of books?"

Cal shrugged. "A shit ton. I can't guarantee you'll understand them all, though."

"I'm smarter than you think," Daisy said, causing Cal to laugh, and me to smile.

"Alright little missy," Cal said. "Get on outta here before you end up stayin'. You might never go home then."

Daisy and I went to leave the trailer, but before she left, she said to Cal, "What's your name?"

"You can call me Cal."

"I'm Daisy. Nice to meet you, Cal." She gave him a smile before going outside.

"Thanks, Cal," I said.

He gave me a curt nod. "Me and you need to have words at some point, about bringing strangers into my yard. That shit coulda went real bad out there."

"I know. I'm sorry."

He stared at me for another second and then sighed. "Go on. Get the girl home. And Ethan?"

"Yeah?"

"You know what you gotta do about the Cuban, don't you?"

I stared at him for a second, then nodded. "I do."

8

I t was almost dawn by the time I got Daisy home. As we stood outside her apartment, I told her once again I was sorry about what happened, and that maybe it would be best if we didn't associate with each other anymore. Perhaps I should move out of the building altogether, I told her. At least that way she would be safe then.

Daisy frowned when I said this. "Don't be silly," she said. "You're my only friend, Ethan. Why would I want you to leave?"

"I can't be your only friend," I said. "What about your friends at school?"

"They're a bunch of phonies. They aren't my friends."

"Listen to you," I said. "You sound like Holden Caulfield."

"Who?"

"*Catcher in the Rye?*"

"I've never read that one. Is it good?"

I nodded. "I liked it as a kid. I think Cal might have a first edition. Ask him to lend it to you."

"You'll take me back there?"

"If you want."

"I do. I like Cal. He's grouchy, but I can tell he's nice."

I smiled. "Okay then. Go and get some sleep, Daisy."

"Ethan?" she said as I was walking away.

"Yeah?"

"Are you going get your friend Scarlet back?"

I nodded. "I hope so."

"Good. Are you going kill the men that took her, like you did Jarvis?" I stared at her, and despite me saying nothing, she said, "Good."

Then she went inside her apartment, leaving me to stand in the hallway for a moment, shaking my head as I considered what a bad influence I was.

～

Thanks to the incident with Carlito's men, my apartment was in a bit of a state, though no worse than usual. The locked bedroom door had been kicked in, but after a quick check, nothing appeared to be missing from inside.

There was no sign of the Hellbastards either, who I assumed were out frolicking somewhere, getting up to no good. Clearly, they weren't around when Carlito showed up here, or I would've heard about it.

Closing the busted front door as best I could, I went and sat down on the couch for a minute so I could gather my thoughts. Foremost in my mind was Scarlet, naturally. Carlito would have her in The Brokedown Palace probably strapped to a chair in the middle of the stage. That's how he liked to do it, he told me once, when he had to torture or interrogate somebody. He'd put the person on the stage and shine a spotlight on them. That way, they could hardly see what was coming, which shocked and disorientated them all the more. I also knew that all of Carlito's crew would be there, as would his dead cousin Eduardo's crew, who would be seeking revenge for their boss's death. There would be two dozen guys there at least, all looking for a piece of the great Scarlet Hood, all looking to have their wicked way with her.

I didn't know Scarlet that well—hell, I hardly knew her at all—but I knew her well enough to know that she was one of the good ones and that she didn't deserve the pain she was no doubt getting right now. No one would try to save her.

No one except me that is.

As I stood up to go into the bedroom, my phone rang in my pocket, and I stopped to answer it, seeing from the caller ID that it was Hannah. "Hey," I said. "How's the girl?"

"Fucked up," Hannah said. "As you'd expect. I drove her to Salem Hospital about an hour ago. She's on the verge of giving birth to the hybrid inside her. I'm not sure what the doctors will make of it. Clare said the hybrids look human, but you never know."

"Did you contact the parents yet?"

"Clare asked me not to. She's an adult, what could I say?"

"Contact them," I said. "They have a right to know their daughter is alive."

"Okay, I will."

"What about the cult leader, Gretchen Carmichael? Anything on her?"

"I ran her name through the system," Hannah said. "She's in her early thirties, from a wealthy family. Her father is a hedge fund manager. She was arrested at the age eighteen for cocaine possession, but apart from that and a few speeding tickets, that's it. Her record seems clean."

"Did you get a location for the boarding school?"

"Yes. It's in Charlesburg, just outside the city limits. When do you want to move on it?"

"I don't know," I said. "There's something I gotta do first."

"What is it? Can I help?"

"I don't think so."

She went silent for a second, before asking, "What's wrong, Ethan? Did something happen?"

I was reluctant to tell her anything because I knew she would try to involve herself, and I didn't want her risking herself over something that had nothing to do with her. But I didn't enjoy lying to her either, so I told her what happened to Scarlet. "Carlito has her at his club," I said. "I'm going to get her."

"You're going there alone?"

"I'll take the Hellbastards with me."

"Fuck that," she said. "You're not doing this alone. I'm going with you."

"You know how dangerous this will be?"

"I don't care. Anyway, you forget what I am, Ethan. I don't go down that easily."

"We must remedy that," I joked.

"Seriously," she said. "Are you at your apartment?"

"Yeah."

"Gimme twenty minutes."

"You don't have to do this just for me, you know."

"Of course I do," she said. "Who else am I gonna do it for?"

I smiled as she hung up. I had to give it to her; she was coming along just fine on her journey of redemption, and on becoming a decent human being. I didn't know many others who would join me in such a dangerous endeavor. Even Cal was staying out of it, though that was fine by me. He'd done his fair share of running into dangerous situations over the years. He'd earned his retirement if you could call what he does retirement. Either way, I wasn't about to hold a grudge. I'd rather he stay alive as die trying to back me up.

While I had the phone still in my hand, I found the number for Pan Demic and Artemis and called it. A few seconds later, Artemis answered. "What's up, Drakester? How's the lovely Scarlet doing? Still reeling from the blinding charisma of the two world's best Technomancers?"

"Not exactly," I said. "She's been taken."

"Taken?" Pan Demic was now on the line too. "What do you mean taken? By who?"

"Carlito Martinez took her. I'm going to get her back, but I need your help."

"Anything," they both said at the same time.

"Can you hack the power grid of The Brokedown Palace?"

"Dude," Pan Demic said. "We could do that in our sleep."

"Alright," I said. "Wait for my text. Then cut the power."

"You got it," Artemis said. "And if you need us to come down there, just call."

"Dude," Pan Demic said. "What the fuck?"

"What?" Artemis said. "We have guns, don't we? Plus, it's Scarlet, man, come on. There's nothing I wouldn't do for her."

"You're right, man," Pan Demic said. "Drakester, you want us to lock and load?"

"No, I don't want you to lock and fucking load. Just cut the power when I tell you to," I said. "I'll handle the rest."

Hanging up on the two mooncats, I put the phone in my pocket before contacting Scroteface.

Yes, boss?

I need you back here. We have a mission.

A real one? Like the old days?

Not exactly, but near enough.

Wait till the boys hear. I'm getting hard, boss.

Too much info. Don't be long.

Walking into the bedroom, I took off my trench and my tie before putting on the police issue body armor that I'd swiped from the precinct a few years ago. While it didn't exactly make me bulletproof, it was better than nothing. Back when I was in Blackstar, we wore fully armored suits that protected us not only from bullets but from teeth and claws, mostly anyway. Nothing was invulnerable and a tooth or a claw would often get through. Plus, if a MURK wanted to pull you apart, the suit wouldn't stop it.

With your self-protection—and your survival—the things that will protect you the most are your skills and experience. Without those two things, all the armor in the world will not protect you against something determined to kill you.

Luckily, I was long enough in the tooth that I had an excellent skill-set and bags of experience. I've been a soldier all my life in one way or another, something Carlito in his arrogance has neglected to realize. If he was as ruthless as he wanted everybody to think, he should've killed me when he had the chance. As it was, it would be a decision he would come to regret. I'd make certain of that.

After tightening the body armor around me, I put my trench back on over the top of it. Then I went to a shelf and opened a military-green metal box, inside of which were several grenades of various types. It would be easy to bust the doors of The Brokedown Palace down and toss in a load of frag grenades, blowing the whole place and everyone in it to hell, but that would also include Scarlet, and I couldn't have that. So I selected a few smoke grenades instead and put them into my trench pockets.

Closing the box, I stared at the guns for a minute before selecting a Heckler and Koch MP5K-PDW with folding stock and extended barrel, my go-to submachine gun for any medium scale assault like the one I had planned. From a shelf next to the guns, I took three forty-round magazines and put them into my right trench pocket. Then I took another mag and slid it into the mag well of the MP5K before placing the submachine gun back on the rack for a moment while I exchanged my service pistol for a Heckler and Koch P30L pistol, loading it with a full magazine of 9mm Parabellum rounds, adding two more mags to the holsters on my belt.

Finally, I went to the medicine shelves and got the jar with the Snake Bite in it, emptying no small amount onto the back of my hand before snorting it up, gasping as the stuff kicked my ass straight away, filling my veins with fire.

After putting the jar back, I retrieved the MP5K from the rack and carried it out into the living room just as the Hellbastards came walking through the door. Cracka and Scroteface were still sporting their cat and dog headdresses. Toast still paraded around in his ridiculous Day-Glo outfit like some monster from the eighties. Reggie was now smoking what smelled like a massive joint, and Snot Skull, well, he appeared to have gotten a tattoo of Animal from *The Muppets* on one of his four arms. I didn't even ask.

"What's up, boys?" I said as they all piled in looking excited.

"We get to kill, boss?" Cracka asked. "Scroteface say we get to kill. Do we, boss?"

"Till your little heart is content, Cracka," I told him.

They all cheered. "Fucking A!" Snot Skull shouted.

"When do we leave, boss?" Scroteface asked.

"Just waiting on someone," I said.

"He waiting on the woman," Cracka practically whispered to Reggie, and they both giggled.

"You have something to say, Cracka?" I asked him.

"You horny for the woman, boss," Cracka said. "We know it."

"Do you now?" I said, smiling despite myself, the effects of the Snake Bite making me grind my jaw and widen my eyes as I stared.

"Yeah, boss," Toast said and then began to swivel his hips in a manner that I suppose was meant to be sexy, helped along by his slimy tongue sliding slowly over his rubbery lips. "You luuuuvvve her, don't you, boss?"

My fatal mistake was hesitating before answering, for as soon as I told Snot Skull to fuck off, they all started laughing and jeering, pointing at me like a bunch of idiot school kids. It was at that point that Hannah walked in, and all the Hellbastards went quiet and stared at her.

"Did I interrupt something?" Hannah asked, looking at the Hellbastards, and then at me.

"No, Miss," Cracka said.

Then Scroteface said, "The boss was just saying—"

"Time to move," I said, cutting him off. "Let's go."

"You alright?" Hannah asked me. "You look a bit flushed."

"I'm fine," I said. "Come on. Every minute we stand around here is another minute Scarlet gets tortured."

When everyone was out and moving down the hallway, I did my best to close my busted front door, making a mental note to get it fixed later, if there was a later for me, for you never know with these missions. Something always surprised you, and if you weren't careful, you could get your ticket punched.

With Hannah and the Hellbastards already heading down the stairs, I moved quickly down the hallway myself but stopped on the landing when a familiar voice called my name. I turned around to see Daisy standing there. "Don't you ever sleep?" I said a little too fast, enough that she frowned and looked at me weird.

"Are you going to get Scarlet back from the bad man?"

I nodded. "That's the plan, yeah."

"Okay," she said. "Be careful then."

"I will. Do me a favor and lock your door till I get back."

"I will."

"Good girl." I smiled at her, seeing Callie for a second, then turned and headed down the stairs to find Hannah and the Hellbastards waiting in the hall.

"What's this, a group meeting?" I asked.

"Just waiting on you," Hannah said. "You have the car keys. Also, Cracka just asked me if you and I had, and I quote, made the beast with two backs yet."

A snigger left my mouth; involuntarily, I have to say. "Jesus, Cracka, where do you hear this shit?"

"TV boss," Cracka said.

"We learn everything from TV," Toast added.

Out at the car, I ushered the Hellbastards onto the back seat before closing the door. Then I opened the trunk and put the MP5K inside. I was about to close it when Hannah told me to wait. She went to her blue sedan and opened the back passenger door, leaning in and emerging a second later with a CA-415 rifle. "Where the hell did you get that?" I asked her. "Not from the precinct, anyway."

"The former Hannah owned a lot of weapons," she said. "This is one of them."

"I hope you know how to use that thing."

"We'll see, won't we?"

Once she placed the weapon in the trunk, I closed the lid and started walking to the front of the car, but stopped when I heard a galloping noise behind me, and then a deep, accented voice shouting, "Wait!"

I turned around to see Haedemus galloping down the street like a beast from somebody's nightmare, half the skin on his body decayed so much you could see through to the flesh beneath, and in many parts, the bone. Despite his Hellish appearance, though, there was something almost comical about him as he bounded down the middle of the street toward the car. He was like that friend that everyone has, the one who makes you smile to yourself every time you see him. So I hear anyway. I've never had many friends myself. Friends can be dangerous in my world, and a liability. I steer clear of them, though they don't always steer clear of me. "What are you doing here?" I asked Haedemus as soon as he pulled up.

"I—I—" He snorted a few times as he caught his breath. "I'm going with you to save Scarlet."

"I see. So she strokes you a few times, and now you wanna be her knight in shining armor?"

"Don't be a dick, Ethan. I didn't see you complaining when I was your knight in shining armor at that vampire club."

"That was Hannah."

"Oh, so it's Hannah now?" He looked past me and gave Hannah a look, who was standing by the front passenger door. "Taking your relationship to the next level, are we? Am I sensing a wedding soon?"

Hannah and I both snorted at the same time. "No," I said. "No wedding."

"Oh, that's right," Haedemus said. "You've been there, done that, got the pants."

"It's T-shirt."

"What?"

"Never mind. You can come along."

"Excellent," he said, then bellowed, "Haedemus to save the day!"

"Jesus Christ," I said. "Just follow us, Mighty Mouse."

When I got into the car, the Hellbastards were thrashing around like a bunch of school kids about to go on their first trip. "Pipe down back there," I said, glaring at them in the rear-view. "And don't fuck up my seats."

"Ready to rock?" Hannah asked me, a slight smile on her face like this whole thing was an adventure to her.

"Yeah," I said, starting the engine. "Let's do this."

9

I would've preferred to wait until nightfall before assaulting The Brokedown Palace, but since we obviously couldn't afford to wait that long, an early morning assault it would have to be.

As I drove slowly along the street, I glanced down at the front entrance to the club and saw that the security gate was closed across the front doors, which was as I expected. Carlito wouldn't want anyone interrupting the party inside, even though that's precisely what my motley crew and I were about to do.

I continued driving on up the street, intending to turn into the back alley, but as I did, I saw a guy standing near the corner about ten feet away, holding a submachine gun. When he spotted us, he recognized me immediately, and his eyes widened as he brought up his weapon.

"Shit," I said, reaching across for my gun, but as soon as I did, Haedemus appeared in the alley as if from nowhere, charging at the gunman, the guy unaware that a hell beast was about to put an end to him.

Which Haedemus did, in gruesome fashion, spearing the guy in the side with his razor-sharp horn, lifting him high into the air as the guy screamed, before slamming him down onto the ground. At which point Haedemus used his two front hooves to bust the guy's head open like a melon.

When he was done, Haedemus turned his head to look at me. His lips peeled back into some horsey version of a goofy grin before giving me a triumphant whinny. "Jesus Christ, he's turning into Scooby-Doo."

"Scooby-Doo, where are youuuu," Cracka said from the back seat. "We love Scooby-Doo, boss."

"That's great, Cracka," I said as I turned the car into the alleyway. "Thanks for sharing."

"No problem, boss."

I drove the car down the narrow alley as Haedemus walked on in front, before stopping outside the back entrance of the club where another of Carlito's men lay on the filthy ground, blood pumping from a massive hole in his chest, a submachine gun lying on the ground beside him. A camera mounted above the door also looked down upon him, but I wasn't worried about that. I'd already told Pan Demic and Artemis to disable the exterior cameras on the way here.

Haedemus came around and leaned his head down to look through the passenger side window at us. "I bet you're glad I came now," he said. "Being invisible in this world has its benefits, no?"

"Good job, Haedemus," Hannah said.

"I'll get you a carrot," I said smirking.

Haedemus made a low neighing noise at me. "Piss off, Ethan. You always have to undermine me, don't you? What is it, penis envy or something? Can't handle the fact that my magnificent member dwarfs your puny human cock?"

Hannah laughed. So did the Hellbastards. "He got you there, boss," Scroteface said.

"Mouthy horse is funny sometimes," Cracka said laughing.

I turned and looked at them. "Y'all finished now?"

"You started it, carrot dick," Haedemus said.

That cracked the Hellbastards up even more. Even Hannah put her hand over mouth as if to cover up the fact that she was laughing, though she wasn't doing a very good job of it.

"Fuck the lot of you," I said, smiling despite myself as I got out of the car, opening one of the back doors so the Hellbastards could all pile out as well.

"So how are we going to do this?" Haedemus asked as I popped the trunk and took out my MP5K, putting the strap over my shoulder before handing Hannah her rifle. "I was thinking you guys go in first, and then I run in when you've taken down all the bad guys, and save Scarlet. What do you think?"

Hannah and I looked at each other. "Nice plan, but no," I said. "I already have a plan."

"Of course you do," Haedemus said. "Let's hear it then, Action Man."

"I'm going to use Cracka to scout the place first," I said. "I'll see what he sees, so I'll get an idea of how many are in there. Then I'll have the power cut, and we'll storm the place, taking down anybody that gets in our way, which will be all of them. Cracka?" I turned to see Cracka and the other Hellbastards playing with the dead guy, Reggie blowing dense clouds of marijuana smoke over the guy's face, thinking it was hilarious. "Leave the fucking dead guy alone. Have some discipline for once." The Hellbastards all stopped their laughing and stood to attention. "You wanted a mission like the old days, here it is. Now stop fucking around. Cracka, get your tiny ass over here."

"I'm here, boss," Cracka said as he stood by me.

I pointed to an air vent set into the wall about ten feet up. "You see that vent up there?"

"Yeah."

"Get your ass into it and check out the inside of the club. And keep your mind clear if you can, I need to see through your eyes. You got it?"

"Yeah, boss. Keep mind clear. Got it."

"Off you go."

The little demon jumped to it, using his claws to climb the wall as deftly as a spider, ripping off the cover to the air vent before climbing inside the small hole.

When he was inside, I crouched down and leaned my back against the car before closing my eyes and whispering a few precisely combined syllables that functioned as a gateway into Cracka's mind first of all—which let me tell you, isn't a pretty place, resembling an R-rated episode of *The Muppet Show*...in Hell—before I locked onto his vision.

He was crawling through the air vents, but despite the darkness, he could still see, his sight having a greenish tinge to it like a night vision camera. Soon, he exited one of the air vents and jumped down onto the floor. From his surroundings, I could tell he was in the kitchens, and I told him to go through the door and follow the hallway, turning right down another hall before going through an entry into the main club.

Before he even got there, I could hear the commotion through his sensitive ears. Men cheering and shouting, occasionally erupting into wild applause fueled by bloodlust, like the crowd at a boxing match when one of the fighters lands a damaging blow.

When Cracka made it out into the club, all I saw through his eyes was a sea of bodies covering the whole dance floor. Men with guns in their hands. Men with knives and swords and clubs and even a cattle prod. "Get to the other side," I told Cracka. "Get up high so I can see the stage."

Cracka ran at speed along the edge of the sea of bodies, before finding a foothold in the wall and climbing up toward the ceiling, eventually coming to rest on one of the lighting rigs, ensuring I now had a clear view of the proceedings.

Down below, there must've been two dozen people, most of them men, but a few women as well who sat at a table with drinks in their hands as they enjoyed the show. On the stage, not strapped to a chair as I expected, but hanging naked from a rope bound around her wrists and tied to one of the lighting rigs above her, was Scarlet. Lit up by a spotlight, she looked barely conscious. Her body was covered in blood from head to toe, oozing from multiple cuts and stab wounds. She had lost so much blood it was pooling around her feet. All over the stage were bloody footprints where people had walked in the crimson fluid, tramping it everywhere.

Standing near Scarlet was Carlito, stripped to the waist, wearing only a pair of bloodstained white pants. At the other side of Scarlet stood a man in a dark blue tracksuit, his fingers adorned with gold rings. He was standing facing Scarlet, swaying back and forth like a fighter facing a punching bag. Through Cracka's eyes, I watched as the guy drew back his right hand and then fired it with all his might into Scarlet's face, spraying Carlito with blood as her head snapped around from the sheer force of the blow.

The crowd went silent for a second as Carlito wiped the blood from his face and then licked his hand. A huge cheer erupted, and the guy with the gold rings turned to the crowd and shook his fist at them before getting down off the stage, people slapping him on the back as he made his way toward a table and sat down, lifting a drink as the others at the table congratulated him on a job well done.

"What did you think of that punch, huh, bitch?" Carlito said to Scarlet, taunting her as he leaned his head in close to hers. "Did it hurt? It sure looked like it did." He laughed uproariously, no doubt full of coke—no doubt they all were— until Scarlet somehow found the mettle to spit blood in his face, drawing a gasp of shock from the crowd.

It was at this point that Cracka's vision abruptly shifted, and suddenly I was looking at the face of Miss Piggy, who was bent over naked in front of me as I fucked her doggy-style while Kermit the Frog watched from the shadowy corner of a candlelit room. "Fuck me, Cracka, you naughty little demon," Miss Piggy was saying. "Give it to me, you saucy little bastard—"

"What the fuck, Cracka?" I said. "Keep your fucking mind clear, I said."

"Sorry, boss," Cracka said. "My bad."

I'd seen enough, anyway. "Stay here and wait for us to come in. Once we do, fuck shit up. Do it for Miss Piggy."

"You got it, boss."

When I opened my eyes, everyone was standing around looking at me.

"Well?" Hannah asked as I waited on my eyes adjusting to the light again. "How many are there? Did you see Scarlet?"

"I saw her," I said. "They have her on the stage, hanging from a rope. I'd say there are over twenty guys in there. They're all taking turns having a go at her."

"What state is she in?" Hannah asked.

"She's not good," I said. "Though she still has fight left in her yet. Probably not for much longer, though. We need to move now. Haedemus?"

"Yes, Ethan?" Haedemus said.

"When I tell you to, I want you to kick that door open. Can you do that?"

"Just say the word, Ethan."

I looked down at the Hellbastards. "As for you guys, you know the drill. Once we get in there—"

"Fuck shit up, boss?" Scroteface asked.

"You got it," I said. "Here." I handed them each a smoke grenade. "You go in first and set these off. Got it?"

"We got it, boss."

I took out my phone and sent Pan Demic and Artemis a

text to get ready. After that, I got Haedemus to position himself by the back door, which he did, facing forwards so he could use his back legs to kick the door.

Hannah stood beside me, her demon Visage hovering just behind her, darker than it usually was. "You sure you wanna do this?" I asked her. "I'm not sure this will be good for you. It'll be a lot of violence and bloodshed."

"I can handle it," she said, that amber glow back in her eyes again, a dark smile on her face.

"Maintain control," I reminded her. "If things get too much, get out of there."

"Stop worrying," she said. "I got this."

Nodding, I took out my phone and texted Pan Demic and Artemis to cut the power, quickly putting the phone in my pocket again as I shouldered the MP5K. "Now, Haedemus!"

Haedemus grunted as he kicked out with his back legs, his massive hooves impacting the steel door and taking it right off its hinges, after which he quickly moved to the side to allow the rest of us to pass.

I took the lead as the Hellbastards all scampered past me with the smoke grenades in their hands. Halfway down the long hallway, we could already hear the baying of the crowd inside as everyone likely wondered why their fun had been spoiled by a power cut. If most of them were the soldiers they thought themselves to be, they would know something was up. Carlito would. He had to have known I wouldn't let what he did stand, and that I would come after him to get Scarlet back.

The Hellbastards made it to the door and pushed it open, running inside the dark club to set off the smoke grenades. I waited in the hallway as I aimed my weapon at the door, giving the Hellbastards time to set off the grenades. After ten seconds, I started moving down the hall toward the door, just as someone opened it and entered the hallway, freezing when he saw me. I let off a burst from the MP5K and blasted the guy back through the door, knowing that as soon as I did, it would be on.

The inside of the club was in pitch darkness when we entered, the place filled with heavy smoke now, making visibility impossible for anyone with normal vision. Blinking rapidly three times, I switched to infrared vision, and the room lit up with a sea of orange and red bodies, some standing still, some running around in a panic. Whatever they were doing, it didn't matter.

Hannah and I opened fire on them straight away, cutting down gangsters left and right, staying on the move as those still standing fired blindly back, having nothing but our muzzle flashes to pinpoint our positions with.

The Hellbastards for their part were diving at whoever was closest to them, biting and clawing at flesh, ripping off limbs, even pulling off heads as their bloodlust soon reached peak levels.

Within minutes, the whole place stank of gunpowder and human offal, the floor turning red in my infrared vision as it became awash with blood.

Haedemus got in on the action too, forcing himself through the narrow club entrance before charging at whoever he pleased, using his razor-sharp horn to spear chests and heads, splitting bodies apart as he discarded them with a shake of his head.

Hannah was the biggest surprise. At some point, she had discarded her rifle and was now using telekinetic power to lift people into the air and rip them limb from limb before they even hit the ground again. In the darkness, I could see the amber glow of her eyes burning brightly, and with each person she ripped apart, she did so with an unholy scream straight from fucking Hell.

And once Carlito's crew realized that Hell had come for them and there would be no escape, they started screaming and begging God to come and help them.

But God was nowhere near The Brokedown Palace. Only death was, and there would be no escaping it for any of them.

Inevitably, some of them tried to run out the front and back doors, but the Hellbastards, knowing the score, already had all exits blocked, and anyone who tried to run soon fell into the Hellbastard's clutches where they were slain without mercy, their blood mingling with the crimson lake that passed for a floor.

Despite the shock and awe of this full-on, bloody assault, Carlito held his ground up on the stage, holding his gun to Scarlet's head. He knew we were there for her, and that as long as he didn't move from her, he'd be safe. Safer than the rest of his crew, anyway.

After throwing some guy over my shoulder who tried to grab me from behind, firing off a burst from the MP5K into his face when he hit the ground, I paused for a second to take out my phone, texting quickly to tell Pan Demic and Artemis to hit the lights again.

Before the power came back on, I blinked rapidly three times to return my vision to normal, and a second later, the previously dark club became flooded with light, the spotlight hitting the stage once more to illuminate Carlito standing behind Scarlet, holding onto her with his gun still to her head.

Even *his* defiant face dropped in shock when he saw the extent of the carnage inside his club. Bodies lay everywhere, many of them in various states of dismemberment, some still alive and crawling through the blood as if trying to make their escape.

The Hellbastards, dripping with blood themselves, made sure no one made it out. Same with Haedemus, who went around stomping heads with his massive hooves.

Hannah kneeled in the middle of the dance floor, her hands cupped as she scooped blood from the cavity of a dead guy's stomach, raising her hands in front of her as she allowed the blood to run down over her face. Her demon Visage loomed imposingly behind her, dark wings outstretched, horns spiraling off toward the ceiling. When she opened her eyes to look at me, I saw the full amber glow in them, and the pure darkness that swirled in her irises.

"Hannah," I whispered, knowing there was nothing I could do right now. The torment she suffered in Hell had risen to the surface, turning her mind dark, and she didn't seem to care. She smiled as blood poured down her face and into her mouth.

"The blood is the life," she kept repeating, laughing to herself as if she found this amusing.

It was all I could do to stop myself from going to her to bring her back from the brink if I could, but my priority now had to be Scarlet.

I made my way toward the stage, my MP5K discarded on the floor, the P30L pistol now in my hand as I pointed it in Carlito's direction. I didn't have a shot, however, for he kept moving around Scarlet's suspended body, knowing I wouldn't take the chance in case I hit her.

"What have you done, Ethan?" he roared as he peeked around Scarlet, surveying the devastation before him. "My fucking crew is all dead, you fuck!"

"Step away from her, Carlito," I said as I advanced closer to the stage, trying to find a shot. "It's over. There's no escape for you now. Step away from her."

"Fuck you, Ethan!" he shouted back. "You've done it this time. You're all going to pay dearly now. Mark my words…"

In the blink of an eye, Carlito just seemed to disappear. One second he was there, the next he was gone. "What the fuck?" I said, wondering how he could've just vanished like that.

Despite not knowing what happened, I rushed up onto the

stage. Going to Scarlet, I stood by her for a second. "Scarlet, can you hear me?"

She whispered something back as blood spilled from her mouth, though I couldn't make her out. At least she was still alive, which was a goddamn miracle considering the damage she had taken. "Someone cut this fucking rope!" I shouted.

Within seconds, Scroteface was up on the stage, his whole body dripping with blood. "Got it, boss," he said and then jumped up high, a single swipe of his clawed hand enough to sever the rope. As Scarlet's weight dropped, I held her up and then let her fall over my shoulder before I shouted for Haedemus, who came to the stage, standing sideways to the stage so I could drape Scarlet across his back. She needed a hospital, but given the circumstances, there was no way I could take her to one. I'd have to take her to Larry's instead and hope that he could treat her. If not, then I would call Jacklyn Turner on the off chance that she would want to even help, though I doubted it, given that I couldn't save her son.

As I was about to tell Haedemus to take Scarlet outside, my Infernal Itch flared up suddenly, heat spreading across the back of my neck and shoulders as my tattoos swirled madly beneath my skin. I froze for a second and then spun around to the sound of heavy footsteps, but there was nothing or no one there.

Or so I thought, for a split second later, what felt like a massive fist punched me right on the chest, sending me flying back off the stage where I landed on the blood-soaked floor, skidding across it for a few feet before I came to a stop close to Hannah, who was still on her knees, bathing herself in blood.

Sitting up as I tried to catch my breath, I said, "What the fuck was that?"

As if in answer, a deep, almost monstrous voice answered from the stage. A voice that I still recognized, despite the drop in pitch. "You're not going anywhere, Ethan," the voice boomed. "None of you are."

"Carlito?" I said in surprise.

On the stage, under the spotlight, there was a kind of shimmering effect for a moment, and then a figure appeared out of nowhere. It was a towering, heavyset figure covered with thick slabs of dense muscle and reddish-brown skin. The creature had massive clubbed feet and hands the size of shovels that were balled into fists. As my eyes moved up the creature's body to its face, I realized with utter surprise that the beast was Carlito. It still had his face, though with massive ears like a rodent, a huge wrinkled nose and a wide mouth full of pointed teeth. "That's right," he growled. "It's me, Ethan."

"What the fuck are you?" I asked him, wondering how the hell I never knew Carlito had this monster inside him. Why hadn't my Infernal Itch detected this MURK before?

"Back in Cuba," he said, "my mother used to tell me about a creature called a chichiricu. My brother and I thought she made it up, to keep us away from the rivers and deep lakes. We were wrong..."

"Great," Haedemus said, backing away from the stage. "Now we have a Cuban lycanthrope to contend with. Quick, someone hand him a cigar, it might shut him up."

"Insolent hell beast!" Carlito growled, and dived off the stage at tremendous speed, landing a punch to Haedemus' jaw on the way down, which was enough to send Haedemus toppling over. As he fell, so too did Scarlet, and she would've been crushed by the Hellicorn's weight had something not kept her hanging in the air as Haedemus hit the deck.

I turned my head to see Hannah still on her knees, but with one hand out as she used her telekinetic power to hold Scarlet up for another second before slowly moving her across and setting her prone body down on the stage. After nodding my thanks to her, I turned to look at Carlito again, but he seemed to have turned himself invisible once more.

"You're all going to die in here!" he called out from across the other side of the dance floor. "I will crush every one of your skulls!"

The Hellbastards were running around crazily looking for Carlito in his beast form, sniffing at the air and floor as if trying to trek his movements, and it wasn't long before they found him, launching themselves at his invisible form as they gripped onto him.

Carlito cried out as the demons began to bite and tear at his skin, becoming visible once more as he ripped the Hellbastards off him one by one like irritating ticks, launching them with his powerful arms so the Hellbastards went flying across the dance floor, wailing as they went until they bounced off tables and walls before finally landing on the floor among the piles of bodies. They didn't seem to be too hurt, but they were wary about attacking again, choosing now to keep their distance.

With Carlito occupied with the Hellbastards, I jumped to my feet and started shooting at him, squeezing off several shots before he cried out with pain and turned invisible again. Ejecting the magazine from the pistol, I dug out a full one from my trench pocket and reloaded, keeping the gun out in front of me as I turned to look for Carlito again.

"You'll have to do better than that, Ethan," Carlito said, sounding like he was off to the left now, which is the direction I swung my pistol as I advanced, stepping over bodies as I did so.

Hannah was on her feet by this point, turning slowly as she appeared to look for the beast that was Carlito. For a moment, I made eye contact with her and hardly recognized her at all. Her eyes were glowing nearly full amber, and her face—dripping with blood—seemed to have distorted into something barely human. I also noticed her hands had become claws, and her skin had darkened a good deal, something I hadn't seen before with her.

There was a pregnant silence inside the club for a long

moment, until the sound of heavy footsteps made me turn around, and I saw the bodies on the floor get crushed under invisible feet. Instinctively, I extended my weapon and started firing, but the footsteps kept coming, and the next thing I knew, I was being grabbed around the throat and lifted off my feet.

Still with the gun in my hand, I kept firing downward, eliciting a scream of pain from the beast holding me before it swiped the gun from my hand and squeezed my neck even harder. The Hellbastards rushed in again, attacking en masse as they viciously punched, kicked, bit and clawed at the creature. If it weren't for them, Carlito would've broken my neck.

As it was, they forced him to drop me as he tried to get the Hellbastards off him once more. "Fucking stinking demons!" he roared as his form became visible again.

As I lay choking, I saw Carlito grab hold of Snot Skull and rip off one of the demon's four arms before flinging the screaming Hellbastard away from him. He tried to do the same with Cracka, but Cracka was too fast and agile, and while Carlito tried to catch Cracka as he danced across his back, Toast unleashed a blast of fire into Carlito's face, causing Carlito to scream and clamp his huge hands over himself to put out the flames.

Within seconds, the smell of burned flesh co-mingled with the stench of blood and human offal inside the club.

Meanwhile, Scroteface clung to Carlito's back as he continually punched the back of Carlito's head, who turned himself invisible again in defense, but it was too late by then.

Snot Skull, never one to stay down for too long, came rushing back again, more pissed off than ever now that he was an arm short. As Carlito staggered back, his invisibility glitching until he was fully visible again, Snot Skull shouted, "Fucking bastard!" and jumped onto Carlito's leg, gripping his thigh before unleashing a stream of acid vomit that slapped down onto Carlito's foot.

Carlito roared in pain as the acid melted the flesh and bone of his foot, but he was still somehow able to stay upright, and using one of his fists, he knocked Snot Skull off his leg.

That's when Haedemus came charging at him from behind and speared Carlito through the back, the Hellicorn's horn bursting from Carlito's chest. As Carlito screamed, Haedemus started jerking his head upward as if he was trying to saw Carlito in half.

"No one sucker punches this pretty mouth and gets away with it!" Haedemus snarled, as angry as I've ever seen him. "I lost another tooth because of you. Teeth don't grow on fucking trees, you know!"

When Haedemus finally slid his horn out of Carlito's back, Carlito toppled over onto the floor, Scroteface and Cracka still clinging to him as he fell onto the bleeding bodies of his crew. He could only lie there, groaning in pain and defeat, most of his right foot now melted off, a massive gash in his chest that leaked dark blood.

To humiliate him further, both Cracka and Scroteface stood over Carlito with their cocks in their hands and pissed their acidic urine all over his face. Carlito tried to move his head away, but couldn't, much to the Hellbastard's amusement. "Eat piss," Cracka said, laughing.

"Agghhhh," Carlito cried, his voice gargled from his chest wound. "You...fucking—"

"Shut up," Scroteface said as he directed his stream into Carlito's mouth, making Carlito choke and gag, which only further amused the Hellbastards.

"Oh-oh, I know," Haedemus said, sounding like he was enjoying himself now. "I could cum all over his face. No wait that might take too long. I know..."

Haedemus turned around and backed himself over the top of Carlito, who was shifting back into his human form again. As he did so, Haedemus unleashed a stream of stinking excrement from his rear end; excrement that was nothing like the grassy nuggets a horse would make. No, this was the half-digested remains of Haedemus' last meal—a stinking stew of human flesh and bone that spilled down onto Carlito's face like so much raw sewage. It was so vile, I had to cover my mouth against the smell, though it didn't seem to bother the Hellbastards, who rolled around the bloody floor in fits of hilarity like it was the funniest thing they had ever seen.

"You crazy horse!" Cracka shouted.

"Ahh, that's better," Haedemus said when he was done. "Now who wants to wipe my ass for me?"

Carlito was fucked by this point: covered in blood, shit and his own vomit, though he still managed to say defiantly, "Fuck…you…all."

"Alright," I said, standing up. "He's done. Did everyone forget about Scarlet?" She still lay on the stage, unmoving, hopefully not dead.

"We're not done yet."

Everyone turned to see Hannah standing there, glowing eyes staring at us. She thrust out a hand and used her telekinesis to lift Carlito off the ground, so he hung in the air, shit and blood dripping down his naked body. "His soul still needs condemning to Hell."

As Hannah—or Xaglath at this point—began to speak in Hellion in a low, deep voice, the floor beneath Carlito soon cracked open and pulled apart to reveal a fiery pit that even the Hellbastard's jumped back from in fear. As I chanced a glance down into the hole which radiated an intense heat and sulfurous fumes, my blood turned cold as I realized I was looking into Hell itself.

Carlito must've realized this also, for he soon started screaming, begging not to be dropped into the fiery hole. But Xaglath, with a sneer on her lips, moved her arm down and Carlito fell screaming into the burning pit, never to be heard from again.

As Xaglath smiled with satisfaction and the rest of us

stood with disturbed looks on our faces, the hole in the floor closed up, much to everyone's relief.

"My goodness," Haedemus said as he looked around at us. "I feel ten pounds lighter after that. Nothing like a good shit, is there?"

10

By the time I bundled Scarlet into the back of my car, I was hardly sure if she was alive or dead. Putting my fingers to her neck, I felt a faint pulse, indicating she was at least alive. But she had lost a lot of blood—pints of the stuff—and I wasn't sure how much longer she'd be able to hold on.

Playing on my mind also was the fact that The Brokedown Palace had over two dozen dead bodies lying inside it, though Hannah—or rather Xaglath—said she would take care of them. "There's plenty of room in Hell for them all," she said with an evil smile that, frankly, freaked me the fuck out. Even the Hellbastards couldn't wait to get away from here, just in case she ended up sending them back to Hell too, which for the Hellbastards, was the worst thing you could do to them, given how attached they'd become to living here on Earth.

The only one who stayed with her was Haedemus, and probably only because he felt peckish after all the activity and excitement, and because his belly now had room after he had emptied the contents of his rotten bowels over Carlito's face earlier, which I still couldn't believe he did. I swear, I think sometimes I've surrounded myself with a bunch of fucking degenerates.

Driving as fast as I could through the early afternoon traffic, I soon made it to The Tattomb without incident. Grabbing Scarlet from the back seat, I kicked the door of the parlor open, scaring the shit out of Larry, who was busy smoking a cigarette as he stared at a paperback, the room empty of customers.

Which was just as well, for if anyone had seen me standing there with a blood-soaked naked woman in my arms, they probably would've shit themselves.

Larry's cigarette nearly fell from his mouth when he saw the state Scarlet was in. "Jesus Christ, Ethan," he said. "I know I told you not to leave it so long next time, but this is fucking ridiculous, son."

"I got nowhere else to go," I said. "Get your shit together."

"Ethan, that girl needs a hospital, not—"

"Just fucking do it, Larry!" I barked as I carried Scarlet into the back room and placed her on the cushioned gurney. Everywhere I looked on her, she was bleeding from some wound or other. *Christ*, I thought, *if she makes it, it'll be a fucking miracle.*

When Larry started examining Scarlet, he just shook his head at the damage done do her. "Ethan," he said. "This is bad. Very fucking bad. I don't think I can fix her."

"Fuck's sake, Larry," I said. "You used to be an ER doctor. I'm sure you've seen worse."

"Maybe so, but in a hospital, I'd have what I needed. Proper equipment, people to assist me." He shook his head. "This girl needs blood and lots of it. And that's just for starters."

"Tell me what you need. I'll get it."

"I just told you. She needs a hospital."

I glanced at Scarlet laying there on the gurney, unconscious, looking like fucking roadkill. Then I shook my head and took out my phone, calling Jacklyn Turner on her cell number, which I'd kept from the last time she phoned me. She'd no doubt be home alone, mourning the death of her only son. As soon as she realized it was me calling, she'd probably tell me to go fuck myself. But I was out of options. Scarlet's injuries were beyond a few simple procedures and a bit of homemade medicine. She needed extensive treatment that only a hospital could provide, or at the very least, a good surgeon with access to the right equipment. "Do what you can for her," I said to Larry as I waited on Jacklyn Turner picking up. "Try to make her stable."

"I'll do my best, Ethan," Larry said, his gloves already on as he examined Scarlet's body.

"Hello?" a voice said down the phone.

"Ms. Turner," I said, turning away from Larry. "It's Detective Ethan Drake here."

"What the hell do you want?" She sounded drunk, depressed. Bitter.

"I need your help, Ms. Turner."

She snorted down the phone. "My help? I asked *you* for help, Detective. Help in saving my son. And you let him die."

"I did everything I could to save your son," I said, doubting my own credibility at the same time.

"Did you, Detective? Did you really?"

I paused before answering. "Yes. I'm sorry, Ms. Turner. Unfortunately, we can't always save the ones we love."

I heard her sniffling down the phone as she lapsed into silence for a long moment. It was tempting to push her out of it, but I resisted the urge and allowed her to have her moment. "What is it you want, Detective?" she asked finally, a note of tired resignation in her voice now. It was a feeling I knew well.

"I have someone here who will die if she doesn't get urgent medical attention," I said.

"And I'm assuming since you called me—a woman you hardly know—that you cannot take this person to a hospital?"

"That's right."

"Does this have anything to do with that…*darkness* my son was involved in."

"Yes, it does."

She went silent for a second, then asked, "What are her injuries?"

I turned to look at Scarlet as Larry was tending to her. "Multiple stab wounds," I said. "A lot of blunt force trauma, extensive bruising, probably internal bleeding. Gunshot on one arm. Burn marks. Fractured ribs. That's just what I can see."

"I'm sorry, Detective, but that person needs a hospital," Jacklyn said. "Even if I wanted to help you, I couldn't."

"Jacklyn," I said. "Please. She'll die."

Again, she went silent for a moment. "Alright, look. There's a doctor in Wilshire General who'll probably treat her, but you'll have to pay him. A lot."

"Fine. Who is he?"

"I'll arrange it. Just get her to Wilshire."

"Thank you."

"I'm not doing this for you, Detective."

"That's fine," I said. "But at least tell me how you know about this doctor, and why you haven't reported him."

"My son wasn't the only one with secrets, Detective. Get your friend to Wilshire. Park around the back of the disused wing. The doctor will meet you there."

"Thanks, Jacklyn. I'll owe you for this."

"You already owed me, Detective," she said before hanging up.

I DROVE AS FAST I COULD TO WILSHIRE GENERAL WITH Scarlet lying across the back seat, Larry in there with her keeping her steady and doing his best to stem the blood flow from her various open wounds.

As instructed by Jacklyn Turner, I drove around the back of the disused wing of the hospital, a wing that was shut down five years ago because of underfunding. In the small parking area, a red-headed man in blue surgical scrubs stood alongside a dark-haired woman, who also wore scrubs. Beside them was a gurney.

When I pulled up, the two of them immediately came to the car and opened the back doors, ordering Larry out. The red-headed man then leaned into the car and briefly checked Scarlet over before asking me to get her out and onto the gurney. The whole thing was a blur as I slid Scarlet out of the car and placed her on the gurney, at which point the man and woman in surgical scrubs rushed Scarlet inside the disused hospital wing.

"What the fuck?" Larry said as he looked at the dilapidated building with its grimy, broken windows.

"You should go, Larry," I said. "Thanks for your help. I owe you."

"You sure you don't want me to stick around and make sure those two strangers know what they're doing?"

For whatever reason, I trusted Jacklyn Turner. "It's fine, Larry. I'll make sure you're paid as soon as I can."

"Don't worry about it," he said. "Just let me know if she pulls through."

"She will."

Larry nodded but said nothing as he walked away.

I THOUGHT I'D SEEN IT ALL IN THIS CITY UNTIL I WALKED INTO the empty hospital wing—which was like a setting from a bad horror movie, dark and rat-infested—to find that one of the old rooms had had a makeover at some point, turning it into a fully equipped operating theater.

Scarlet now lay on an operating table surrounded by state-of-the-art machines and gleaming trays filled with shining surgical tools. The red-headed man seemed to take the lead as the doctor, with the dark-haired woman assisting him. Both seemed highly capable and experienced, I'm glad to say, and soon they had Scarlet hooked up to various drips and machines. She seemed to get the same care and attention here in this grimy shit hole as she would've gotten in Salem Hospital. It said a lot about Wilshire's continual decline as an institution that this unsanctioned operation was going on within its walls, albeit walls that were no longer in use, except it seemed, by these two otherwise normal medical professionals.

I stood outside in the dark hallway looking through the glass in the door as I thought about entering the room. But I decided against it, knowing my presence wouldn't be welcome. Scarlet's life was out of my hands now. It was up to the doctors to try to fix her, and they didn't need me hanging around distracting them.

So I found an old plastic chair in the dank hallway and sat down, rummaging inside my trench until I found the small hip flask there, which I'm glad to say was full. After taking a swig, I took out my phone and called Hannah's phone, but there was no answer, and the call soon went to voicemail. The same thing happened the second and third time I called her. After the third time, I knew she wasn't going to answer, so I stopped trying after that. I'd seen the way she was back at The Brokedown Palace. I'd seen *who* she was—Xaglath, the demon she had become after her fall to Hell. My worry now was that Hannah had slipped irrevocably back into being the demon she used to be. Despite telling me she could handle it, the violence and bloodshed at the club had drawn Xaglath out of her again. If Hannah wasn't answering her phone, it was probably because Xaglath was still in control.

The real question was: what was she going to do with that control now that she had it?

It didn't take me long to drink all the whiskey in the hip

flask, so once it was gone, I took out the Mud bottle and deposited two full doses into my mouth. My extreme tiredness, combined with the drugs and alcohol in my system, soon made everything around me take on a surreal, nightmarish quality as I continued to sit in the dark hallway, the only real light being the glow from the lights inside the operating theater where the doctors continued to work on Scarlet.

Sitting with my eyes half-closed, the dirty walls around me seemed to move with the shadows cast across them, the floor beneath my feet undulating in a way that made it feel like I was in the belly of some beast.

My eyes closed for an indeterminate amount of time, and when I opened them again, the shadows all seemed to have gathered in one spot in the dark corridor, coming together into some shapeless form that could have been a distillation of death itself, an entity created from the souls of everyone I'd ever killed, gathered together so they could stand there in common judgment of me.

My only defense against it was to close my eyes so I could no longer see it, but even as sleep pulled me down into its embrace, there was no escaping the nightmarish visions that came rushing out of my subconscious like waiting demons. In my dreams, they taunted me with visions of my dead daughter as she stood before me with her guts hanging out, soon joined by her mother, who stood with half her face in bloody tatters, though I could still make out the look of blame and hatred on her disfigured features.

"It should've been you," they said, over and over. "It should've been you…"

"I know," I said. "I know. I'm sorry…"

My wife and daughter, they came together then, twisting themselves into some monster that rushed toward me to slash at me with its claws. Screaming, I tried to defend myself, even though I knew I deserved every ounce of the monster's terrible wrath…

"Hey, buddy."

I snapped my eyes open and almost went for the figure standing before me, who stepped back away from me in fear. It was the red-headed doctor, his blue scrubs now streaked with blood as a surgical mask hung around his neck. I stared at him, wide-eyed, as I regained my bearings and caught my breath. "What?" I said.

The doctor regarded me warily as he spoke. "Your friend is in stable condition," he said. "We patched her up as best we could. She still has internal damage, but she should live."

I nodded as I wiped sweat from my face. "Thanks, Doc."

"No need to thank me." He handed me a piece of paper. "Just make sure the bill is paid. I expect the money in the account within twenty-four hours. If you don't pay up, there'll be severe consequences for both you and your friend. You understand?"

"Nice bedside manner, Doc."

"You wanted that, you should've gone to Salem," he said. "Your friend can stay here for another six hours tops until she regains consciousness. After that, you'll have to take her elsewhere."

"Sure thing. Thanks, Doc."

Nodding, the doctor walked back into the theater again, leaving me to wonder how I would pay the five-figure sum written on the piece of paper he'd given me.

11

I didn't know where else to take Scarlet after her six hours were up at the hospital, so I ended up taking her to my trailer at Cal's scrapyard. She was barely conscious when I carried her out of the disused hospital wing—her wearing only a hospital gown—and helped her into the back seat of the Dodge. She groaned her sister's name a few times on the way to the scrapyard, but apart from that, she said little else.

When I got to the yard, I carried her into the trailer and lay her down on the single bed. Her face was a swollen mess, and her body was covered in bandages, but at least she was alive, and as far as I could tell, in recovery. The doc told me she would need aftercare in the form of fluids and lots of rest. Medicinally, there were things I could do to help speed her recovery. I could apply ointment to her wounds to help them heal faster, and I could give her specific tinctures and home-brewed medicines to help with her internal injuries.

When I was sure she was comfortable, I left to get the supplies I needed from Cal, but as I did, Scarlet grabbed my hand, her grip still weak, though stronger than I expected. "Ethan…" she whispered.

I leaned over and put my face close to hers. She smelled like iodine. "Yeah?" I said.

She could barely open her eyes enough to see me, and her voice was faint. "Thank...you..."

I smiled down at her. "That's okay. Just rest now and get better."

"Charlotte?" she whispered.

"We'll find her. Don't worry."

She barely nodded before closing her eyes again. "Find her...Ethan."

I left Scarlet and went to find Cal, thinking he would be in his trailer, which he wasn't. So after checking the smithy and not finding him there either, I went to the only other place where I thought he could be, and that was his underground bunker behind his trailer.

Finding the steel doors unlocked, I pulled them open and walked down the steps to the bunker which was just four large shipping containers buried underground, the inside walls cut out to create one massive space. This is where Cal kept his vast library of books, organized in rows of free-standing shelves that collectively hold thousands of tomes. Cal also had an armory and an apothecary down there.

As I weaved my way through the bookshelves to the open space on the other side, I wasn't surprised to find Cal sitting behind a large antique reading table, his eyeglasses on as he peered into some dusty book.

Who I *was* surprised to see, however, was Daisy, who was sitting on the opposite side of the desk with a dusty tome of her own. Cal noticed me first, looking up and staring at me for a second before saying with a smile, "Well, look what the cat dragged in."

When Daisy turned her head and saw it was me, a broad smile crossed her face, and she got up and came to me, taking me by surprise by hugging me. "You're alright," she said, ignoring the fact that my clothes were covered in blood. "Where's Scarlet? Is she okay? Did you save her?"

"Scarlet's in my trailer," I said. "She's in bad shape, but she'll be okay."

"Oh," Daisy said. "How hurt is she?"

"Enough," I said. "What are you even doing here? *How* did you get here?"

"I got worried when you didn't come back to the apartment building," she said. "So I got a cab here to Cal's to see if he'd heard anything."

"Well, you don't have to worry," I said smiling at her, flattered as hell by her concern, but also worried that she was being drawn into my world, and we all know what happens when people get drawn into my world—they get hurt.

"Are you injured?" she asked. "You're covered in blood."

"It's not mine."

"You got it done then?" Cal asked, taking off his eyeglasses.

I nodded. "It wasn't pretty, but yeah, we got it done."

"We?" he said.

"My partner, the Hellbast—" I stopped and looked at Daisy, almost forgetting that she was still an Unaware.

"The Hell what?" she said.

"Nothing," I said. "Don't worry about it."

"I'm not stupid, Ethan," Daisy said as she went back to sit at the reading table.

"I didn't say you were," I said.

"I've heard the noises from your apartment. I've heard you talking in there."

"You've been listening outside my door?"

"Not all the time," she said. "Just sometimes."

I looked at Cal, who was sitting with a knowing smile on his face. "Like she said, she ain't stupid."

"I've noticed things," Daisy went on. "Strange things that made little sense before, but now they do."

"You mean now that Cal has brought you down here," I said, throwing Cal a disapproving look.

"Yes," she said. "Coming here has filled in the blanks. Plus, Cal explained to me what's going on."

"Did he now? That's idiotic of Cal to do so."

"Don't be mad at Cal," Daisy said. "I already knew there were monsters in the world from all the books I read. All those writers had to get their inspiration from somewhere, right? Cal tells me you call the monsters MURKs." She looked at Cal. "What does that stand for again?"

"Monsters, Unnaturals, Reapers, and Killers," I said, leaving out the Kunts part. "You don't seem put out by any of this, Daisy."

"Were you when you found out?" she asked.

"Not really, if I'm honest. It fit my view of the world."

"Exactly," Daisy said nodding as if she just realized this to be true herself, which given her life and the upbringing—or lack thereof—that she'd had, it was no surprise that she would grasp this new form of dark enlightenment with both hands. The fact that there were monsters in the world—and a form-less Darkness behind everything—no doubt explained a lot to her. I felt sorry for her, though, for this knowledge she now possessed was a burden, and one she would have to shoulder for the rest of her life, even as most of the world remained blind and ignorant to it.

"Anyway," I said, moving now toward the corner of the room dedicated to the apothecary. "There's stuff I need to get for Scarlet."

"Can I help?" Daisy asked, getting up to join me as I stood staring at the rows of shelves containing scores of medicinal ingredients and ad hoc medical supplies.

"You can grab that IV stand over there," I said as I took a bag of saline solution from a shelf, a jar of ointment and some bottles of medicine.

"I can be Scarlet's nurse if you like," Daisy said. "I look after my momma all the time."

"I'm sure you do," I said.

"You don't like my momma, do you, Ethan?"

"Like has nothing to do with it," I said as I turned away from the shelves armed with supplies. "You deserve better, that's all."

"She's good sometimes," Daisy said. "Like for my last birthday, she took me to see the *Avengers* movie. She left halfway through and didn't come back, but you know——" She shrugged as if this was normal behavior on her mother's part. "She tries."

Not hard enough, I wanted to say, but didn't. What was the point? It wouldn't change anything.

"Here," Cal said, handing Daisy a thick leather-bound book. "You can continue your education while you sit with the assassin."

"Scarlet is an assassin?" Daisy looked delighted by this news as she took the book. "That's *so* cool."

I shook my head at Cal. "Me and you need to have words later," I told him.

"Yeah yeah," he said. "You're not the only one who needs guidance, you know."

"I'm not sure Daisy needs the kind of guidance that you or I can offer," I said.

"Let me be the judge of that," Daisy said, book under one arm as she held the IV stand in her other hand.

"Let the girl be the judge," Cal said with a smile.

"You're enjoying this," I said. "You think you have someone else to mold." I looked at Daisy. "Don't fall for his grizzled charm. It's all a sham to get you to trust him, and then he'll try to break you."

"Break me?" Daisy said, looking slightly worried now.

"He's kidding," Cal said, knowing full well that I wasn't. "I'm too long in the tooth now to be breaking anyone. Just think of me as the wise old owl you can come to for guidance and advice."

"Fucking hawk more like," I muttered.

"Don't curse in front of the kid," Cal said. "You're setting a bad example."

"Right, well, I'll leave setting the bad example to you then," I said.

"God, you two are like an old married couple or something," Daisy said. "Can we tend to Scarlet now? I want to ask her about all her kills when she wakes up."

"Her kills?" I shook my head. "God, I've created a friggin' monster."

When we got to my trailer, Scarlet was still out of it on the bed. "Poor thing," Daisy said as she took in Scarlet's injuries. "Those bastards."

"Yep," I said as I hooked Scarlet up to a saline drip.

"I hope you killed them all. Especially the one who held a gun to my head. What happened to him?"

"Believe me," I said. "He won't be bothering anyone ever again, at least not in this world."

"So he's dead?"

"Worse."

"What's worse than dead? Has he gone to Hell or something?" She laughed a little at this but stopped laughing when I looked at her. "Oh shit, he has, hasn't he?"

"Don't worry about it," I said, handing her the ointment. "Do you think you can put this stuff on her wounds and reapply the bandages?"

Daisy nodded. "Sure."

"If she wakes up, give her some of this medicine. I'll leave it on the table here."

"Where are you going?"

"Home to sort myself out, and then into work. I got stuff to do. Are you okay to stay here for a while?"

Daisy nodded like she was happy to stay. "Sure. My momma thinks I'm at school, anyway."

"Won't you get in trouble for not being there?"

"In school?" She made a snorting noise. "I'm like a ghost in that place. Hardly anyone will notice I'm not there, and the ones who do won't care."

"What about your teachers?"

"That's who I'm talking about."

I shook my head and then stared at her a minute as she began to carefully peel back a bandage on Scarlet's stomach and then apply a little of the ointment over the sutures. Daisy was a good girl, I had to admit. Considering what she had to contend with at home, she seemed to be remarkably well balanced, though I didn't doubt she had her insecurities like the rest of us. How could she not with a mother like hers?

Although, at least she had a mother. Mine was dead by the time I was five, and in the time before that, my mother was away more than she was at home. The crazy thing was, I never stopped loving her. I mean, she was my mother, right? No matter what they do, you still love them. Same with kids, you always love them…even when they're dead. Especially when they're dead.

"I appreciate your help, Daisy," I said. "You're a good girl."

Daisy smiled, a little embarrassed, but also pleased by what I'd said. I guess she didn't hear compliments often. "Thank you, Ethan," she said.

I left Daisy with Scarlet and told her I'd come by later and take her home, even though she seemed happy enough not to go back home at all. She had a purpose, and she felt useful, a feeling she didn't want to give up. And I had to admit, I enjoyed having her around, despite the danger involved for her. I mean, if it was Callie, would I want her involved in this life; this life of darkness, and murder and mayhem and sorrow? Maybe, maybe not. People do what they want to do, and no one else can stop them. I certainly did. So does Daisy. Probably Callie would've too. I mean, look who her dad is.

When I got back to the apartment, the Hellbastards were there, crowded onto the couch, drained it seemed as they watched *Dinosaurs*, an old puppet show from the nineties. "Hey, boss," they said, one by one, hardly looking at me.

"Tired, boys?" I asked them.

"Yeah," Scroteface said, his tabby cat headdress gone now, which he must've lost in the melee at The Brokedown Palace.

"How Miss Scarlet?" Cracka asked. He seemed to have held onto his Chihuahua headdress, although the two front legs had been ripped off.

"She's okay," I told him. "She'll live."

Cracka smiled as much as a demon with a mouth like his could smile. "Yayyyy," he said in a little voice that could almost have been cute if it wasn't for the rest of him.

"Mission accomplished," Snot Skull said.

"Sorry about your arm, Snot Skull," I said.

"It'll grow back," he said.

"Right," I said. "That's good."

"We had fun earlier, boss," Scroteface said. "When's the next bloodbath?"

"I'll let you know," I said. "What about Hannah? Has anyone seen her?"

"We left her there," Reggie said, puffing on a joint. "She said to tell you something, though."

"What did she say?" I asked.

"She said to tell you she was going to take care of some old business," Scroteface said.

"We didn't hang around, boss," Toast said. "She was opening portals to Hell."

"Fuck that noise," Reggie said.

"She scary bitch," Cracka said, then looked at me. "Sorry, boss."

"It's okay, Cracka," I said, knowing he wasn't wrong. "What about Haedemus?"

"Mouthy horse stay with her," Cracka said and then tittered to himself. "He shit on that man's head."

All the Hellbastards let out a snigger without taking their eyes off the TV.

"I'm glad you had fun, boys," I said. "Enjoy your program. You earned it."

I left them to it, heading into the bedroom to strip off my clothes, which were covered in blood. "Another trench ruined," I sighed as I dumped it in the corner of the room.

12

On the way to the precinct, I stopped at a thrift store and found a dark trench that fit me, even if it was well-worn. Not being the height of style at the best of times, I didn't mind a little scruffiness.

As I left the store, the heavens opened, and rain started drenching the city once more, making me glad I had a new coat. Inside the car, I tried calling Hannah's phone again, but it was going straight to voicemail, so I texted her instead:

WHATEVER YOU'RE THINKING OF DOING
DON'T!

Going by what the Hellbastards had told me, I suspected that Hannah's demon personage would go after one of the Yakuza members who had wronged her. I hoped that wasn't the case, for if she were, she'd be opening up a whole can of worms and things would undoubtedly get bloody down the line. They always did. Not that there was much I could do about it now. I just had to hope Hannah gained back control from the demon before she did anything foolish.

When I got to the precinct, the officer at the front desk said the captain had left a message for me to see him as soon as I got in. Thanking the officer, I sighed and went straight to Captain Edwards' office, finding him in when I got there. "Drake," he said when I knocked on the door and opened it. "Come in. Sit down."

"You wanted to see me, sir?" I asked, wondering what this was about.

Edwards huffed slightly as he sat staring at me with his hands on his desk. "A while ago a report came in of heavy gunfire at a blues club downtown, a place called The Brokedown Palace. Do you know where that is?"

I nodded. "Of course."

"I know you do because you were seen near it just before the gunfire was heard."

"I don't think so, sir," I said, wishing I'd taken a dose of Mud before I came in here. "I've been out investigating a case with my partner all day. The pregnant girl that came in here last night?"

"Yes, I heard. Some crazy cult chick."

"There's more to it than that, sir."

"Yeah, there always is with you, Drake."

"Meaning...sir?"

"Meaning, I don't like how you and your partner swan around this place doing whatever the fuck you like, with no oversight."

This again. Fucking hell. "You mean without *your* oversight."

Edwards leaned forward. "This is my precinct, Drake. Don't fuck with me."

"I'm not, sir," I said. "I'm just doing the job assigned to me by the commissioner."

"Did he assign you to The Brokedown Palace?"

"No, sir. I wasn't near there. What's supposed to have happened?"

"Nothing, that's just it," he said. "We had multiple reports from ear witnesses saying it sounded like World War Three was going on there. Funny thing is, when a patrol car went to check it out, they found nada."

I shrugged. "Maybe the music was too loud."

Edwards glowered like he wanted to jump across his desk and strangle me. "Couple of dealers nearby saw you drive into the alley behind the club around the time of the gunfire. What were you doing there, Drake, and what the hell happened? There's evidence all over the club that something big and bloody went down, but there's not a single body anywhere. No owner, nothing."

"Weird," I said. "Sounds like an investigation for my unit."

Edwards shook his head as I stared at him straight-faced. "You used to be a good cop, Drake."

"I still am, sir."

"Maybe, but you're also a loose cannon," he said. "I can't have loose cannons running around my precinct."

"Look, sir," I said. "I'm saying this with the utmost respect, but you need to accept how things are and just let me and my unit get on with it."

"On with what?" he barked. "Doing whatever the fuck you like?"

"With saving fucking lives!" I shouted, shooting forward in my chair. "With dealing with the shit that no one else here wants to deal with! I gave you fucking ten years of service, Edwards. I think I've earned the right to be left alone to get on with my fucking job, and if you have a problem with that, take it up with the commissioner. In the meantime, stay out of my fucking way and let me do my job." I got up out of my chair and stomped to the door.

"Your days are numbered here, Drake!" the captain shouted after me as I walked out the door. "Nobody talks to me the way you just did and gets away with it. Nobody!"

～

A WHILE LATER, AS I SAT AT MY DESK IN THE SUBBASEMENT, I wasn't surprised to get a phone call from Commissioner Lewellyn. "Hello?" I said as I sat with my feet on my desk.

"Ethan," Lewellyn said. "What the hell are you playing at, winding Captain Edwards up like that? He wants your badge."

"I'm sure he does, sir."

"This isn't a joke, Ethan. He's petitioning to have you thrown off the force."

"On what grounds?"

"Insubordination."

"He's just puffing his chest out. He'll calm down."

"You better hope he does. There's only so much protection I can give you."

"I know, sir," I said, nodding to myself.

"Anyway, on a more positive note, I'm happy with the work you and Walker have been doing," he said. "You're stopping some dangerous people."

"That was the whole idea. Anything else, sir?" I said, taking my hip flask out and opening it. "I'm in the middle of something important here."

"Yes, there is, actually," he said. "That guy from Blackstar called again, Eric Pike."

I rolled my eyes. "What did he want?"

"He seems to have heard about this latest case you're investigating, the one involving the pregnant girl."

"What about it?" I asked, taking a swig from the hip flask.

"He wants you to steer clear of it," he said. "The balls on this guy, right?"

"It's Blackstar. They carry their balls in a wheelbarrow, sir."

"It sure seems that way. Anyway, I asked him why and he said he couldn't comment, but that there'd be repercussions if we didn't drop the case."

"What did you say?"

"I told him to go fuck himself…again."

"Good call, sir."

"I hope these guys aren't going to make trouble for us, Ethan."

"Don't worry about it, sir. They're just saber-rattling. There's not much they can do."

In reality, there was plenty Blackstar could do—to me, to the department, even to Lewellyn himself, but I wasn't about to tell him that.

"Alright, Ethan, I'll take your word for it. And Ethan?"

"Yes, sir?"

"Keep your fucking head down, for God's sake."

"I'll try my best, sir."

When I hung up the phone, I sat and thought about Blackstar for a moment. When it came to MURK activity in this city, I knew well that Blackstar thought they were the only ones who should be dealing with it. They had their reasons, but mostly, it came down to power and control. Wendell Knightsbridge was the founder and CEO of the company. Wendell was a smart man, but manipulative with it, and he thought he was above everyone, spending most of his time at the Blackstar facility in a fenced-off area just past the city limits, far from prying eyes. Fueled by his burning desire for more power, knowledge, and control, Wendell built Blackstar from the ground up, soon gaining the nickname of The Magician because of his social sleight of hand and manipulative ways. The entire company and everyone in it was an extension of Wendell's ego; a tool he used to fulfill his dark desires. I knew from experience that nothing ever impeded those desires, and if he thought either me or my unit was getting in his way, he wouldn't hesitate to wipe me off the board. He probably already had a chip on his shoulder that I had bested him when I left the company on my own terms, which no employee ever did. It therefore wouldn't take much for

Wendell to give the order to have me taken out, so I would have to tread carefully.

In the meantime, I had a hunch as to how I could locate Scarlet's sister, Charlotte. Scarlet had said that Charlotte had been adopted and also that there'd been no signs of struggle when she was taken from the forest. From that, I extrapolated that Charlotte had some connection with the person who turned up and took her away. It was possible, even likely, that the person who took Charlotte away was her biological father. It was the only reason that would explain Charlotte's willingness to go along with him.

This man had turned up and had somehow convinced Charlotte that he was her father, coercing her into leaving with him. Given the circumstances, it was the only thing that made sense to me. I still had to prove it which meant finding out the identity of the biological father and then tracking him down. To do that, I would have to go through official channels and wade through a load of red tape and bureaucratic apathy, which could take days. Or, I could go and see Pan Demic and Artemis, and they could get me what I needed in a fraction of the time with no awkward questions. I chose the latter option as I left the subbasement and went on my way.

WHEN I GOT TO BANKHURST AND ENTERED THE PENTHOUSE, IT surprised me to find that Artemis was alone. "Where's your bum-buddy?" I asked as I took a seat next to him at his workstation.

"Pan Demic's mom is in hospital," Artemis said as he sucked what looked to be a smoothie through a straw.

"What's wrong with her?"

"She has cancer, dude. I don't think she has much time left if you know what I mean."

"I'm sorry to hear that," I said as I took a cigarette out and lit it up. "How's Pan Demic taking it?"

"How do you think? He's fucking devastated, man." He took another suck on his straw. "There might be a silver lining, though. I hacked one of the Big Pharma companies and found out they're sitting on an honest to God cure. Can you believe that? The fuckers would rather let people die than cure them. So I stole their fucking formula, and now I'm having the cure made up myself."

"Let's hope it works."

"Yeah, and if it does, I'll release the formula online." Artemis bent down to the coke mirror on his desk and snorted a line through a silver tube, snorting and rubbing his nose before continuing. "Better than that, I'll have the cure made up and distributed *everywhere*. There's nothing those Big Pharma fucks can do to stop me either."

"You'd be surprised what resources they have," I said, blowing smoke out at the same time. "Just be careful."

"Always, Drakester, always. So what can I do for you on this fine day?"

"I'm glad you asked," I said. "I need you to dig into some records for me."

"No problem. How's Scarlet by the way? I can't believe I forgot to ask you. This whole Pan Demic thing is fucking with my head." He bent down and did another line, offering the mirror to me, which I declined.

"You sure it's not the fucking coke messing your head up? Between you and Pan Demic, you must keep the cartels in business just by yourselves."

Artemis laughed. "Yeah, we do a lot of this shit. Keeps the sinuses clear, you know what I mean?"

I shook my head at him. "You're fucking nose will fall off before long."

"Fuck it, if it does, I'll get a new one." He sounded serious.

"Anyway, Charlotte Hood. I need you to find her adoption records. Go back to 2001. Charlotte was adopted when she was only a few months old."

"Ah," he said, already typing furiously on his keyboard, bluish magical energy glowing under his palms and arcing off his fingertips. "The lovely Scarlet's little sister."

"That's right."

"How is she? You rescued her okay?"

"Yeah, she's not in great shape, but she'll live, I'm sure. Thanks for your help on that."

"Sure thing, Drakester. Any time."

As Artemis continued to work on his computer, I put my feet up on the desk and leaned back in my chair as I continued smoking, my mind turning briefly to the events at The Brokedown Palace. I'd hardly had time to process what had happened, though to be honest, I wasn't much for sitting around ruminating on stuff, especially missions. I'd done so many over the years that they had become commonplace, like going out for breakfast or dinner. You did it and came home, end of story. What was done was done, so thinking about it constantly wasn't going to accomplish anything.

Although I have to say, I was more than a little surprised when Carlito revealed his true nature. I knew the bastard had been good at keeping secrets, but not that good. My Infernal Itch had never once reacted to him, which meant he had kept his inner monster buried so deep my sixth sense couldn't even detect it. And what goblin-like thing was he? A fucking chichiricu or something he had said. Some obscure Cuban lycanthrope from legend. I had never heard of one until Carlito transformed into it. Not that it did him much good. As powerful as he was, he was also outmanned. I felt sorry for him toward the end, especially when Haedemus shit all over his face. I tell you, that fucking Hellicorn has no morals, but then I suppose he's in good company.

"Ctrl+Alt+Success, Drakester," Artemis said, interrupting

my reverie as he sat back in his seat and used a finger on each hand to point at the large computer screen. "Check it out. That shit was buried *deep* like someone didn't want it found." He smiled smugly as he snorted. "They never factored in me, though."

Leaning forward, I stared at the screen, looking at what appeared to be a record of registration from Social Services for Charlotte Hood, only her name wasn't Charlotte Hood, it was Charlotte Webb. "You're sure this is her?" I asked.

"Positive," Artemis said. "I checked the birth records first, but there were none."

"No birth certificate?"

"That's what I said."

I frowned as I stared at the screen, wondering why Charlotte's birth was never registered like most other newborns. And if that was the case, why didn't her biological parents want her officially registered? "So how did you happen upon this DSS record?"

"Well, you said Charlotte was adopted when she was just a few months old," Artemis said. "Which means she would've been placed into the care of the state first. A little digging and —" He gestured toward the screen. "Bob's your uncle."

"So there's still no record of who the biological parents were?"

"Not that I can find," he said. "It does say on the form that she was handed over by Fairview PD. Your buddies at the precinct must've stumbled across her somehow."

"No shit," I said, rubbing the coarse beard on my chin as I wondered about what must've happened. Cops came across kids all the time who were suffering from abuse or neglect. I'd come across my fair share over the years. If someone at the precinct had found Charlotte during an investigation, then there had to be a record of it in the central database. I just had to look and see what came up.

"Anything else I can do for you?" Artemis asked.

"No," I said, standing up. "I got what I needed. I can take it from here. Thanks Artemis."

"You're welcome, Drakester. Tell Scarlet I said hi."

"Will do, and good luck with the cure for Pan Demic's mom. I hope she pulls through."

"She will," Artemis said, taking another blast of coke. "And so will a lot of other people soon enough." He grinned, his nose dusted with white powder. "Just changing the world, Drakester, one step at a time."

Yeah, I thought on my way out. *More like one snort at a time.*

Back in the car, I was just about to start the engine when a call came through from dispatch, giving a report of a dead body that was hanging in the center of Little Tokyo. As soon as I heard the report, I froze for a second as I stared out the window. Something about the incident gave me a bad feeling, and I knew it had something to do with Hannah, or rather Xaglath. Was this the "old business" she had mentioned to the Hellbastards?

Only one way to find out, I thought as I started the engine, swung the car around, and sped off toward Little Tokyo.

13

A while later, I stood in Serenity Square smack in the middle of Little Tokyo. Surrounding the square were neon-edged pagodas that stood alongside more modern buildings, many of which were businesses that catered to the tourists who came through Little Tokyo in their droves, just one stop on their whistle-stop tour of the whole city. Many of these tourists stood around now holding up their cameras and phones as uniformed officers kept them back behind the lines of the crime scene that had not long been cordoned off.

The rain had just started to fall when I got there, the morning light—as dull as it was—still hurting my over-tired eyes. Smells from the food stands peppered around the outside of the square filled the air, along with the smell of cigarettes and, also—strangely—cherry blossom, even though the cherry blossom trees dotted around were bare at this time of year, nothing more than skeletal sculptures on which crows and other smaller birds sat looking on at the spectacle unfolding before them.

In the center of the square was a massive statue of a samurai, made of bronze and correct in every detail when it came to depicting the elaborate armor of the samurai, his helmet and his long sword. The samurai statue was meant as a tribute to Ishida Yagami, a long distant ancestor of the Yagami crime family, who also headed up the Yakuza clan in this city. It was they who had the statue erected many years ago, though I doubted they thought it would ever be so blatantly debased as it was now.

For impaled on the end of the statue's long Katana was a body, the sword piercing the chest of the dead person; the body slid to the middle of the sword. The body itself appeared to belong to a man, though it was difficult to tell since every inch of skin had been removed, apart from the face that is. Looking at the impaled corpse was like looking at a slab of hung beef that glistened red and raw in the morning rain. I didn't recognize the face of the dead man, but I knew instinctively that he had to be Yakuza. Whoever had killed him had impaled him here to send a message to the Yakuza, a message they had no doubt received loud and clear by now.

As the forensic team, led by Gordon Mackey, did their work, I walked across the square to where Jim Routman stood with his hands dug deep into his coat pockets as the rain started to come down heavier. When he saw me, he frowned. "What are you doing here?" he asked, his tone making it clear that this was his crime scene.

"I heard the call over the radio," I said, coming to stand beside him as I gazed at the bronze samurai. "Has the body been ID'd yet?"

Routman stared at me for a long moment like he wasn't sure if he even wanted to talk to me or not. "Yeah," he said after a bit. "It has."

"He's Yakuza?"

Routman nodded. "Yeah."

I shook my head slightly upon hearing his conformation. "What are you thinking, Jim?" I asked as a uniform shouted and tried to keep the press away behind us.

"I'm thinking it's probably some gang war. This is a statement of intent."

"Intent?" I glanced at him. "To do what?"

"What do you think?"

"You expecting more bodies?"

"Wouldn't you?"

I nodded, saying nothing.

"Someone wanted to make a bold statement, and they fucking made it alright." Routman hunched his shoulders against the cold rain. "The Yakuza will be out for blood after this."

"I'm afraid they already are," I said almost to myself.

"What?"

"Nothing."

"Do you know something about this, Ethan? Is that why you're here?"

I shook my head. "I told you, I was just nearby. I had to see if it was of interest to my unit."

"Your unit." He snorted with some derision. "It's just you and that Jap, Walker. That's hardly a unit."

"Don't talk about my partner like that, Jim."

"Why? She's a Jap, isn't she?"

There was a slight smile on his face as I stared at him. "Where's your bum buddy, Stokes? Oh yeah, he's fucking dead."

Routman's face dropped as his lips pressed together in anger. "You know something, Ethan? You can be a real cunt at times."

"Takes one to know one, Jim."

"Do me a favor and get the fuck out of here," he said. "This is my crime scene, not yours."

"I'm going, don't worry."

"Hey," he shouted after me as I walked away. "Tell your Jap partner to come and see me. I figure she might know something about this shit, being a *Jap* and all."

I stopped dead next to the bronze statue, the Yakuza guy's corpse hanging to my right and just above me. My hands balled into fists as I thought about turning around and beating the shit out of Routman for his disrespect, but I doubted beating up another cop would go over well with the press watching on, or the brass back at the precinct. I'd just be giving Captain Edwards the excuse he was looking for to get me thrown off the force. No, I would play the long game with Routman. He had it coming, but just not today.

As I was walking away, my phone rang in my pocket. Taking it out, I saw it was Hannah calling, and I answered it as I ducked under the police tape and pushed my way through the crowd of rubberneckers. "Hannah," I said. "Where the hell are you?"

"In my apartment," she replied, sounding like herself again, albeit a depressed version.

"You know where I am?" I stopped next to an empty bench and turned around to view the dead Yakuza guy again. "I'm in Serenity Square looking at a dead Yakuza impaled on the sword of a bronze samurai warrior. You know anything about that, Hannah?" When she said nothing, I pressed her further. "Hannah? Answer me."

"I'm sorry, Ethan," she said. "I couldn't control her. She just took over, and I couldn't control her."

Shit, I thought. "You mean Xaglath? She killed this Yakuza guy?"

"Yes."

"Fuck's sake."

"I couldn't—"

"Yeah, you couldn't control her. You already said."

"I couldn't."

"Couldn't or wouldn't?"

"What?"

"We both know you have a beef with the Yakuza, that you're *one of them*. You wanted revenge. Is this the start of it?"

Again she went silent for a long moment, and I started walking back to my car. When I reached the Dodge, she finally said, "Can you come over so we can discuss this?"

"Sure, why not. Where are you at?"

When she gave me an address that was just a few streets away, I got in the car and drove there, ending up in a street that seemed to function as some scaled-down Sex District, with rows of neon signed seedy porn shops and small clubs that offered live sex shows. Hannah's apartment was situated above one of the porn shops.

When she opened the door, I was shocked to see the state of her face. She had one large gash that went from her left eye socket across her nose to her right cheek, and another cut across her forehead. Both cuts were clean like they were done with a sharp blade.

"Jesus, Hannah," I said as I walked into the apartment, which was even smaller and more rundown than my apartment in Bricktown. The smell of damp permeated the stale air, the paint peeling off the mostly bare walls in many places. Dirty blinds covered the living room window, which didn't stop the light from the neon sign hanging outside spilling into the gloom, alternating between red and blue hues.

"I know," Hannah said as she closed the door behind me. "The place is a shit hole. I intend to get a better place soon."

"I was talking more about your face," I said as I stared at her. "Did the Yakuza guy do that?"

"Turns out he was handy with a knife." She touched her untreated wounds with her fingers as if they didn't hurt. "The cuts will heal soon enough."

"I fucking hope so. You can't go into work looking like that."

"Maybe I should get some Band-Aids?" she joked as she sat down on a worn fabric couch that looked like it belonged in the alley out back.

I shook my head as I sat down next to her, staring around the room for a moment. There were a few pictures on the walls of Hannah with an older woman who I assumed was her mother. Also on the wall was a set of Japanese swords next to a picture of Hannah in her police uniform, looking fresh out of the academy. Apart from that, there didn't appear to be much else in the place. Not even a TV. "You don't have a TV."

"Hannah sold her TV to pay for drugs one time. She sold most of her stuff, actually."

"But not the swords."

"No, she kept all of her weapons. The rest are in the bedroom, locked up in a closet."

"At least she had her priorities right."

Hannah laughed slightly as she sat in the same clothes she wore to The Brokedown Palace, which were still covered in blood. "How's Scarlet?"

"In recovery at Cal's place," I said. "She's lucky to be alive."

"I'm glad to hear that."

I turned to look at her as I took out a cigarette and handed her one, which she took. "So what happened?" I asked. "Did Xaglath take over and then decide to get started on this revenge plan you've been thinking about?"

She nodded as I lit her cigarette for her, followed by my own. "That's about the height of it, yeah. That guy in the square, he's one of Kazuo's Kumi-in, or soldiers. He was one of the men who stopped Susan, Hannah's mother, at the airport that day and brought her back to Kazuo."

"So you're starting at the bottom and working your way up, is that it?"

She nodded. "I'm not going to lie to you, Ethan. Whether my demon side was in control or not, I was still going to do this. Kazuo has to pay for what he did to Hannah and her mother, for what he did to *me*. I may not have been physically present at the time, but it still feels like I was, and I can't ignore that."

"So you're going to keep going until you get to Kazuo?"

"Yes."

"Alone?"

"If I have to."

"What about your former demon self? Is Xaglath going to help?"

She shrugged. "I don't know. Maybe, if I need her again."

"And what happens if she decides to stick around after, permanently I mean? What happens to Hannah then?"

"That won't happen."

"You don't know that. I saw you at The Brokedown Palace. You were——"

"Pure evil?"

"You said it."

She took another drag on her cigarette before stubbing it out in a metal ashtray that sat on a scuffed coffee table in front of us. "I can control it," she said.

"I'd like to believe that," I said. "But I know what's it like to lose yourself to darkness. It gets harder every time to find your way back until eventually, you don't find your way back at all."

"You did."

"Did I?"

She took my hand and smiled, her beauty marred by the open wounds on her face. "I know darkness, Ethan, and you're not it."

"So what am I then?"

Sitting closer, she said, "You're just a man in a lot of pain. A man who lost the people he loved the most."

I looked away as I stared at the pictures on the wall, at Hannah's mother, a dark-haired beauty in her own right, standing next to a young Hannah, who had the same haunted look in her eyes even then; the same look she had now. "You might be right," I said. "And that's why I understand this need for revenge that you have."

"Because you have the same need?"

"Yes."

"Are you any closer to finding out who killed Angela and Callie?"

"Scarlet said she would help me track down the wolf who killed them. I think maybe he was a dog soldier."

"Dog soldier?"

"A werewolf mercenary. The murders would be too random if the wolf was acting alone. For the most part, were-wolves don't just break into strangers' houses and kill them. They're careful about who they hunt, and aren't so open about doing so."

"Do you think whoever killed them was hired by someone else? Any idea who?"

"I could give you a long list," I said, stubbing my cigarette out in the ashtray. "I've made a lot of enemies in my time."

"I don't doubt it," she said, smiling.

"What's that's supposed to mean?"

"Nothing, just that you have a way about you."

"A way?"

"You know what I mean," she said, squeezing my leg, and I smiled at her, a smile that was tinged with sadness by the damage done to her face. I knew she would heal, but it still hurt to see her that way.

"Here's what I know," I said. "If he doesn't already, Kazuo will find out it was you who killed his man and left him out there for everyone to see. Before long, you'll be his top priority, and you'll have Yakuza coming at you from everywhere."

"So, what are you saying?"

"That you need to forget about going after the underlings and making statements, and just go after Kazuo himself."

"Go straight for the throat, you mean."

"Exactly. But even then——" I paused as I shook my head.

"What?"

"Even if you kill Kazuo, you'll still end up with the rest of the Yakuza clans coming after you. There'll be no end to it."

"So I'll just take them all out."

"I'm not kidding here. If you stop now, maybe Kazuo doesn't find out it was you who killed his man. Maybe you can still walk away from this."

She shook her head. "I can't. Sooner or later, Kazuo is going to come knocking. As far as he's concerned, I'm still part of his Yakuza family, and I'm still his daughter despite everything."

Jesus, I thought. *Why is everything always so fucking complicated?*

"So you don't have a choice, do you?"

Resting her head against my shoulder, she said, "I don't expect you to get involved. I'll do things on my own."

"I know you will," I said as I put my arm around her. "And that's what I'm worried about."

Hannah and I both agreed that she should stay in her apartment, at least until her face had fully healed, which given her demonic/celestial abilities, shouldn't take long. I thought it best that she lay low for a while anyway until the heat had died down a little.

When I got outside, it seemed to have stopped raining, though the sky was still dull and overcast. There was also a definite tension in the air, which was to be expected, given what happened. The Little Tokyo residents would be on edge now, knowing that the Yakuza would be on the warpath, threatening information out of people, spreading fear in their efforts to find out who had hit one of their own. It was a selfish act on Hannah's part, killing the Yakuza guy. I understood why she did it, but I was annoyed that she had given no thought to the consequences. Her revenge trip, despite what she believed, didn't just affect her. Her actions would ripple out, causing unseen problems for other people who had nothing to do with anything. Pretty soon, the clan would be marching through Little Tokyo and beyond, rattling business owners, other criminals, drug dealers and whoever else they thought would have information on who killed their man, and they wouldn't stop until they found out what they wanted to know. Sooner or later, they would find their way to Hannah, if she didn't find her way to them first, that is. Either way, the times just got more dangerous.

I was about to get into the car when someone called my name, and I looked to see Haedemus come wandering out of an alley. He walked slowly, seeming depressed as he stood by the front of the car. "What's up with you?" I asked him.

"Oh nothing," he said, shaking his massive black head slightly. "I just feel like I'm in the midst of an existential crisis."

"Are you serious?"

"Why wouldn't I be? Honestly, Ethan, you need to stop thinking of me as some dumb animal. As I keep telling you, I've been around for millennia. I've seen things, I've done—"

"Yeah, yeah. Do you want to go to the beach?"

Haedemus almost froze as he stared at me with his red eyes. "Are you serious?"

"I just said so, didn't I?"

"You better not be fucking with me, Ethan. If you are, I'll—"

Closing the car door, I cut him off. "I'm not fucking with you." I locked the car up and walked over to him, grabbing his mane before mounting him. "Let's go before I change my mind."

"Oh, Ethan, you've made me so happy. I feel like crying here."

"Please don't."

"Should we bring a picnic?"

"What? No, we're not bringing a fucking picnic. What are you going to bring anyway, intestine salad? Pickled brains?"

"Okay, maybe I'll grab a bite while we're there. I'm sure there'll be a beach bum around somewhere."

"You still have bodies stashed in the scrapyard. You don't need to eat any beach bums."

"The bodies you speak off are a little ripe at this stage. I prefer fresher meat."

"Beggars can't be choosers."

"Is that what you said before you fucked my Mistress?" He laughed like he found this hilarious.

"Jesus, really?"

"Come on. You don't know a joke when you hear it?" He snorted to himself as he started walking down the street, both of us oblivious to the people and traffic surrounding us, invisible to it all.

"Some joke."

"God, you humans are so sensitive. I'm actually glad you two are together, you know. I'm hoping it will stop her from becoming Xaglath again. I take it you know what she did?"

"Yeah, I saw. Were you there?"

"Obviously. I helped her do it."

"Of course you did."

"Don't judge me. I was only doing what I was told. I suppose you have a problem with it, do you?"

"I don't know yet. Maybe."

"You're afraid of her losing her newfound humanity, aren't you?"

"Something like that."

"Not long ago I wouldn't have cared. But now——"

"Now, you do?"

"I'm almost ashamed to admit I'm beginning to like it here. I don't want to end up back in Hell again. And if Xaglath takes over, we'll inevitably both end up in Shitsville once more."

"I guess we'll have to make sure Hannah stays as Hannah then."

"How do we do that?" he said. "I mean, you're fucking her, so what should *I* do? Be the voice of reason? Whisper positive affirmations in her ear? Like, 'You are no longer a bad demon, you are a kind and gentle soul at peace with yourself and the universe.' Isn't that the kind of bullshit you humans like to come out with to each other? I tell you, there wasn't much of that talk in Hell. It was more like, 'Dear God make it stop, and 'What did I do to deserve this?'" He snorted with some derision. "I'll tell you asshole; you pissed off God, that's what. I mean, duh!"

"Yeah," I said, lighting a cigarette. "We're a pathetic bunch at times."

"*All* the fucking time, you mean. Though you are not without your good points on rare occasions. Like now, with you taking me to the beach. It's a genuinely kind and considerate gesture."

"I guess that's something you aren't used to."

"No, not really. In Hell, kind and considerate means not stepping on some damned soul's head as you walk by, or just calling them a bastard instead of a shit-eating cunt."

I stifled a laugh as I shook my head. "You know, Haedemus, for a creature that hates humans so much, you're very like one yourself."

"Well, you know, Ethan…hang around scum for long enough, and you become scum."

"You think we're all scum?"

"Don't you?"

"Maybe, as a species. As individual souls…"

"Ahhhh," he cooed. "You think some humans are special

little snowflakes, don't you? Oh, Ethan, you're so adorable at times."

"Fuck off."

Haedemus chuckled to himself as he trotted out of Little Tokyo, leaving the neon pagodas behind. "I'll say this. My stay here thus far would've been far less tolerable without you, Ethan. You keep me entertained."

"Gee, thanks, Haedemus," I said. "It's like my whole life has been leading up to this moment; the moment you tell me I'm just here to keep you entertained."

"Screw you. I was trying to be nice."

"Just speed it up. I haven't got all day."

Haedemus broke into a gallop, and before long, the city and its people were no more than a blur as we sped by, with me doing my best to hold on as Haedemus swerved this way and that to avoid vehicles and pedestrians who inevitably got in our way sometimes.

A while later, as we were heading into Bayside, Haedemus slowed to a trot as we made our way through the middle of a long line of traffic heading into the nearby Industrial Zone. The rain was coming down heavy again, and I was soaked to the skin. "What the fuck are we playing at going to the beach on a day like this?" I said.

"It was your idea," Haedemus said. "Don't even think about backing out now. I don't care if it's raining or not. I still want to breathe in the ocean air."

I was about to argue that we should turn back when something to the left caught my eye. A man had jumped up onto the roof of one of the cars in the line of traffic. It was raining so hard now that I could barely make the man out, dressed as he was in dark clothing.

As Haedemus started to pick up speed again, the man raced across the roofs of the parked cars with a speed and dexterity that almost belied belief, causing my Infernal Itch to go haywire, the tattoo ink racing excitedly across my skin, the back of my neck burning with warning.

But before I could pull on Haedemus' mane to slow him down, the racing figure launched himself off one of the cars and flew through the air toward me, timing his attack with perfect precision, his body impacting mine just as Haedemus rode by.

My attacker grabbed onto me in mid-air, taking me down as Haedemus carried on down the street. As my attacker and I both fell, I bounced off a parked car and landed on the wet asphalt, my skull cracking off the ground as I fell into a momentary daze.

My attacker was on his feet straight away, standing over me as the rain continued to pound down. Doing my best to focus, I could make out a young guy, no more than twenty, dressed in a dark suit with blond hair and blue eyes that were cold and calculating. As I went to reach for my pistol, my assailant stamped on my arm, pinning it to the ground, causing me to shout in frustration. "Who the fuck are you? What do you want?"

Still with his foot on my arm, the dark-suited man crouched down, rain dripping off him as he stared down at me, a look of mild curiosity on his face rather than the aggression or arrogance that I expected. In my dazed state, I thought there was something weird about the guy, as he seemed to be completely lacking in emotion, his movements almost robotic in their precision. As he crouched down, he put his other knee on my solar plexus, pressing the wind out of me, making sure I couldn't get up. "Drop your investigation, or there will be consequences," he said, his voice free from inflection, sounding flat and matter of fact.

"What investigation?" I barely said as he put more of his weight on my solar plexus, forcing most of the air out of my lungs.

"The one involving the pregnant girl."

Now I realized that this male model wannabe must be part of the cult that Clare was talking about. Maybe he was even one of the grown-up offspring of the demon the cult worshipped. Given what Clare had said about them, he seemed to fit the bill. "Go…fuck yourself."

As soon as I said it, I balled my fist and punched the guy in the balls as hard as I could, but incredibly, he never flinched. He just smiled instead.

Then another voice sounded from behind him. "Hey fuck-pot," Haedemus said, now standing behind the hellot, or whatever the hell he was. "Get off my friend right now before I stick my horn right up your fucking asshole, and believe me, that's not something you want."

My assailant never even looked at Haedemus. Instead, he kept his gaze on me. "Drop the case," he said, and then slammed his knee down onto my ribs, causing me to cry out as at least one of them cracked. "Or suffer the consequences."

He leaped off me then onto the hood of the car I was squashed up against. When I got up to look for him, he had gone, the rain and the gathering crowd making it difficult to see anything. Taking out my badge, I flashed it at the rubber-neckers and told them to move it along, which they soon did once they realized there was nothing to see.

"I suppose this means we're not going to the beach now?" Haedemus said.

"No," I said, holding my ribs and wincing. "We're not."

Haedemus raised his head to the darkened sky as if addressing God himself. "I suppose you think this is funny, do you? Well, fuck you. Ethan and I will have our beach trip, you'll see."

"You can just go on your own, you know," I said. "You don't need me to hold your horn for you."

"It wouldn't be the same," Haedemus said, turning his head away slightly as if to hide his upset. "I wanted us to share a nice moment to feel a little connection for once."

I patted his side, my hand almost slipping into a gaping hole in his flesh. "The stars will align at some point, buddy, don't worry."

"Thank you, Ethan," he said. "Your sarcasm is really appreciated. I don't know what I'd do without you."

"Don't mention it, buddy."

14

_____

After a painful journey back to Little Tokyo, I told Haedemus to hang around and keep an eye on Hannah, just in case her demon self decided to go walkies again. And while I was at it, I called Hannah herself and told her about the guy that attacked me and to stay alert just in case the cult sent someone after her as well.

Sitting now in the Dodge, I took a double dose of Mud to dampen the pain in my ribs, which I didn't think were broken thankfully, but at least one was fractured, so I wouldn't be sneezing properly for a while.

Taking out my phone, I called Salem Hospital to find out how Clare was doing, thinking the cult might send someone after her too. But it was too late, for they already had by the sound of it. The hospital front desk told me that Clare was gone, along with her newly born child. No one saw her leave or knew where she might be. She had vanished, and so had her baby.

"Fuck," I said after hanging up the phone, sinking back in my seat as the Mud hit me hard, turning the rain running down the windshield into something like a shimmering portal, that if I fell into it, would take me far away from here, perhaps to oblivion where nothing could ever bother me again. A bullet to the head would do the same thing, but there was a reason I hadn't gone down that road.

Reaching into my trench pocket, I took out Callie's locket and stared at it in my hand, moving the delicate silver chain around with one finger. "Callie, sweetheart…"

As soon as I said her name, I heard her voice in my head; listened to her joy-filled laughter, followed by an image of her smiling face, her bright blue eyes filled with so much love and affection…

Clenching my fist over the locket, I wiped away a single tear that was running down my cheek. Putting the necklace back in my pocket, I started the car and sped off toward the precinct, my jaw set as I stared straight ahead at nothing.

~

THANKS TO THE MUD AND THE ISOLATION OF THE PRECINCT subbasement, I felt like the only person alive as I sat at my desk going through police reports from 2001 as I tried to find any that referenced an infant found at the scene.

As I read through the reports, my vision occasionally blurring out as I stared at the computer screen, a twinge of pain in my side would remind me of the assault I'd suffered from my assailant earlier, who was apparently a member of the cult Hannah and I were investigating. And going by the guy's physical abilities and strange emotionless detachment, I also figured he was one of the demon/human hybrids that Clare had talked about—a super hellot if you will. I hoped the bastard was there when we got around to raiding the cult headquarters at the old boarding school.

It was tempting to get a team together now and hit it after dark, but I didn't want to make a move until Hannah was ready to come back to work. If she walked into the precinct looking like she'd gone a few rounds with knife-wielding maniac, awkward questions would be asked. And Routman, being who he is, would probably try to connect Hannah to the murder of the Yakuza because of it. So the raid on the boarding school would have to wait.

In the meantime, I carried on my search for Charlotte Hood's birth parents, hoping I would find some reference to them in the reports I was going through.

After a while, I came across a report that seemed to be what I was looking for. Detectives were sent to an address in the Eden gated community to investigate reports of possible kidnapping and torture. The report didn't mention where the initial information came from, but when detectives got to the house, they came across the bodies of multiple women, as well as several dead infants. According to the report, the basement had been turned into a makeshift laboratory, though to what end, the report didn't say. Detectives also found a recently born baby in the house, apparently being looked after by the main suspect, whose name I didn't know because it was redacted in the report, along with other information it seemed, including what happened to the baby after it was taken away, though I already knew what happened to it thanks to Artemis.

What wasn't redacted, however, were the names of the two detectives who conducted the investigation. Detective Brian Philips was one.

And Detective Jim Routman, the other.

"Son of a bitch."

I FOUND ROUTMAN IN THE BULLPEN SITTING AT HIS DESK drinking coffee from a stained FPD mug as he spoke to one of the other Homicide detectives about the murdered Yakuza soldier. "Go through the video footage," Routman said to the much younger detective, a new guy I didn't know, obviously having just transferred over from somewhere. "There has to be something on there."

The younger detective nodded, throwing me a mild look of disdain before walking away as if Routman had told him all about me. "You have video footage?" I said as I perched on the edge of Routman's desk.

"What are you doing here?" Routman asked. "You get lonely down in the subbasement or something?"

"No, I came to speak to you about something."

"If it's about the Yakuza case, I'm not at liberty to talk about it."

"Don't be an asshole, Jim. What footage did you get your hands on?"

"Why are you so interested?" he asked, staring at me.

I shrugged like it didn't matter. "I'm not, I was just wondering, that's all. I'm still a cop, you know."

"You could've fooled me."

Letting his comment slide, I asked him about the case from 2001. "You and Philips went to a house in the Eden gated community and found multiple bodies, and a newborn baby. Do you remember that?"

Routman looked surprised for a second, and then uncomfortable as he slid forward in his seat and started to read over some report on his desk. "Not really. That was a long time ago." He tapped his temple with his finger. "The old memory isn't what it used to be. You know how it is."

"Not really," I said. "Come on, Jim. This is important. I need to know about the suspect whose name is redacted on the official report."

Routman continued to stare at the report in front of him like he was reading it, even though I knew he wasn't. "I'm kinda busy here, Ethan. I got a murder to solve, so I don't have time to discuss old cases with you."

"Why was the name redacted, Jim?" I said, continuing to

press him. "Who killed those women and infants? What was going on in that house?"

Sighing, Routman shook his head and put the report down on his desk. "What does this have to do with anything?"

"It relates to another case I'm working on."

"How?"

"I'm trying to find a missing girl, and I think she's the same girl you and Philips found at that house."

Routman looked disturbed when I told him this, and I knew it was because he hated the idea of one of his past cases unraveling and undoing all his good work, as he saw it. "Only you could dig this shit up," he said. "Why would you think it's the same girl?"

"I did some digging," I said. "The girl was handed over to Social Services. Her name was Charlotte Webb. Now I'm thinking that was her biological father in that house. Did he artificially inseminate one of the women or something? Was the girl part of some fucked up experiment?"

Routman looked around him for a second as if he was afraid others were listening. "Come with me," he said, getting up, and I followed him into the men's restroom. Once inside, Routman checked all the cubicles to make sure no one else was there with us.

"We're alone," I said. "Spill."

Leaning against one of the sinks, Routman lit a cigarette, even though smoking was banned in the building. "What I'm about to tell you didn't come from me, are we clear?"

I nodded. "Sure."

He sucked hard on his cigarette before blowing a large plume of smoke into the air. "Alright, Philips and I, we were told to go to this house in Eden—that jumped up gated community for all those rich, entitled fucks— to check out a house after somebody reported it was an illegal laboratory for human experimentation."

"Who reported it?"

"Don't know. The captain at the time—your buddy Lewellyn, actually—never said. He just told us to go to the house and check it out. So we did, taking a team with us. And we found—" He stopped to take another drag on his cigarette, his eyes haunted by the memory of what he was talking about. "The SWAT guys busted the door in, and the first thing that hits us is the smell. You know what it's like, right? It's hard not to gag. So we search this huge fucking house, and eventually, we find a basement that's like...somebody's fucking nightmare. Full of hospital beds and all kinds of lab equipment. We found the bodies of three dead women on the beds, and in the subbasement, we found another six bodies, all women, and all in different stages of pregnancy."

"Jesus," I said, shaking my head, taking out a cigarette and lighting it.

"As I said, the smell was just awful, but that wasn't even the worst of it." He stopped to take a drag of his cigarette, glancing at himself in the mirror for a second before quickly looking away, his eyes haunted by bad memories. "We also found incubators in there, eight of them, and inside seven of them...Jesus—" He stopped again like it was too much. "There were babies inside. Seven babies, and all of them... Christ, I can't even think about it." Routman made the sign of the cross as if to protect himself from the awfulness of the memories.

"What about the owner of the house, the person who was doing all this?" I said.

"He was in there," Routman said, his voice strained now. "We restrained him as soon as we hit the basement. He didn't even put up a fight, though he kept shouting about his daughter, the only baby in that charnel house that was still alive. He kept saying she was important, that she was special, that she was going to change the world. We just thought the guy was some fucking sicko. We didn't pay his ranting any attention. The baby was taken away for Social Services to deal with."

"And the guy? Who was he?"

Routman stared at me a moment. "His name was redacted for a reason. Why don't you ask your buddy, Lewellyn?"

"Come on, Jim," I said. "Save me the fucking trouble, will you? The baby you saved is all grown up now, and I think she's in danger. I think this guy has her."

"Fine," Routman said. "I'll tell you, but you never heard it from me, got it?"

I nodded. "Sure."

"His name was Jonas Webb."

"Jonas Webb?" The name sounded familiar, and it took a moment of wracking my brain to remember why. "Wasn't he some big-name scientist, the owner of a pharmaceutical company?"

"That's right, at least until his wife and three kids were murdered in their home one night." He shook his head. "I was on that case. It was a fucking massacre. Never caught who did it."

"So this Jonas Webb guy goes crazy after that or something?"

"Seems that way, although we never got the chance to interview him. Men in dark suits came and took him away shortly after his arrest."

"Men in dark suits?"

"Yeah, like corporate guys, but with guns. Big Pharma guys, is my guess. That's the last I saw of Webb. He ended up being committed to Danvers Asylum. He's been there ever since."

"Wait, you're sure he's still there?"

"Unless he's escaped, and I didn't hear about it, but I doubt it. You know Danvers, once you're in, there's no getting out." He stubbed his cigarette out in the sink before throwing the butt in the waste bin. "So it seems to me like your theory is wrong, Ethan. Jonas Webb is rotting in a padded cell right this minute, so he couldn't have kidnapped anybody."

~

AFTER SPEAKING WITH ROUTMAN, I RETURNED TO THE subbasement and called Hannah. "Hey," I said when she answered. "I just spoke to Routman. He's saying he has video footage of the square in Little Tokyo. How likely is it that you're going to be on it?"

Hannah stayed silent for a moment, then said, "I don't know."

Not the answer I was looking for. "You're fucked if your little act of revenge was caught on camera, you know that, right? Routman will put you away."

"You think a prison could hold me?"

"Don't get fucking cocky, Hannah," I said, annoyed at her cavalier attitude. "We don't need this fucking hassle. Our partnership will be over."

"I know, I'm sorry."

"You couldn't have picked a less public place?"

"That would've defeated the purpose of what I was trying to do."

Rubbing my forehead, I sighed down the phone. "Jesus, Hannah. Sometimes I don't know where I stand with you."

"What do you mean?"

"I mean dealing with you is like dealing with someone with multiple personalities sometimes."

"Isn't that...everyone?"

I gave a small laugh as I shook my head. "Alright, look. I'll get my tech guys to look into the footage. If there's anything incriminating on there, they should be able to wipe it."

"Thank you, Ethan," she said. "I'd be lost without you."

"How's your face?"

"It's healing. I should be ready for action by tomorrow."

"Glad to hear it." I told her about Clare and how she had gone missing from the hospital. "We need to hit that boarding school soon so we can put an end to this cult and hopefully save Clare, assuming they haven't killed her already."

"I hope not. I liked her."

"If they have, there's nothing we can do."

"What are you doing in the meantime?" she asked. "Would you like to come over for a drink? There's a lot of old vinyl records here you might like. I don't know much about music, but we could listen to them together."

"As good as that sounds, I can't," I said. "I'm still trying to track down Scarlet's little sister. I have a lead now that I'm going to check out."

"You need any help?"

"I got this. Just stay in your apartment for now. I'll see you tomorrow."

"Okay." She didn't sound happy about it. "I guess I'll see you tomorrow then."

"Bye, Hannah."

"Ethan?"

"Yeah?"

"Be careful."

"I will," I said after a pause, and then hung up the phone.

After the call, I sat for a moment, staring into space before pouring myself a whiskey and typing the name Jonas Webb into the computer's search engine. Surprisingly, the search returned very little information about the man. It was as if someone had gone to great lengths to make it seem that Jonas Webb had never even existed. The most I found on him was a brief entry in Wikipedia that outlined his career as a scientist and geneticist. In the late nineteen-eighties, Webb founded a pharmaceutical company and became a billionaire almost overnight thanks to a drug to treat depression that outsold even Prozac. There was a brief mention of his family's tragic slaughter, and then nothing after that. No mention of his arrest or the fact that he now resided in an insane asylum.

The article did mention, however, that Jonas had a brother, a man named Robert Webb, who was a professor of chemistry at Fairview University. If anyone could fill me in on what happened to Jonas Webb, it was his brother. A quick search in the police database got me an address for Robert Webb that was near the university. I decided to pay the man a visit, but first I had to go and see the terrible twosome about the possibly incriminating video footage of Hannah, or rather Xaglath.

I left the precinct by the front entrance and walked to the Dodge parked just down the street. Night had long fallen, and there was a brisk breeze in the air, the sky threatening more rain by the look of it.

When I reached the car, I noticed the motorbike parked behind it, a motorbike I recognized. Seeing me coming, the rider took their helmet off. "Going somewhere?" Scarlet said.

I was surprised to see her. I didn't think her capable of even getting out of bed, never mind riding a motorbike. "What are you doing here?" I asked, coming to stand next to her. "*How* are you even here?"

"The medications you told Daisy to give me helped," she said, her face looking drawn and pale, not to mention covered in dark bruising still.

"I doubt it helped that much. You have severe internal injuries, for Christ's sake. You should still be resting up."

"I'm fine. Besides, I can't lie around when I know Charlotte is out there somewhere. Have you found out anything else?"

"Yes," I said. "Quite a lot. Why don't you come with me and I'll tell you everything?"

On hearing this, her battered face lit up with hope. "You know where she is?"

"Not quite yet, but I'll know soon. We're close."

"How close?" she asked as she got off the bike, her face registering the pain she was still in.

"Very close," I said. "Where's Daisy? Please tell me she's still not with Cal."

"I dropped her off at her place before I went to the storage unit I have here in the city to get some clothes."

"Glad to hear it."

"She's a good girl. She thinks highly of you."

I shook my head. "Fuck knows why."

"Don't sell yourself short," she said as she opened the car door, pausing to stare at me across the roof. "You're there for her. Sometimes that's all that matters."

I thought about my lonely childhood, and about how no one was ever there for me, not until I met Cal. Before that, it was just the boys home and a long line of authoritarian figures who thought they could control and dominate me, most of them finding out to their detriment that they couldn't do any such thing. "She's not a replacement for my daughter if that's what you're thinking," I said.

"I don't think that. No one could replace your daughter, Ethan, any more than anyone could replace my sister. It helps to have people, though."

"So who do you have, besides your sister?"

She looked silently across at me, her eyes full of physical and emotional pain, before giving me a plaintive smile and getting inside the car, leaving my question to hang in the air unanswered.

~

ONCE I TOLD SCARLET WHERE WE WERE HEADING, SHE ROLLED her still swollen eyes. "Really? You're going to let me get fanboyed again by those conspiracy-obsessed death metal freaks?"

"You're too hard on them," I said, smiling. "They're good kids, and besides, they love you."

"Oh, I know."

I laughed. "They think you're Jane Wick."

"I don't even get the reference, so…"

"You don't watch movies?"

"I don't own a TV."

"Good call. I just keep mine for the Hellbastards. They'd be lost without their daily dose of *The Muppet Show*."

"I saw those little guys in action at the club. They're vicious."

"Yep, that's why I keep them around. Better than any gun most times."

"You know," she said, staring out the window at the rain that had just started. "I didn't think I would make it out of there alive."

"You thought I was just going to leave you there for Carlito to have his way with you?"

"It felt that way when he was running a blowtorch across my back."

"I'm sorry that happened to you," I said as I pulled onto the expressway leading across the river. "It took balls to do what you did."

"It took balls to come and get me after."

"It was nothing we couldn't handle. How much did you see?"

"It was all a blur, to be honest. Bits and pieces."

"Probably just as well."

"What do you mean?"

"Nothing, it doesn't matter. It's over now."

"If you say so. Are you going to tell me what you've found out then? About my sister?"

"Sure."

As we sped down the expressway, I told her everything. About Jonas Webb and his crazy experiments, and about how he was committed to the insane asylum. I also told her about Jonas' brother Robert, who we'd be paying a visit soon.

"I had no idea," she said, shaking her head. "It explains a lot, though. I always knew there was something different about Charlotte. Her physical capabilities are beyond human, but I always put it down to freak genetics and all the training I gave her."

"Well, you're right about the freak genetics," I said, lighting a cigarette and cracking the window an inch. "Jonas Webb created Charlotte for some purpose that we don't know yet. I'm hoping his brother will shed some light on the subject."

Scarlet put a hand on my leg and smiled across at me. "Thank you," she said.

"What for?" I directed my stream of smoke out the window before looking at her.

"For getting me closer to Charlotte. I'm not sure I would've managed the same on my own."

"I'm a detective," I said, smiling. "It's what I do."

"By the way," she said. "Was I in a hospital at any point? I have vague memories of two people in surgical clothing poking and prodding at me."

"Yes, you were," I said. "You were dying on me. You needed professional medical attention that I couldn't provide. Luckily, I knew someone who set me up with a couple out of hours doctors."

"Out of hours?"

"Off the books." Reaching into my pocket, I took out the piece of paper the red-haired doctor had given me and gave it to Scarlet.

"What's this?" she asked, looking down at the slip of paper.

"The bill."

"Oh," she said.

"Yeah," I said. "It's a lot. It also needs paying soon."

"Don't worry. I have it."

"I guess you do, after doing all those hits. Do you ever think of retiring?"

"Do you?"

I shook my head. "No."

"There you go then."

∼

A WHILE LATER, SCARLET AND I WERE STANDING BEHIND PAN Demic and Artemis as they sat in their customized chairs, snorting coke as usual as the death metal blasted away in the background, which Pan Demic informed me was Morbid Angel's classic first album, *Altars Of Madness*. "I can make out the lyrics in this one," I said.

Pan Demic spun around then after a huge snort of coke and started singing, *"Bleed for the devil, Impious mortal lives, Feel the enticing power, Fill the chasm of your soul..."*

"Nice," I said. "I guess Morbid Angel knows about hellots too."

"Oh yeah," Pan Demic said, smiling and nodding. "I see what you mean there, Drakester. Nice."

Beside him, Artemis was too busy staring at Scarlet to engage in the usual banter, a sad look on his face, his eyes like saucers from all the drugs. "I can't believe they did that to your beautiful face," he said.

"Relax, Artemis," Scarlet said, as she finished paying her hospital bill via one of the computers. "I'm fine."

"Is it okay to say you look even *sexier*?" Artemis said. "I mean, the color on all that bruising, it's—"

"Dude," Pan Demic said, cutting him off with a stern look.

"You have a fetish you want to share with us, Artemis?" I asked.

"A fetish?" he mumbled, swinging around to face his computer screen once more. "No, I just…no."

Pan Demic gave Artemis a look before shaking his head. "Anyway, moving on," he said. "Drakester, I should inform you that we have the whole Brokedown Palace Massacre on video. Full disclosure and all that."

"The Brokedown Palace Massacre?" I said. "Are you serious? And I don't remember giving you permission to video anything."

"Relax, Drakester," he said. "There's only one copy. It's Ctrl+Alt+Safe With Us."

"I don't Ctrl+Alt+Give A Fuck," I said. "Wipe it."

"Drakester," Pan Demic whined. "It's some of your best work. I might even add that it tops Scarlet's Restaurant Mafia Massacre." He turned his head to look at Scarlet, who had a wry smile on her face at this point. "Not by much, though. The Hellbastards tipped the scales in this case. Those little guys are fucking crazy, man. Drakester, where can we get some? Like right away?"

"Believe me," I said. "Even if you could summon the little bastards, you'd never be able to handle them. They'd snort all your coke and fuck your place up."

Pan Demic and Artemis grinned at each other. "Sounds awesome," they both said at the same time.

"No, it doesn't," I said. "Are you two wasters going to help me out here or not? The video footage, remember?"

"This conversation isn't over," Artemis said.

"We want Hellbastards!" Pan Demic pronounced.

"And we shall have them!" Artemis said.

"You'll have my fucking foot up your ass in a second if you don't get on with it," I said.

"God, Drakester," Artemis said. "You're so strict at times. Are you like that when you have sex as well? I'll bet you're one of those dominant types, aren't you? All like, flipping bitches over and slapping their asses hard as you pull their heads back, making sure they feel your every manly thrust."

Scarlet burst out laughing, and I don't know if it was the surprise of hearing her laugh or what Artemis said or both, but I burst out laughing too, and then Pan Demic and Artemis joined in until we were all busting a gut.

"Alright," I said when I'd stopped laughing. "Just get on with it."

It took them a few minutes, but they eventually found the footage that had been uploaded to the precinct computer system. It showed a clear view of the samurai statue in Serenity Square, beginning in the daytime as crowds of people flowed in and out of the square, and transitioning into the nighttime as Artemis fast-forwarded the video. Soon, the square was practically empty as the time on the footage approached midnight. Then at two minutes to midnight, the Yakuza soldier just appeared out of nowhere, impaled on the giant samurai sword. "What the fuck?" Artemis said, rewinding the footage, slowing it down to try to see what happened.

"It's okay," I said. "You're not going to see anything."

"What?" Pan Demic said. "I don't get it."

"She was riding the Hellicorn," I said. "The Hellicorn is invisible to Unawares, including digital cameras it seems. Thank fuck."

"Who were you looking for?" Artemis asked. "And what is this Hellicorn you speak of? It sounds awesome."

"Never mind the Hellicorn," I said. "Never mind any of this."

"You're not even going to tell us who impaled that guy?" Artemis said.

"You don't need to know," I said.

"You said she," Pan Demic said. "Do you mean your partner?"

Despite me staying stony-faced, Artemis said, "Your

partner is fucking scary biscuits, Drakester. We saw her on the Brokedown Palace Massacre video. Is she like a demon or something? I don't think you saw what she did to all those bodies after you left. You wanna see?"

"No thanks," I said. "We need to be going. Thanks, boys, and wipe that fucking video. I mean it."

As Scarlet and I headed to the door, Pan Demic called out, "Hey Scarlet, sleep on this one. Tears are the by-product of the soul. Whatever essence that rests in any true human, excretes the salty fluid as waste. That's how you can tell the automatons. Taste their tears. Just water."

Scarlet stared at Pan Demic like she didn't know what to say, shaking her head when words failed her.

"It's okay," Pan Demic said. "Just let it sink in."

"Yeah," Scarlet said. "I'll do that. Thanks…Pan Demic."

Pan Demic smiled before turning back to his computer. "Don't mention it."

15

The Cathedral Quarter is the oldest part of Fairview. Most of the population here can trace its heritage back to the indigenous people of the city, and to its first settlers. It's a cramped district filled with meandering cobbled streets and old stone buildings that stand in the glow of wrought-iron street lamps, giving it the appearance of a place out of time, or a place long forgotten by the rest of the city.

As Scarlet and I drove farther into the district, it became harder to negotiate the narrow streets and alleyways. While I did my best not to scrape the Dodge against enclosing walls, Scarlet looked out the window at the various historical landmarks we passed, which the Cathedral Quarter was full of. Smack in the center of the district was Blackwood Cathedral, a huge building and a grand example of classic gothic architecture in the shape of a Latin cross.

The address I had for Robert Webb was a historical townhouse a few streets away from the cathedral. After navigating the narrow roads, I finally pulled the Dodge up outside Webb's house.

"It's quite beautiful in its own way, this place," Scarlet said as she stared out the window toward an antiquated, masterfully sculpted fountain across the street that sat in a little square of its own, surrounded by various boutiques and art galleries.

"This is your first time here?" I asked her, sitting for a minute while I finished my cigarette.

"Yes. It's like something from a fairy tale."

"Don't let the quaint appearance deceive you," I said. "This place is filled with darkness and terrible secrets as much as the rest of the city. Probably more so, given how far its history goes back. All the old money is here, along with the skeletons and inbreeding that goes with it. I'm not surprised you haven't done any hits here."

"Why?"

"Because people here handle their own business, that's why. They don't like outsiders."

"You think that's what happened with Charlotte's father?" she asked.

I nodded. "My guess is Big Pharma had him committed so he couldn't ruin the reputation of a multi-billion-dollar company. Hopefully this guy Robert will shed some light on that."

"Let's go and talk to him then."

As Scarlet exited the car, I got out as well, dropping my cigarette butt on the pristine cobbled street and grinding it underfoot, ignoring the disapproving look of a man out walking his dog just down the street.

Walking up to the door of number forty-five, I rapped it with my knuckles and stood back waiting, with Scarlet standing beside me. A moment later, a man answered, opening the door just enough so he could get his head around to peek out at us. "Yes?" he said. "Can I help you?" He seemed to be in his early sixties, tall with a gaunt face and white hair. His blue eyes were suspicious and a little afraid as he stared out at us.

"Robert Webb?" I said.

The man nodded. "That's right."

I unclipped my badge from my belt and held it up for him to see. "I'm Detective Drake with the FPD. I want to ask you a few questions if that's alright."

"What about?" Webb asked, staring at Scarlet now, and the cuts and bruises all over her face.

"Your brother Jonas."

Webb said nothing for a moment as he stared at me, and for a second I thought he was going to close the door on us, but instead, he opened it fully and stood back to let us in. Thanking him, Scarlet and I walked into the hallway and followed Webb into the front room where he had a fire roaring in the fireplace and classical music playing softly from an expensive-looking stereo in the corner of the small room, most of which was taken up by bookshelves, and not a TV in sight. "Excuse the mess," he said as he cleared folders and papers from the couch so we could sit down. "I was grading papers before you called."

"You teach at the university nearby?" I asked.

"Yes," he said, still standing as Scarlet and I sat down on the couch, the smell of pipe tobacco and brandy in the air. Dressed in plaid pants and red smoking jacket, Webb looked every inch the teacher. "I'm a chemistry professor there. Can I get either of you a drink?"

"No, thank you," Scarlet said, regarding Webb with some suspicion it seemed. She sat perched on the edge of the couch as if ready to pounce on Webb at the slightest provocation. Webb could hardly bring himself to look at her, either out of fear or shame, I couldn't tell which.

"I didn't catch your name," he said to Scarlet as he stood in front of the fireplace.

"My name is Scarlet. Scarlet Hood. Perhaps you know me?"

Webb stared at Scarlet for a second before sighing and sitting in an armchair positioned by the fire. "I'm not going to lie," he said. "I know who you are, Ms. Hood. I also know why you are here."

"Do you? Why?"

"You're here about your sister, Charlotte. Isn't that right?"

"Do you know where she is?" Scarlet edged forward a little more on the couch, causing Webb to shrink back slightly in his seat.

"Relax, Scarlet," I said. "Let's take this nice and easy. We didn't come here to bully, Mr. Webb. I'm sure he'll tell us everything." I looked at Webb. "Isn't that right, Mr. Webb?"

"Robert," he said, seeming to relax a little as he got up and retrieved his pipe from the mantle, sitting back down again as he started filling it with tobacco from a pouch he produced from his jacket pocket. "Call me Robert. And to answer your question, Ms. Hood, I don't know for sure where your sister might be, but I have some idea."

"Where?" Scarlet pressed.

"She's with my brother, I imagine," he said.

"Jonas?" I said. "He's not in Danvers?"

"He was," Robert said. "He escaped about a month ago."

"Why did no one report it?" I asked.

"The same reason his name was kept out of the public eye all those years ago," he said. "To avoid a scandal."

"So no one's looking for him?"

"People are looking for him, alright. People that want to silence him for good."

"You have a problem with that?" Scarlet said.

"Yes," Robert said. "Jonas is my brother. I don't wish him dead, despite what he did. He wasn't in his right mind when he kidnapped all those women. His entire family had been slaughtered. He was insane with grief."

"You're making excuses for him," Scarlet said, shaking her head with disdain.

"Not excuses," he said as he lit his pipe, puffing fragrant smoke into the room. "Jonas' actions were abhorrent. Unforgivable even. But that doesn't mean I will assist in killing him, which the company men want me to do."

"Company men?" I asked.

"Agents of the pharmaceutical industry, an unscrupulous business I warned Jonas not to get involved in many years ago."

"What happened to Jonas' family?" I asked. "Any idea who would've killed them?"

Robert Webb sighed slightly and shook his head. "Do you believe in monsters, Detective?"

"What kind of monsters?"

"Vampires."

I nodded. "Do you believe in them?"

"I really can't say. I've seen many strange things in my time, things I still can't explain, but I've never been face to face with a monster, so like a good scientist, I reserve judgment pending further proof. Regardless of my beliefs, however, it's what Jonas believed that matters, and he believed that a vampire murdered his wife and three children as they slept. Jonas was always more open-minded about these things than most, and when he noticed the strange marks on the necks of his family and the exsanguination of the bodies, he concluded that it was a vampire who killed them. The police, of course, thought otherwise and dismissed Jonas' conclusions as the mad rantings of a grieving man. Regardless, Jonas never changed his mind, and he became obsessed with finding a way to wipe out all vampires from the face of the earth."

"Is that what the experiments were for then?" I said. "Is that why he kidnapped those women and forced them to have babies?"

Robert nodded with some sadness. "Yes, I'm afraid so. Those poor women didn't deserve what happened to them."

"What was your brother trying to achieve with those experiments? Why did he need babies?"

"I confess to knowing very little about Jonas' experiments," he said. "During that time, he had no contact with anyone, including me. When I called at his house, he would tell me to go away, that he was fine and that he just wanted to be left alone. I thought he was grieving, so eventually I stopped calling, thinking he would come around in his own time."

"And he came around, didn't he?" Scarlet said. "You could've stopped it all if you'd tried harder."

"Perhaps," he said. "But then your sister wouldn't have been born either, would she?"

Scarlet stared hard at Webb for a long moment before shaking her head and looking away, knowing there wasn't much she could say on the matter.

"During his arrest," I said. "Jonas kept ranting that Charlotte was special somehow. I take it he genetically enhanced her?"

"I don't know, Detective," Webb said. "I didn't speak to Jonas again until after he was committed. His once brilliant mind had deteriorated badly by that stage. I'm sorry to say he was utterly insane. He spoke very little, and what he did say was rambling nonsense, centered around his lust for revenge, however long it took. He said he would wait until the time was right, and then he never spoke another word to anyone since."

"And now he's escaped," I said. "Nice going for a madman."

"Jonas may be insane, Detective, but I don't doubt he's still smarter than you or I could ever hope to be. His brilliant talent has just been turned toward more unsavory pursuits."

"Like my sister, you mean?" Scarlet said.

"I don't know," Webb said. "I haven't heard anything from Jonas since his escape."

"You haven't even tried to find him?"

He shook his head. "Whoever Jonas is now, he's not the brother I once knew. That's not to say I want him dead, but I don't want to see him either."

"Why?" Scarlet asked. "Because you're afraid of him? Or because your guilt won't let you?"

Webb smiled plaintively. "Both, I would say."

"You said you had some idea of where Jonas might be," I said. "Can you tell us where?"

"Jonas was a secretive man," he said. "He had property all over the place, secret bank accounts and various lab facilities that only a select few knew about. However, there is one place in particular where I think he might be and that is an underground bunker in the mountains outside of Redditch Village. The pharmaceutical industry is rife with espionage and dirty dealings, so Jonas did his most important work at the secure bunker where no one could steal it. If I had to guess, I'd say that's where he is now." He looked at Scarlet. "It's where he probably took your sister."

"God only knows what he's doing to her," Scarlet said. "What he's *done* to her."

"I can't comment on that, I'm afraid," Webb said. "What I can tell you is that Jonas will probably have armed security guards at the bunker. He'll know the company men will be after him, so he won't take any chances. Knowing my brother, he'll have access to whatever resources he needs to complete whatever plan he has in motion. His plan for revenge most probably, however crazy it may be."

"You better not be lying to us," Scarlet said, on her feet now as she glared over at Webb. "If I find out you're sending us on a wild goose chase, I'll come back here and kill you."

"I don't doubt that you will, my dear," he said. "I sincerely hope you find your sister."

"Come on," Scarlet said to me. "Let's go."

I stood up. "Thanks for your help," I told Webb.

"Are you going to kill my brother?" he asked, looking at me.

"We're going to get Charlotte back," I said. "Whatever happens after that is up to him."

Webb stared into the fire. "Perhaps it would be best if someone were to put poor Jonas out of his misery."

"As I said, that's up to him."

Scarlet threw me a look that said she disagreed, but she remained silent.

"Before you go," Webb said, grabbing a sheet of paper and a pen and beginning to write on it. "You'll need the access code to the bunker. The one time Jonas took me to see the place, he used his wife's birthday as the code. He may have changed it now. If so, you'll have to find your own way in." He handed me the piece of paper with the access code written on it, which I folded up and put in my pocket. "Drive through Redditch Village and keep going for about two miles until you come to a gated access road on the right-hand side. Follow the access road up the mountain until it forks off. Take the right fork, and it will bring you to the main entrance."

"Got it," I said. "Thanks."

As we were leaving, Webb said, "Tell Jonas I'm sorry."

Scarlet stopped and looked back at him for a second. "Tell him yourself when you meet him in Hell."

Outside in the car, I said, "That was a bit harsh, what you said there."

"He stood by while his brother did unspeakable things," Scarlet said, seething with anger. "He's just as bad."

"Evil happens when good men stand by and do nothing."

"Exactly."

"Don't worry," I said. "He'll get what's coming to him."

"Fucking right he will," Scarlet said. "I'll make sure of it."

WE DIDN'T DRIVE IMMEDIATELY TO JONAS' MOUNTAIN HIDEOUT. Instead, Scarlet got me to drive to the storage unit she kept downtown first. If Jonas had security like Robert said he might have, she said we would need to be prepared, which meant arming up first.

Which wouldn't be a problem, for the storage unit she took me to was like an Aladdin's cave of deadly weapons, housing everything from military-grade guns to a vast selection of knives, crossbows, compound bows and even a shelf filled with various poisons. On a rack to the left hung a collection of tactical outfits. Scarlet looked through them for a moment before stripping off the clothes she had on until she stood in just her black underwear. When she caught me looking at her, she pulled a face and said, "Sorry, I forgot you were here."

"Touché," I said smiling.

"Help yourself to whatever you want," she said as she began to put on a black leather outfit that appeared to be reinforced in places with thicker leather and probably Kevlar as well.

"Cool. Does that include the outfits?"

She smiled. "I don't think they'd suit you."

Smiling back, I turned to the guns and ran my eyes over the racks of rifles and submachine guns before selecting a custom Noveske Rogue Hunter with a ten-inch barrel and suppressor, putting four extra magazines into the pockets of my trench.

When I turned around again, Scarlet was putting on a dark red tunic over her black leather outfit. "What's with the Red Riding Hood get up?" I asked her.

"A girl can't look good when she's killing people?" she said.

"There's no law against it, I guess."

"Actually, it was my grandmother's thing. She would wear red for luck while she hunted."

"Your grandmother was a hunter?"

"Yes, before a pack of werewolves attacked the cottage. One of them almost killed her, which is why she now resides in a coma." She smiled sadly. "My grandmother taught me everything I know about hunting and killing."

"She sounds awesome. I'm guessing that's also why you have a thing for hunting werewolves?"

"Yes. I haven't forgotten your dog soldier either. I'll find him for you, once we get Charlotte back. It's the least I can do, after everything you've done for me."

"I appreciate that," I said, looking deep into her green eyes for a moment as something passed between us; a connection, perhaps even a longing on her part. I sensed she felt alone in the world, especially without her sister. Nor was she used to being so open with someone else, which appeared to make her uncomfortable as she moved to a shelf and lifted a quiver full of arrows, which she slung onto her back. She then added two pistols to the holsters on her thighs before finally selecting one of the black, compound bows from the rack.

"You any good with that thing?" I asked.

In a flash, she drew an arrow from her quiver and had the bow loaded and pointed at me before I could even blink. "What do you think?"

16
_____

I t was after four a.m. by the time we drove past the city limits on our way to Jonas Webb's secret mountain lair. As the view changed from industrial to agricultural, the road bent and turned up a small hill until it ended in a quaint little hamlet known as Redditch Village, which was hidden in a labyrinth of greenery. Stone cottages stood few and far between and gradually huddled together as we neared the main square. Each of their windows boasted a colorful and well-tended flower box, but still the place looked *wild*. To add to the strangeness of the place, we even spotted some people standing around outside their cottages, their faces glistening with sweat as if they had just finished toiling to some mysterious end. "What the hell are they doing out at this time?" Scarlet asked.

"They're a mysterious bunch in this village," I said. "They do their own thing."

The nocturnal villagers stared at us as we drove by, their faces full of suspicion as we invaded their quiet little hamlet, shattering the silence with the roar of the Dodge's engine.

"And I thought the city folk were weird," Scarlet said as we finally drove out of the village, the residents still watching us from far behind.

"Rural folk, especially Redditch villagers, are a whole other kind of weird," I said. "It's like *The Wicker Man* out here."

"The what?"

"Jeez, haven't you watched *any* movies?"

"Not in a long time. The last movie I saw was *Evil Dead II*. My friends and I watched it on a sleepover, the night before my parents were killed."

"At least you've seen one classic."

As per Robert Webb's instructions, we followed the road outside the village for roughly two miles until we came across the gated access road. I pulled the car up near the gates, and we both got out. "We should walk from here," I said.

Scarlet nodded as she went to the trunk and took out her bow before handing me the Rogue Hunter submachine gun. "You know how to pick a lock?" she said, nodding toward the large padlocked gates.

"Of course," I said. "Don't you?"

"Obviously. I'm an assassin."

"Oh, I see. You just want to feel superior when it takes me longer to pick it, is that it?"

She smiled. "Something like that."

"Well," I said, reaching inside my trench for the leather pouch containing my lock picks. "You might be pleasantly surprised." I walked over to the steel gates and began to work on the padlock holding the thick chain together. A minute later, I was still at it.

"You were saying?" Scarlet said.

"Shh," I said. "It's a security lock. They aren't the easiest."

"You mean your skills aren't the best?"

"No…I'm just a little rusty…shit."

"Here, let me." Scarlet pushed me aside as she took the

lock picks from me. Ten seconds later, she had the lock open. "Never let a man do a woman's job."

"Okay, I'm impressed," I said, taking the tools back off her and returning them to my pocket. "You should teach a class or something."

"You should take a class or something."

"Ha-ha."

She laughed as she pulled the gates open so we could squeeze through. "Let's go, Rusty."

I threw her a look. "You cheeky bitch."

"You said it old man, not me."

"It's old man now, is it? Jesus, I'm gonna have to teach you a lesson when this is all over."

Standing there smiling, she said, "I'll look forward to it."

Our eyes met for a second, and then I smiled and shook my head. "Come on, let's go."

We walked up the gravel road in silence for a bit as we got our bearings, the road steep and slippery from the rain. Tall pine trees flanked us on both sides, encasing us in darkness. Now and again, I would switch my vision to infrared as I looked ahead for signs of life, but aside from a lone fox, I saw nothing else.

As we neared the fork in the road that Webb had told us about, I realized that Scarlet had stopped behind me. "What's up?" I said in a hushed voice, going to stand by her.

"What if she's not here?" she said. "What if we're wasting our time?"

"Then we keep looking," I said.

She sighed and shook her head as if my response wasn't good enough. "And what if she *is* here? What if this Webb guy has done something awful to her? What if Charlotte isn't Charlotte anymore? What if she's some...monster?" Tears formed in her eyes as she spoke, and I put a gentle hand on her shoulder.

"Whatever it is, we'll deal with it," I said. "You're not alone in this, Scarlet."

Scarlet stared at me with wet eyes for a second, and then took me aback by coming forward and kissing me, her soft lips pressing into mine for a few seconds before she pulled away. "I —I'm sorry," she said. "I don't know what came over me. I—"

"It's okay." I stood awkwardly for a second, trying not make a big deal out of it. "We should probably keep moving."

She nodded as she wiped the tears from her eyes. "Yeah, good idea."

We took the right fork in the road and crept along in silence. As we did, I would glance at her occasionally, seeing her for the lonely soul that she was, thinking it took one to know one.

"Hold up," Scarlet whispered. She had her hood up as I stopped beside her. "There, up ahead."

About fifty yards up the winding road, there were three vehicles parked on a wide ledge—two black SUVs and a VW camper van. "At least we know he's here," I said, glancing at her, seeing the relief on her face, but still the dread underneath. "I'm guessing the SUVs belong to the security team. Maybe eight guys. Ten at most. What do you think?"

"I think you're right," she said as she loaded her bow with a steel-headed arrow. "Shouldn't be a problem."

"What are you doing?"

"Up ahead. By the entrance."

Peering up ahead, I soon spotted an armed guard standing in front of a set of huge steel doors fitted into the side of the mountain. But before I could even say anything, Scarlet unleashed her arrow, and a second later, the arrow penetrated the guard's skull at a forty-five-degree angle, knocking him sideways onto the ground. "You really can use that thing," I said.

"We should be clear now," she said. "Everyone else should be inside."

Moving quickly, we made our way up to the entrance to the mountain facility. On the way up, I set the submachine gun to full auto and planted it into my shoulder, ready to fire in case any more guards appeared, but none did. Before we reached the entrance, however, I stopped Scarlet and pointed to the camera positioned above the steel doors. Nodding, Scarlet loaded her bow again and fired an arrow at the camera, the steel tip penetrating the body of the camera and staying there. "Nice. You'll have to give me lessons sometime."

Scarlet gave me a slight smile, and we both walked up to the keypad set into the rock to the side of the doors. I didn't need to look at the piece of paper in my pocket, for I'd memorized the number as soon as Webb gave it to me. After pushing in the six-digit code, the heavy steel doors immediately began to open, drawing apart at a steady pace.

While I stood to one side of the doors, Scarlet stood to the other. As expected, two guards soon came to investigate. Leaning around the door as it continued to slide open, I let off a burst from the Rogue Hunter and shot the nearest guard in the chest, at least one bullet penetrating the guy's throat, the suppressor keeping the noise to a minimum. Almost at the same time, Scarlet unleashed an arrow from her bow that hit the other guard in the forehead, dropping him instantly.

With two guards down, Scarlet and I nodded to each other as we moved inside the facility, her with her bow already reloaded, me with the Noveske shouldered and ready to fire if any more guards appeared.

We walked into a long, wide corridor with concrete walls and floor, lit up by strip lights. We were halfway down the corridor when two more guards—one at each side of the opening up ahead—leaned around and fired at us with their submachine guns.

Staying close to the wall, I dropped to a crouch and fired a burst at the guard straight ahead of me, who had already ducked back behind the wall. Keeping my gun pointed, I waited on the guard to appear again. As I did, I heard the whoosh of another arrow unleashed from Scarlet's bow, and out of the corner of my eye, I saw the guard on her side fall to the floor. When the guard nearest to me leaned around the wall again, I shot him in the head before he could even pull the trigger.

Glancing at Scarlet, we both started moving again. I changed the magazine on my gun just as another guard fired on us from up ahead. Once again I ducked as bullets whizzed past my head, but before I could even return fire, Scarlet took the guy down with an arrow.

Keeping up our advance, we were almost at the end of the corridor now as it opened into an enormous room. More guards awaited us there, all of them firing at us with bursts from their automatics. Most of them seemed to be on the left-hand side, so I dived across the corridor to Scarlet's side where I would be less of a target. There was also a stack of wooden crates there that we used for cover. "I counted about five guards out there," I said.

Scarlet loosed an arrow at a guard who dared show himself up ahead, hitting him in the chest. "Make that four," she said.

Inside the open room, there was a walkway that went around the far walls leading to another corridor. The room we were at seemed to be the main room, however, for I also caught a glimpse of computer equipment and what appeared to be a large transparent box near the left side of the room.

Then from out of the room, a voice shouted, "Don't let them in here!"

"I assume that's Jonas," I said.

Scarlet said nothing as she let fly another arrow, this one hitting a guard who was trying to sneak around the walkway.

Edging past Scarlet, I peeked around the corner to see where the rest of the guards were. I caught sight of two of them standing by the see-through box, and another was making his way boldly toward us, a pistol raised in front of him as he started to squeeze off shots, his bullets taking chunks out of the surrounding walls.

From the corridor across from us, more guards came running down toward the room. Scarlet was already on them, firing arrows at a rapid rate, hitting at least two men that I saw.

But my attention was now taken by the lone guard still making his way toward us like he didn't give a fuck if he got shot or not. He was a big fucker, heavily built with a face like stone. Leaning around the corner, I fired off a burst, and the guard dived to the side to avoid getting hit. When I next squeezed the trigger, there was nothing but clicking, and I quickly pulled out the empty magazine and tossed it away.

But as I went to grab a full magazine from my trench pocket, I realized the guard was now sprinting toward me, not even a gun in his hand anymore. A split-second calculation told me I wouldn't have time to reload. He'd be on me before then, which he nearly was already. He roared like a bear as he practically dived at me, forcing me to drop my gun to defend myself.

By that point, the room ahead had flooded with more guards. Scarlet was doing her best to take care of them, firing off arrows at an insane rate while trying to avoid getting shot.

As bullets flew all around us and the smell of gunpowder filled the corridor, I was driven back by the manimal who'd attacked me, losing my footing as I stumbled and hit the deck.

As I fell, Manimal fell with me, and he immediately started raining down punches, his massive fists smashing into my skull as I crossed my arms in front of me to deflect the blows.

After taking a few good hits, I was able to pull the bastard into my guard, wrapping my legs around his waist and pulling his head down into me.

With his block head close to my face, I turned toward him and bit down on his ear, holding it with my teeth for a second before jerking my head sideways, ripping off the ear before spitting the severed appendage out of my mouth.

Manimal screamed as his blood flowed down over my face, but I held him in position with one hand as he struggled to break my guard. Luckily for me, Manimal was all aggression and no technique. A more skilled fighter would probably have broken my guard. As it was, I could jam my thumb into the bloody hole where his ear used to be. Gritting my teeth, I forced my thumb in as far as it would go, pulling his head toward me, my thumb driving deep into his eardrum as he started screaming with the pain.

It sometimes happens that you can cause a person *too* much pain in a fight, and your opponent ends up getting a massive adrenaline rush that nullifies the pain and causes them to go all Hulk on your ass. Which is precisely what happened in this case, and it's why I hate fighting anyone on the ground. I'm usually a straight-back-to-my-feet kind of guy when I hit the deck, but in this case, I had a raging assailant on top of me preventing me from doing that.

Manimal got his adrenaline burst and went fucking crazy, ripping his head away and pulling out of my guard. As he leaned back, his face a mask of pain and rage, I could only watch as he went for a knife strapped to his belt.

The next thing I knew, I had a massive Bowie knife coming toward my skull, the gleaming tip of the blade mere inches from my forehead as I gripped Manimal's wrists to stop the knife from descending any farther.

It was a tricky situation. I had my sidearm, but if I took my hand away from Manimal's wrist to grab the gun, I wouldn't be able to hold the knife back with just one hand, and the next thing would be that I would have a brand new adornment to my skull and a one-way trip to the Void.

So as gunfire and shouting sounded in the background, I went for the only option left open to me, and that was to use my magic.

I say magic, but it's not really. Or maybe it is, depending on your definition, I don't know. All I know is, Blackstar gave me these tattoos that somehow work a kind of magic that allows me to fuck with people's minds. Not make them do things necessarily, but confuse them, make them forget things. I don't know how it works, nor do I care. The magic is in the ink, that's all I know.

Still using the space between my thumb and forefinger to push on Manimal's wrist—while still gripping the same wrist with my other hand—I turned the fingers of my left hand out to the side so that my palm became exposed, just as the ink made its way down my arm and out onto my hand. There, it began to swirl as the magic within it intensified and began to focus itself. All I needed now was for Manimal to look at my hand. One glance would be enough for me to hook him.

The problem was, though, he was wholly focused on my face instead. He was one of these sadistic fuckers who like to look in a person's eyes as they kill them. They get off on seeing the fear and then watching the lights go out for good.

But there was no fear in my eyes, I can tell you that much, even when Manimal growled through gritted teeth, "Fucking die, you fucker!"

The tip of the Bowie knife was half an inch from my head now. As strong as I was, there was no way I could push back against the massive downward pressure for much longer. So unless Scarlet was going to kill this guy for me—which I didn't see happening, given she was being shot at by the other guards—I would have to do something, and quick.

Here, I applied Occam's Razor to the problem. More often than not, the simplest solution is always the best solution. This applies particularly to fighting, where the simplest moves are nearly always the most effective.

So I said, "Look at my hand, asshole."

Sometimes people can't help but do what you tell them. By

giving simple commands or asking simple questions, you engage their brain in a way that they can't control. You're plugging directly into their deeper wiring, bypassing their conscious thought.

So when I told this asshole to look at my hand, that's exactly what he did. Just for a split second, but long enough for his attention to be hooked by the swirling ink, to the point where he couldn't look away.

Immediately, he eased off the pressure as his full attention was taken by the gracefully moving ink patterns swimming around my palm like fish in a pond.

"You don't even know what you're doing here," I told him, out of breath. "You can't even remember your own fucking name."

As Manimal sat back with a look of extreme confusion on his face now, I pushed him off me and got up into a crouch, drawing my sidearm at the same time. Scarlet was behind the boxes, having just fired an arrow at a guard on the walkway. There was one more that I could see standing just around the corner. Pointing my gun in the guard's direction, I fired four or five rounds, and the guy staggered back before falling to the floor.

"I think that's all of them," Scarlet said, staring at the man who had just tried to kill me as he kneeled on the floor in a state of extreme confusion, his bloody face registering his rising panic. "What did you do to him?"

"Where am I?" Manimal said. "I don't know who I am—I—"

I saved him the trouble of trying to remember his own name by putting a bullet in his head. "Fuck that guy," I said, breathing hard.

Scarlet threw me a quick smile. "You're getting on in years, Detective. Maybe you're not fit for this anymore."

"Fuck you," I said, wiping sweat from my forehead. "Let's go and get your sister and get out of this fucking rat hole."

17

D ead guards littered the cavernous room as Scarlet and I
entered, training our weapons on the man standing
next to a bank of computer equipment. A man we presumed
to be Jonas Webb. He was tall like his brother, though much
leaner, his physicality almost skeletal. A shock of wild, white
hair topped his gaunt face. Eyes that were sunk deep into their
darkened sockets gave him a ghoulish appearance, as did his
pasty white skin, which doubtless hadn't seen much sunlight
during his eighteen-year incarceration. He wore a long, white
lab coat with nothing but a pair of black slacks underneath.
There weren't even any shoes on his feet.

To me, he looked every inch the lunatic they purported
him to be. As he stood staring at us, he held a twisted smile on
his face, showing teeth that were yellowed and almost black in
places. In his wild eyes, I saw very little in the way of sanity.

"Big sister!" he announced in a voice that made him
sound like he had lost most of his capacity for logical
discourse. "Big sister has arrived, but it's too late. Too late, Big
Sister! Too late!"

"Too late for what?" I said as I held my gun on him, but

before he could answer, I heard Scarlet call out Charlotte's name.

Turning, I looked toward the huge box in the center of the room. I could see now that it was in fact of steel construction, the frame anyway. The rest consisted of thick plate-glass windows and a heavy steel door that opened and closed electronically.

Scarlet had moved around to the side of the box and was staring through the window at her sister, who was inside, though her form was steadily being obscured by a rising cloud of greenish gas.

"What the fuck are you doing to her?" Scarlet shouted. "Open the door!"

Jonas Webb's response was to laugh crazily to himself. "You're too late," he said. "She will become wrath, and no one will stop her. She will carry out my revenge just as I've created her to do."

I stepped forward and held my gun inches from Webb's head. "Open the fucking door. Let her out."

"I've waited eighteen years for this moment," Webb said as he stared at the box, hardly even acknowledging me or the fact that I had a gun to his head. "Eighteen years of sitting alone in a padded cell, with only the thought of getting my revenge to keep me going. They thought they could break me, silence me, lock me up and throw away the key."

He finally turned his head to look at me with his wild, sunken eyes. "They underestimated me. They always have. Now those monsters will finally meet their match. They will have nowhere to run, nowhere to hide. My creation will hunt them all, flush them all out into the light and kill every last one of them until their vile species no longer exists. No more innocent blood will they take. No more innocent families will they massacre to feed their disgusting bloodlust."

Scarlet was banging on the thick glass, calling her sister's name. As the gas filled up the chamber, Charlotte fell to the floor and started violently convulsing. "What are you doing to her?" I demanded of Webb.

"Starting her final transformation," he said with some pride. "She is becoming the perfect specimen that I always intended her to be. The perfect killing machine. No one will stop her now."

"The code for the door," I said, pressing the gun against his head. "What is it?"

Webb started laughing as if at some great joke that only he knew about. Then he suddenly stepped away from me, and I saw his hand slide into his coat pocket and pull out a small pistol which he immediately pressed against his right temple. "My work is done!" he proclaimed.

"Don't!" I shouted.

"Time to be with my family now."

When Webb pulled the trigger, his blood and brains splattered over the computer equipment next to him before he fell to the floor, dead.

"No!" Scarlet screamed.

"Fucking asshole," I said through gritted teeth, wondering now how the hell we were going to save Charlotte when Webb was the only one who knew the code to open the door to the box she was trapped in.

Scarlet dropped her bow to the floor as she took a submachine gun from one of the dead guards. She then went around to the side of the box and fired a burst at the glass. But the glass was so thick that the bullets just ricocheted off it. "Stop," I told her. "Before you shoot yourself."

"Fuck!" She threw the gun to one side and grabbed her hair with both hands, her face a mask of helplessness and frustration.

At this point, the box was completely filled with greenish gas, making it impossible to even see Charlotte inside. With no code to open the door, the only thing I could think to do was to summon the Hellbastards. After speaking the words of power out loud, all five of the demons soon materialized around me.

Cracka was already bouncing with excitement. "Oh yeah, what's this place?" he said, immediately running to one of the dead guards to jump up and down on his chest.

"Cracka!" I shouted. "Stop acting like a kid at a fucking playground and get over here!"

For once, Cracka didn't protest and did as I told him. The Hellbastards could see I was in no mood for fucking around.

"What's going on, boss?" Scroteface asked me.

Ignoring him, I looked at Snot Skull. "I need that door open," I told him, pointing at the box. "Melt the control panel. Hurry!"

"Yes, boss," Snot Skull said and scurried over to the door, jumping up and gripping onto the steel with his claws as he vomited acid over the keypad.

As he did that, I turned to the others. "The rest of you try to break that glass. Go!"

The other four Hellbastards ran past Scarlet and faced the side of the box. Scroteface then began to punch the glass with all his demonic strength. As he did, Toast shot fireballs from his mouth to try to weaken the structural integrity of the glass. Reggie's main power was invisibility, which wouldn't do him much good in this situation, so he joined Scroteface and Cracka in battering on the glass with their fists.

"How we doing?" I said to Snot Skull as I went to the door. The acid he had vomited over the keypad was eating into the metal, the fumes making my eyes water. Soon, the wiring under the metal casing began to spark as acid and molten metal spat out everywhere.

Standing back, with Scarlet now at my side, we waited on the door to short circuit and somehow open, but it never did. Even when the acid melted the entire keypad and the electronics underneath, the door remained shut.

"Why isn't it opening?" Scarlet said, sounding like she was

on the edge of a nervous breakdown. "I can't lose my sister. I won't!"

"Snot Skull," I said. "Start melting through the door. Go!"

Obeying my order, Snot Skull climbed up the box to the top of the door and began to puke acid all over the surface. The door was so thick, however, that I knew it would take a while for the acid to eat through.

Meanwhile, Charlotte was still inside undergoing some transformation that, according to Jonas Webb, would make her into some kind of killing machine.

A monster.

Around the side of the box, the other Hellbastard's were still at it, banging like crazy on the glass, which was now blackened by Toast's constant firebombing. They seemed to be making some progress, however, as cracks soon started to appear in the glass.

I was about to tell them to keep at it when a hand suddenly slammed against the glass from the inside of the box, and the Hellbastards stopped what they were doing to stare at the dark figure now materializing through the green smoke.

Scarlet came around to stare, her face full of fear and dread now that she knew Charlotte was at least still alive, though in what state, it was impossible to tell at this stage. The hand pressing against the glass appeared to be black like it was covered in some outer coating or second skin, and the nails had thickened and lengthened into claws.

"Oh Jesus," Scarlet breathed. "What is she? What has he done to her?"

The hand pressing against the glass retreated after a moment, pulling back into the thick green smoke where it disappeared for what felt like a long time. Scarlet, the Hellbastards and I could only stand staring at the glass as we waited on Charlotte to appear again, which she did, but not in the way we expected.

A pregnant silence fell upon the room for a long moment,

and then the glass on the side of the box shattered as something came crashing through it, causing the Hellbastards to scatter, and me and Scarlet to jump back in shock.

In front of us now, amidst a carpet of broken glass and a cloud of slowly dissipating green smoke, was a black figure that appeared to rest on all fours, the limbs stretched and bent in a way that gave the figure the appearance of a spider. If this was Charlotte, she was not the girl she was before. Adding to her grotesque appearance were four legs that came from her back. Black, spindly things that rested either side of her, making her look like a giant spider. Her skin was no longer skin, now transformed into something resembling an insect-like exoskeleton. Her face still seemed human, at least in shape, but her eyes were black as coal, her once blond hair now long and wild and as dark as her skin. When she opened her mouth, she revealed that she had long white fangs that appeared to drip poison.

"No," Scarlet said, shaking her head, her mouth open in horror. "Oh God, no—"

The Hellbastards growled at Charlotte—or whatever she was now—and began to circle her as though they were about to attack, claws at the ready as they snarled at her.

"Scroteface," I said. "No!"

But it was too late. The Hellbastard's jumped on Charlotte to try to take her down, but in doing so, they put her on the defensive, and she started going crazy. Thanks to the spider legs on her back, she could move across the floor at great speed, grabbing the Hellbastard's one by one and throwing them away from her.

When she grabbed hold of Cracka, she held him with both hands and opened her mouth wide so her dripping fangs could extend to their fullest extent.

Realizing what she was going to do, I raised my gun and fired a shot, the bullet catching her in the arm she was using to hold Cracka. With a screech of pain, she dropped Cracka, and the little demon scurried away from her.

Charlotte focused on me then, baring her fangs, her black eyes as cold and emotionless as any insect.

When she ran at me, I raised my gun again, intending to empty what was left of the magazine into her, but as I went to shoot, Scarlet dived in front of me, shouting, "No, don't!"

But Charlotte had already begun her attack, one of her clawed appendages slicing through the air in a wide arc, a blow intended for me, but which caught Scarlet instead.

The next thing I knew, Scarlet was staggering back into me, holding her throat with both hands as blood spurted through her fingers.

"Scarlet!" I shouted, realizing what had happened. "No!"

Still holding her, I laid her back on the floor as gurgling sounds issued from her mouth. When she took her hands away from her throat, a huge jet of blood squirted from her neck and hit me in the face. With horror, I realized her carotid artery had been severed by the blow. In seconds, the floor around her was pooled with crimson fluid.

To stem the bleeding, I wrapped both hands around her neck, but the wound was so deep it was impossible to do anything for her. Her mouth opening and closing like a fish out of water, she stared up at me with wide eyes, and all I could do was stare back as the life ebbed from her at alarming speed.

As much as I wanted to help her, I knew I couldn't. I'd seen similar wounds before. Once the carotid was severed, that was it. Without immediate medical intervention, you'd be dead in minutes.

Scarlet knew this. As I kept my hands clamped on her neck, she gripped my wrists and kept staring up at me as the light faded from her eyes and the gurgling sounds eventually stopped.

In what seemed like no time at all, she was dead.

"Scarlet…" I said. "No…oh fuck…no…"

My eyes were full of tears as I turned my head to stare at the monster that was Charlotte. She had backed off a bit as she glared in my direction, her head moving from side to side as she appeared to take everything in. Her black eyes seemed confused, even a little afraid. Then the blackness on her skin began to peel back, revealing the human skin underneath. As the spider legs on her back retracted, her eyes changed to their former color, the bottomless blackness now replaced with their original dark blue.

Soon, I was no longer looking at a monster, but at a confused, naked girl with tears in her eyes and grief in her voice.

"Scarlet?" she said, quietly at first, and then louder as she crawled toward her dead sister. "Scarlet! Oh no!"

"She's dead," I said in a flat voice, still in a state of disbelief myself. "You killed her."

Charlotte loomed over her older sister, her face distraught, unable to believe what she'd done. "It wasn't me," she said. "I couldn't …control myself." She looked down at her bloody hands. "I'm …a monster now."

Standing, I left Charlotte to cry over her sister as I crouched against the wall, lighting a cigarette as I stared emptily at the floor.

"You alright, boss?" Scroteface said, approaching me, the other four Hellbastard's beside him.

I shook my head. "No, Scroteface. I'm not alright."

Neither of the Hellbastard's said anything more as they sat down next to me in silence.

Then, as I stared over at Scarlet's lifeless form, I saw Charlotte's spider legs emerge from her back, coming to rest on the floor so they took the full weight of her body along with her two human legs. As she bundled Scarlet's body into her arms, I stood and said, "What are you doing?"

Charlotte looked at me with sad, almost innocent eyes. "I'm leaving with my sister," she said.

"What? Where will you go?"

"I'm taking her home."

As she went to scurry off, I shouted for her to wait. Going over to her, I gazed down at Scarlet's bloodied face for a moment, and then leaned down and kissed her gently on the forehead before running my hand over her face to close her lifeless eyes.

"I'm sorry, Scarlet," I whispered.

"Why did you come here?" Charlotte asked with anger in her eyes now. "Why did you bring my sister here?"

"We came for you," I said. "Scarlet came here to save you."

Fresh tears spilled from Charlotte's eyes as a mix of emotions passed across her face, and for a second, she looked like she wanted to kill me. "Who are you?"

"I'm no one," I told her. "Just a friend of Scarlet's."

At that, she scurried off with her sister in her arms.

That was the last time I ever saw Scarlet Hood.

18

When someone dies, even if they die right in front of your eyes, there's this sense of disbelief that you can never quite get over, at least not for a long while. The person is still fresh in your memories, and they still feel a part of you. When my wife and daughter died, it took me weeks to fully accept that they were gone. In the meantime, I was left with the sensation that they were still around somewhere, even though I knew they weren't.

I felt the same about Scarlet.

Some hours after her death, I found myself in The Brokedown Palace, sitting at the bar, drunk and alone. In the dark.

When I drove back from Jonas Webb's mountain lair, I decided I wanted to be alone somewhere. For whatever reason, The Brokedown Palace came to mind. I knew it would be empty, and that the bar would still be stocked. So I went there and broke in, taking a seat at the bar so I could drown my sorrows, just like I'd done the night Callie and Angela were killed, kick-starting the process of repressing my emotions, which was all I knew how to do in the face of grief.

I'm not going to say Scarlet's death was my fault. It wasn't. No one could've predicted what would happen. No one could've known the kind of monster that Charlotte would turn into. I doubt even Webb knew precisely what he was doing when he made Charlotte. If he had lived to see it, Charlotte's transformation would've been a surprise to him too. Or maybe not. We'll never know.

Scarlet's death wasn't my fault.

I had to keep telling myself that, because every ounce of me wanted to believe that it *was* my fault she was dead. Maybe if I hadn't shot at Charlotte and put her on the defensive? Maybe if I'd been faster in my reactions, I could've pulled Scarlet out of the way? Or maybe if I hadn't let Webb kill himself, he might've been able to control the situation and stop it degenerating into the disaster that it was.

Maybe, maybe, fucking maybe…

My phone rang. Half drunk and full of Mud, I fished it out of my pocket and saw it was Hannah calling. I had several missed calls from her in the last few hours. She probably wanted to know if everything was alright. If I was okay.

I stared at the phone until it stopped ringing, before placing it down on the bar. I don't know why I didn't want to speak to her. I just didn't. All I wanted to do was drink and—

The phone rang again. A different number this time. An unknown number.

"Fuck off," I said and rejected the call, before pouring another shot of whiskey into my glass from the bottle I'd salvaged from behind the bar.

The inside of the club still stank of death. There were bloodstains everywhere. Bullet holes peppered every surface. Broken glass covered the bar. Turning in my seat, I stared up at the stage and remembered seeing Scarlet hanging there like some female Christ figure, being punished for the sins of others as well as her own. She martyred herself to save Daisy. To save me. Just like she did at the mountain facility. She dived to stop me from shooting her sister, and in the process saved my worthless ass.

"It should've been me," I mumbled to no one.

Don't cry, Daddy. Please don't cry.

"I'm sorry, sweetheart…"

The phone vibrated on the bar, startling me slightly. Picking it up, I saw there was a text from the number that I'd just cut off. The text said:

ETHAN, IT'S ERIC PIKE. WE NEED TO TALK. I HAVE INFORMATION REGARDING THE MURDER OF YOUR WIFE AND DAUGHTER. PLEASE CALL ME BACK SO WE CAN MEET.

I stared at the phone for a long time before finally picking it up and texting back:

THE BROKEDOWN PALACE. TAKE THE BACK ENTRANCE.

I hadn't seen nor spoke to Eric Pike since I left Blackstar ten years ago. We were friends once, or at least comrades in arms in the combat department of the company, even fighting alongside each other in the Secret War, spending weeks trying not to die as we and hundreds of other soldiers fought against an army of invading demons. Pike and I were about the only ones left standing after it all. Knightsbridge was so impressed, he asked me to be his head of security. When I turned him down, Pike took up the role instead. He was more suited to it than I would've been. He was sneaky, and more of a company man than I was. He also cared about impressing the boss, which I never did.

In any case, I'd had no contact with Blackstar or any of its employees since leaving the place, so I was surprised to hear from Pike. I was even more surprised when he mentioned he had information on the murders of Angela and Callie. It made me wonder what his game was, or rather Knights-bridge's game, for Pike didn't make a move without Wendell's say so. If he was coming to see me, he was coming to see me on Wendell's behalf. The question was why.

I was soon about to find out, for it didn't take long for Pike to come walking into the dark club. The lights were at a minimum, just enough to see by. Pike cut an imposing figure as he walked across the bloodstained dance floor toward me. He was about my height with a muscular build, though he seemed smaller than he was back when I knew him. His hair was still blond and slicked, and in his expensive black suit, he looked more like a salesman than head of security. His mouth was wide, and when he smiled, his whiter than white teeth were prominent. He stopped by the edge of the dance floor for a second as he looked around. "You really know how to pick 'em, Ethan," he said in his gravelly, Southern drawl. "What the hell happened here?"

"I'm surprised you don't know," I said, glancing over my shoulder at him.

"Well, we heard something went down, but we aren't quite sure what. We weren't surprised to hear that you were involved, though. You seem to be getting your hands dirty a lot these days."

"You know me, Eric," I said, pouring myself another whiskey and lighting a cigarette. "I try to help those who can't help themselves."

"Bullshit," he said, coming to sit on the stool next to me, his bright blue eyes on me now. "This is me you're talking to. You just can't leave well enough alone, can you? Was being a cop not enough for you?"

"I don't know what you mean, Eric."

"You're sticking your nose in where it doesn't belong, Ethan." He reached across the bar and found himself a shot glass, then filled it with whiskey from the bottle beside me. "Jonas Webb. What did he have to do with you?"

"What did he have to do with *you*?" I shot back.

"We were watching him to see what he'd do after his escape. Thanks to you, his little creation escaped as well. Now we have to hunt her down. What were you doing there, Ethan? Those were my men you killed on that mountain."

"Those guys were Blackstar?" I said, surprised. "Shit. If I'd known, I'd've shot them twice."

"Fuck you, Ethan." He downed his whiskey and slammed the glass on the bar. "Wendell isn't happy you interfered. Nor is he happy you called in an anonymous tip to the local Sheriff's Department."

"Someone had to clean up."

"Yeah, us. Now we have to cover up *your* fucking mess and Webb's."

"So what? It's what you're good at."

Pike shook his head at me. "Still the same asshole as always."

I lifted my glass and tipped it at him. "Right back at you."

Laughing now, Pike poured himself another shot, but let it sit on the bar as I downed another. "What are you drowning your sorrows about? What was that Hood woman to you?"

Squeezing my glass tight, I said, "Forget it."

"Was she a friend of yours? I didn't think you had friends."

"I said forget it."

"Fair enough. Anyway, that's not why I'm here."

"You said you had information for me. Or was that just bullshit?"

"No bullshit. Wendell asked me to look into things, so I did."

"Wendell? Why the fuck would he care?"

"You made an impression on him. You know he valued your services. He's not the ice-cold monster you make him out to be."

"So says his number two."

"Fuck you, Ethan. You'd still be a low-life hunter if Wendell didn't take you in. He gave you skills and a purpose."

"His purpose, not mine. There's a difference."

"See, that was always your problem, Ethan. You were never a team player."

"Don't you mean a shill?"

"You saying I'm a shill?"

"Yep."

Pike stared at me, unamused. "Well, it beats being a lousy cop."

I laughed to myself. "At least I have my integrity."

"Oh, Jesus Christ," he scoffed. "Don't start with the famous Drake integrity routine. There's no such fucking thing. We do what we do, and that's it. Integrity has nothing to do with it. Fucking naïve bullshit."

In no mood for arguing with him, I said, "Alright, Eric, what did your blazing detective skills turn up then?"

"More than *your* blazing detective skills did, it seems like."

"So out with it then." I turned to face him as I took a drag on my cigarette, noticing for the first time that he had more lines in his face than I remembered.

"Well, since you asked so nicely." He made a face at me before picking up his shot and downing it in one, grimacing at the taste. "Given the evidence and the wounds on the body, I came to the same conclusion as you. That it must've been a werewolf who killed them. Solomon also corroborated this."

"You still talk to Solomon?"

"Rarely," he said. "Wendell still uses him for certain things. I fucking hate the guy, as you know. He creeps me out, especially now with all this necromancy bullshit. As if he wasn't twisted enough."

"I can't argue with you there," I said, refilling my shot glass, putting the bottle back down after he declined another refill of his own glass. "He's more twisted than ever."

"I'm surprised you have any dealings with him at all. You hated him as much as me."

"I know, but he comes in useful sometimes. It's not like I hang out with the guy. Anyway, you were saying."

"Yeah, so I figured the wolf was probably a dog soldier

and went from there, using company resources to try to track him down."

"And I take it you did? You wouldn't be here otherwise."

He nodded. "It took me a while, but I found the bastard. Turns out he's a careful motherfucker, but not careful enough."

I swallowed, my mind ablaze with the possibility of finally confronting the man who killed my angels. "So who the fuck is he? And more to the point, where can I find him?"

"Not so fast there, killer," he said. "There are conditions attached to this information."

I shook my head and sighed. "Isn't there always? Wendell's conditions?"

"What do you think? He never gives anything away."

"Don't I know it? What conditions?"

"This case you're working on, the one involving the pregnant girl, Clare Jenkins, and the cult she was a part of."

"What about it?"

"You have to drop it."

"Fuck you."

"Really? You'd rather pursue the cult than know the identity of your family's killer?"

I poured another shot and downed it straight away, turning to face the bar now. "Why are you so interested in this case?"

"Because we are," he said. "There are things happening in this city you don't know about. You've been out of the loop for too long, Ethan."

"What things?" He said nothing as he merely stared at me. "Come on, Eric. If shit's happening in my city, I have a right to know. You're not the only one who has to shovel said shit."

"Are you going to drop the case?"

"Clare Jenkins went missing from the hospital. Did you take her?"

"No comment."

"She's just a kid. An innocent kid."

"Like I said, no comment."

"You're a fucking asshole."

"Takes one to know one. Are you going to drop the case or not? Because if not—" He went to get up. "I'll just roll on outta here and take my information with me."

Asshole. Always squeezing people. He was Wendell's man, alright. "Wait."

Pike paused as he stared at me for a second and then sat back down. "I'm glad you see sense. I mean, what's more important than finding your little girl's killer, right?"

Once again, I squeezed my glass tight. "Just tell me what I need to know."

"Sure," he said. "Once I have your word that you'll drop the case."

I turned my head to look at him, hating how he held all the cards. At least for now. "You have my word."

He smiled. "Well alright then. The guy you're after is one Derrick Savage. He's a merc mostly, but he also does contract hits if the price is right. And I'm guessing in your family's case, the price must've been right."

"No shit. Do you know who hired him?"

"You'll have to ask him that yourself." He reached into his pocket and took out a piece of paper and slid it across the bar to me. Picking it up, I saw the paper contained directions to a cabin in the Great Woods. "I'm sure he'll be glad to see you."

"How did you find him?"

"I told you, company resources. Not much gets by us, as you know. We asked around, greased the right palms, twisted the right arms…you know how it goes. We went to a lot of trouble for you, Ethan, on Wendell's behalf."

"Why does he care? We didn't exactly part on good terms."

Pike shrugged. "I guess he still has a soft spot for you. You were his number one operative. Hell, you should've had *my* job."

"Yeah, thank fuck for small mercies."

Laughing, Pike poured himself another drink. "One for the road," he said, downing it before standing up. "I'll leave you to your drinking, Ethan."

"Before you go," I said, turning to face him. "You mentioned that shit was happening in the city. What shit?" Pike grimaced for a second as if he didn't want to tell me anything. "Come on, Eric, it's me. You can tell me."

"Alright," he said after a moment's deliberation. "I guess you'll find out for yourself eventually. There seems to be a new power at play, one we haven't figured out yet, but one which Wendell is very excited about."

"What power?"

"Wendell calls it the Creation Rift," he said. "It seems there are so many Fallen concentrated in this city now, that their combined celestial powers are...changing things."

"Like how?"

"It's more people than anything else. The Creation Rift is slowly awakening certain powers in certain people."

"Like supernatural powers?"

"Yeah, kind of. Ordinary people are taking on the characteristics of figures from myths and legends. We call them Mytholites."

"Catchy. Did Wendell make that up?"

"You know Wendell," he said smiling. "And his flair for the dramatic. Anyway, these Mytholites, they're starting to pop up everywhere. The other day we came across a guy who was robbing stores with a fucking bow and giving the money to the down at heel in Bricktown, much like Robin Hood. There's also a woman out there who thinks she's Medusa, with the power to turn people into stone. There's another guy with the characteristics of Hades, though we know next to nothing about him. Another who thinks he's Jack the Ripper and who's currently on a killing spree. You get the idea. Your friend Scarlet was a Mytholite. She just didn't know it. Most of them don't, at least not yet. Many have powers, but they don't understand where these powers came from, or why they have them. Many of them don't know yet that they're walking incarnations of figures from myth and legend. They're individuals as well, you see. Their identities get mixed up with the identities of the character from myth they are taking on. Anyway, there's still a lot we don't know. Like I say, it's a fairly recent development, as far as we're aware anyway."

"Great," I said. "So now I have fucking Mytholites to deal with as well as MURKs. And let me guess, Wendell wants to tap the potential of these Mytholites for his own gain, am I right?"

Pike smiled. "Business is business, Ethan. That'll never change."

"I guess not."

"Anyway, I got shit to do," he said. "Remember our deal. Steer clear of the cult." He smiled the smile of a salesman who'd just closed a deal. "And happy hunting."

When he left, I remained at the bar, poured myself another shot and sat staring at the piece of paper that Pike had given me.

Derrick Savage, I thought. An appropriate name for a werewolf who didn't mind slaughtering innocent women and children.

"Motherfucker," I growled, crumpling the paper in my hand, enclosing my fist tight around it. "I'm coming for you."

19

I drank that much in The Brokedown Palace, and my body and mind was that drained, that I ended up falling asleep at the bar, waking up some hours later with a raging headache that even another dose of Mud couldn't shift. When I finally stumbled outside, closing the door behind me again, it appeared to be somewhere around early evening. Not dark yet, but it was getting there.

Down the alleyway, something rustled amongst discarded bags of trash, while above, something large flew silently overhead, casting a deep shadow over the Dodge for a second as it passed by.

Standing there trying to breathe fresh air into my lungs, all I was doing was inhaling the stink of the city, which after a few breaths, turned my stomach and I bent over as I vomited over a dead, maggot-infested rat. Wiping my mouth and grimacing at the foul taste there, I staggered toward the car and got inside, resting my head against the seat for a few moments as I fought not to fall asleep again.

Which I would've done had my phone not buzzed me awake. Holding it up, I saw it was Hannah. This time I answered. "Hey," I said, my voice dry and gravelly.

"I've been trying to call you," Hannah said. "Are you okay?"

"Not really."

"Did something happen?"

I stared out the window for a second before answering. "Scarlet's dead."

Hannah went silent for a long moment before asking, "What happened?" in a quiet voice.

I shook my head as if I hardly knew myself. "Things went bad."

"I'm sorry, Ethan. Are you hurt?"

"I'm fine. Where are you?"

"I'm at the precinct."

"Doing what?"

"It's nothing," she said like she didn't want to tell me.

"Hannah. What's going on?"

"Clare Jenkins' body was discovered a little while ago," she said. "She was found floating in the river. Too early to tell if it was suicide or murder."

"Jesus Christ."

"I'm handling it, though. You should probably take some time, get your—"

"I don't need time. I'll be there shortly."

"You're sure?"

"I just said so, didn't I? Don't ask me again."

"Okay. I'll see you when you get here then."

When she hung up the phone, I stared at myself in the rear-view mirror. I looked like shit, and I still had Scarlet's blood all over me. As I couldn't go into the precinct looking like I did, I started the car and headed to my apartment to get changed and freshen up.

When I got there, Daisy was sitting out on the landing, a book in her hand. As soon as she saw me, she put the book down and stood up, about to come to me until she saw all the blood on my shirt and coat.

"Ethan," she said. "What happened? Where's Scarlet? She said she would meet you. Where is she?"

Sighing inwardly, I thought, *Christ, this will be hard.*

"Ethan?" Daisy was staring at me, a look of worry on her face now, her dark eyes already filling with tears as she no doubt sensed that something bad had happened to Scarlet.

I went over to her and crouched down, putting my hands on her shoulders as I looked into her eyes. "I'm sorry, Daisy," I began. "But—"

"No," she said, tears rolling down her cheeks now. "Don't say it."

Tears welled up in my own eyes as I stared at her. "There was nothing I could do, sweetheart."

Her face crumpled then as the tears increased, and she threw her arms around me as she bawled into my shoulder. All I could do was hold her as the tears ran down my cheeks, so many thoughts and emotions going through me I hardly knew what to do. It wasn't just Scarlet I was thinking about, or Daisy, but also Callie and the grief I felt the night I'd found her. It was all coming back to the surface as I gritted my teeth against the tide of emotion that threatened to overwhelm me.

After a few minutes, Daisy broke away from me and sat down again, her back against the wall as she drew her knees tight against her chest and wrapped her arms around her legs, doing her best to sniff back the tears. I stared at her for a moment before going to sit next to her, resting my head against the wall.

We sat like that for a long time, sharing in our grief, made worse for me because I thought to myself that Daisy didn't deserve this kind of emotional battering. She got enough of that from her mother. The worst thing I ever did was draw her into my orbit.

"What happened?" she asked. "How did she die?"

"It doesn't matter," I said, shaking my head.

"It does. Tell me."

Sighing, I gave her a brief rundown of the events at the mountain hideout, leaving out the precise details of Scarlet's death. Daisy didn't need to know that Scarlet died horribly with her throat slit nearly to the bone. "I wish I could've saved her," I said. "But I couldn't."

Daisy lapsed into silence again for another while as she processed everything, then she said in a quiet voice, "She was going to teach me how to fight. She said she would before she left."

All I could do was give her a sad smile as I squeezed her knee gently. "You should steer clear of me, Daisy. Go to school, keep your head down, get good grades and then get the hell out of this city and don't look back."

"You don't want to speak to me anymore?" she asked, the devastation in her face nearly setting me off again.

Before I could answer, the door to her apartment opened and her mother stepped out into the hallway, wearing nothing but a pink satin nightdress, holding a glass of something in her hand, probably vodka. "Daisy," she said. "Get away from him. Now."

"But Momma—"

"I said now!"

Sighing, Daisy stood up and did as she was told, trudging over to her mother, who ushered her into the apartment, Daisy giving me a forlorn look before disappearing inside.

Her mother then pointed a boney finger at me. "You stay the hell away from my daughter, murderer."

Standing up, I just stared at her and nodded. There was no point in saying anything to her. Besides, she was right. Daisy shouldn't be hanging around with someone like me. In that sense, at least her mother was looking out for her, or perhaps she was just jealous that Daisy seemed to want to be around me at all. In any case, I walked straight past her, hearing her close the door to her apartment just as I reached mine.

~

When I opened the door, I was hit with the massive stench of dank marijuana. "Jesus Christ," I said as I walked in, the living room enveloped in a haze of thick smoke. On the couch, the Hellbastards sat in a stoned stupor. All of them, not just Reggie. They were passing a joint as thick as my index finger from one to the other as they watched some cartoon on the TV. They barely noticed me even as I stood staring down at them by the side of the couch. "Having a little downtime, boys?" I said.

Reggie, who held the joint, jumped at the sound of my voice, and the others all turned their heads slowly to look at me, their buggy eyes half-closed, their jaws slack. In Cracka's case, his long forked tongue was hanging out the side of his mouth like it was trying to escape. Even Scroteface was pulling strange expressions and occasionally twitching as he did his best to stare at the TV.

"Boss is home," Snot Skull announced to the others, but in a whisper that could barely be heard above the sound of the TV.

Then Reggie looked up at me and slowly extended his arm to offer me the joint. "Smoke boss? It's a heavy-duty indica. We think it might be laced with something. Not sure what. Heroin maybe. Or LSD."

"Both," Scroteface whispered.

"Jesus Christ," I said. "You guys are getting worse. Where do you even get this shit?"

"Stash house up the street, boss," Reggie said.

"That's handy," I said as I looked at Scroteface, who was moving his head in circles like he was watching a fly buzz round and round. "What the fuck's up with Scroteface?"

"I think he's trippin', boss," Reggie said. "I think I am too. Did you dye your hair green?"

"No, Reggie," I said. "I didn't."

"Then I'm trippin'," he said, staring at the TV once more.

In the ensuing silence, Cracka freaked everyone out by jumping to his feet like a wasp had just stung his balls, shouting, "By the power of Grayskull!" in his small voice with his tongue still hanging out. As everyone stared—the other Hellbastards wide-eyed like they didn't know how to react—Cracka started singing the theme tune to *He-Man and the Masters of the Universe*, or trying to anyway. Most of it was garbled nonsense, but he hummed it with gusto, finally finishing by punching the air with his fist and shouting, "I have the powerrrrrrrrrr!"

When he was done, he sat down again and stared at the TV like he was the only one in the room.

Everyone, including me, continued to stare at Cracka for another minute. Then the other Hellbastards shook their heads and carried on with their smoke session as if nothing had happened. "I'm just gonna leave you guys to it," I said, slinking off. "I gotta go to work. Just try not to go outside or anything, alright?"

"Sure boss," Reggie said, seemingly the least stoned among them.

Before I turned away, Snot Skull rotated his head in my direction, his black eyes almost staring through me. "Scar-let," he whispered, then smiled, revealing all of his needle teeth.

Frowning, I shook my head at him before disappearing into the bedroom, wondering when the moment would come when I would finally go utterly insane.

WITH ANOTHER BLOODSTAINED SHIRT TOSSED IN THE TRASH and a fresh one on, I left the Hellbastards to their cartoons and weed-fueled trip on the sofa and drove straight to the precinct. When I got there, the media were crowded around the front public entrance and Routman was standing on the steps looking down on them, taking the opportunity to shine in front of the cameras, doing his best to play the role of the grim, determined cop as he spoke about the murders of three prostitutes, which I knew nothing about. But apparently, someone had murdered the three women by butchering them Jack the Ripper style, making me think about what Pike had said. Maybe this killer was one of these Mytholites that he had mentioned? Not that I cared about fucking Mytholites at this point. I had enough to deal with.

Routman assured the media that we were indeed now looking for a serial killer, which the media had already dubbed The Ripper Tripper, because apparently the bodies of the prostitutes showed inordinately high levels of LSD in their systems, a detail I was surprised but not surprised to hear discussed in front of the media. It used to be such telling details were kept in-house and away from the media, at least until the perp was caught. Now it seemed like everything was being directly uploaded to the hungry media, which in turn fed the bottomless appetites of the mass consumers who needed fresh news every day…hell, every fucking second.

"Should we watch out for a man in a cloak wearing a top hat?" some joker asked from the media crowd, causing everyone to start laughing, including Routman, even though I knew he wouldn't really find that remark funny in the least.

Shaking my head, I walked around to the side entrance and entered the precinct, making my way down to the subbasement where I knew Hannah would be. When I got there, she was sitting at her desk, appearing to stare at her hand as she held it palm up in front of her face. It was only when I got closer that I noticed there was something floating near the center of her palm. A tiny flame, glowing with intense brightness as it lit up her face, which held an almost serene smile. "Hi," she said, her smile unwavering as she looked up at me. "It's beautiful, isn't it?"

I had to agree. There was a purity to the little flame that

I'd never seen in anything before, but also a vastness of potential just waiting within it to be tapped somehow. It calmed my anxiety just looking at it and almost made me forget that Scarlet hadn't long died in my arms. "Yes, it is," I said. "What is it?"

"The Light of God." She continued staring at it as though she believed the Creator was within the flame. "Can you feel His presence?"

Staring at the flame, I hardly knew what to say. "I—I'm not sure."

Her smile turned to one of slight sadness as she looked up at me, the flame in her palm now extinguished. Standing up—the vague image of her Visage wavering just behind her, a winged being of light—she put her arms around me and held me there as I stood stiffly for a second before finally responding by putting my arms around her shoulders and holding her too. The same sense of tranquility and peacefulness that I felt from the flame, I also felt in her now. She understood, somehow, that I didn't want to talk about it. She understood that I needed to know she was there for me, even though I didn't realize I needed to know that until she put her arms around me. When I closed my eyes, I reveled in the respite from the pain, knowing it probably wouldn't last long.

And indeed, several moments later, when she finally let me go, the pain returned soon after, seeping in again like it had just popped out for a smoke break, all like, *I'm back motherfucker. Did you miss me?*

"You seem unusually…angelic," I said to her as I sat on the edge of her desk, noticing the lack of scarring on her face now. "Any reason for that?"

She smiled as she sat in her chair. "I was thinking about you," she said. "Thinking about the pain you would be in; the grief you'd be feeling. I wondered how I could help you and —" She shook her head like she couldn't explain it. "I don't know, I just started to feel different, and then I remembered things from my time as an Elohim in the celestial Heavens. It feels now like God is flowing through me again. It might just be temporary, like before when I saved you. Even if it is, I don't mind, for I got to make you feel better, if only a little bit."

As much as I appreciated what she did, it was also weird seeing her in such a spiritually aware state, especially after witnessing her as evil incarnate not two days before. It was jarring, which she seemed to sense as her smile began to fade. So I stood up and then leaned down toward her, taking her porcelain face in my hands before softly kissing her on the lips. "You're exactly what I need right now," I said.

Her smile returned. "Okay, then. How about we take down some bad guys?"

"Sure," I said, smiling. "Why the fuck not?"

We both stood, and then she said, "By the way, did Scarlet scream when she died?"

I stared at her in shock. Her Visage was now demonic; dark and winged and menacing. She quickly looked away and covered her mouth with her hand, bending over slightly like she was going be sick. Her looming Visage turned to me as though smiling, eyes glowing faintly within it. When Hannah took her hand away from her mouth, she said, "Ethan, I'm sorry, I—"

"Forget it."

"No, I—"

"I said—" I paused for a second to set my jaw and control my anger. "I said forget it."

She shook her head, more at herself, and turned around so her back was to me. "I'm sorry," she said quietly.

I stared at her for a moment, before saying, "I'm going to talk to the captain about getting backup to raid the boarding school. You should get ready."

~

STILL SHAKING MY HEAD AT HANNAH'S UNPREDICTABLE taciturn nature, I walked into the captain's office to speak with him, unsurprised that he acted hostile from the get-go. "What is it, Drake? You run out of holy water or something?" He barely smiled as he glared at me.

I resisted the urge to tell him to go fuck himself, as much as I wanted to. I was only there out of courtesy. Whatever I needed, all I had to do was go straight to Lewellyn. But as Edwards could make life difficult for me, and because I knew he was rallying to get rid of me altogether, I thought I should choose not to go above his head for a change. "No, sir," I said, remaining calm. "I need a team so my unit can raid a cult hideout."

And yes, I'm well aware of the deal I made with Pike. But fuck him, and fuck Blackstar. This was about justice, not self-interest.

Edwards stared at me for a moment, a look of disbelief on his face. "You have some balls, Drake, coming in here and asking for my men to help you out with one of your so-called cases."

"So-called, sir? That girl they took out of the river a while ago was probably killed by this cult."

"So you say. The report says she committed suicide."

I rolled my eyes. "It would say that, wouldn't it?"

"So now you're questioning the credibility of the forensics team and the experienced investigators who came to that conclusion?" He shook his head. "Get out, Drake. I've got work to do here."

"I came in here out of courtesy," I said, struggling to hold down my anger. "You know I can go straight to Lewellyn. Why are you making this difficult?"

Edwards clacked his pen down and stood, coming around his desk to face me. "Let me be clear, Drake," he said, his eyes boring into me. "For as long as I'm in charge of this department, you will never get any help from me or anyone else here. You got that? Your fucked up little unit means nothing to me or any of my men. You're a fucking joke, Drake. A burnout, and everyone knows it. There's simply no place for you or your weird-ass partner in this department anymore. As far as I'm concerned, it's time for you to go. I've already set the ball in motion. It's just a matter of time."

Balling my fists by my sides, I wanted to hit him, and he knew it. He almost dared me to. But we both knew if I did, my tenure as a cop would be over the second my knuckles connected with his face. "Don't think I won't fight you on this," I snarled.

Snorting, he smiled with disdain. "I wouldn't expect any less from you, Drake. That doesn't mean you'll win. Quite the opposite. Now, if you'll excuse me, I have real work to do. See yourself out."

Seething with anger, I stormed out of Edwards' office and went to the men's restroom. Inside, I lit a cigarette and paced the floor as I tried to calm down.

What the fuck am I still doing here? I thought to myself. *Why don't I just leave the force?*

I didn't need this shit. Didn't need to take shit from cunts like Edwards anymore either. But as usual, I also wondered what the hell I would do if I wasn't a cop. Go back to Blackstar? Not fucking likely. Or I could become a PI. Maybe. It's something I've considered a few times. At least I'd be my own boss, then. Maybe it was an idea I'd have to give serious thought to since Edwards wasn't backing down. And as Lewellyn's influence and resolve only stretched so far, I had to accept the fact that my days as a cop were now numbered.

20

After my altercation with Edwards, I phoned Lewellyn, but I kept getting his voicemail. After three attempts to get through to him, I finally said fuck it and went to get Hannah. "Let's go," I told her in the subbasement.

"Did you speak to the captain?" she asked. "Did he approve a backup team?"

"Does it look like he did?"

She shook her head but said nothing. Sighing, I walked out of the subbasement, and she followed behind me, the two of us not speaking until we were inside my car.

"I'm sorry about earlier," she said. "Are you mad still?"

"I'm not mad at you," I said, realizing she couldn't help who she was. "I know you didn't mean it."

"I didn't. Xaglath is still very much a part of me, and I can't seem to get rid of her."

I lit a cigarette and blew the smoke out the window. "We are who we are, Hannah," I said. "The best we can do is try to control our darker urges. There's no getting rid of them, unfortunately."

"I *am* trying."

Putting a hand on her leg, I said, "I know you are, though

maybe this job isn't the best environment for you, given that it
brings out your demon side more often than not."

"What are you saying, Ethan?"

"I'm saying maybe you should consider another line of
work." I turned to stare out the window at the passing traffic.
"Our days at this precinct are numbered anyway."

"Why? What did Edwards say to you?"

"He wants rid of me. Of us. And I don't think there's
much we can do to stop him."

"What about Lewellyn? Surely he can do something."

"Lewellyn has made it clear there's only so far he's willing
to go," I said. "He'll not stand by me if the pressure is that
great, which it will be, because Edwards has significant reach
within the force. Edwards will make sure Lewellyn's career
suffers if he stands in his way. And Lewellyn wants to be
mayor too much to let that happen. So we're fucked. Which is
why I'm saying you might want to start looking elsewhere for
another job."

"I wouldn't know what else to do."

"I'm sure there's a lot you can do if you put your mind
to it."

"Really? Like what? Working in a bank? Serving burgers?
Answering phones in a call center?" She laughed at the very
idea of those jobs. "Not going to happen."

"So what are you saying?" I asked her.

"Maybe we should work for ourselves," she said. "Become
private eyes."

"I've already thought of that. It's an option, I guess."

"Seems like the only one to me."

"We'll see," I said, throwing my cigarette out the window.
"Shit, maybe we could join the fucking FBI, become G-men."
I laughed at the thought.

Hannah laughed as well, though the idea didn't seem so
bad to her. "Look," she said. "I know you think I'm this
fucked up, schizo bitch or whatever, but you know, you're not

in great mental shape either, are you?" She stared at me as I laughed, somewhat taken aback by her bluntness. "Anyway, what I'm trying to say is, we have each other, and we should maybe keep it that way, don't you think? Not like we're married or anything, but more like, you know——"

"Partners?" I offered.

She smiled. "Yes, partners. I mean, what do you think about that?"

"I think you're fucking crazy if you want to keep being partners with me. But you don't die easy, so there's that." When she just stared at me, I said, "Relax, I'm just fucking with you. Sort of. We can stay partners, yeah. Why the fuck not?"

"Why the fuck not," she repeated, holding her fist out toward me.

"Seriously?" I said. "Fist bump? Okay…" I bumped fists with her and she smiled.

"It's a done deal then," she said.

Shaking my head, I started the engine. "Why does it feel like I just got married?"

∾

WE WERE GOING TO HIT THE CULT AT THE BOARDING SCHOOL. It was on, despite some shoddy deal that I made with Pike in bad faith, and despite what the captain said back at the precinct. The cult, led by Gretchen Carmichael and backed by Blackstar it seemed, had claimed the lives of who knew how many innocent women and men—including poor Clare Jenkins—and so the cult, along with Carmichael, had to be stopped.

More than that, they had to pay. They weren't going to face justice any other way, were they? And was this not the reason I had agreed to head up Lewellyn's two-man unit in the first place? To stride into the darkness where no one else would go and extract justice from it? More importantly, to get at least *some* justice for the victims that nobody cared about? Fucking-A-right it was.

As we needed to gear up, I thought it might be easier to visit Scarlet's storage unit rather than drive all the way to my apartment. Besides, I didn't want to risk bumping into Daisy again and then having to explain to her what I was doing just so she could worry about me all over again. I wanted to keep Daisy out of the madness, and as such, I was even considering moving out of my apartment so Daisy would never have to see me again. So I could never put her in danger again.

It was a sombre experience visiting Scarlet's storage unit. Just seeing her outfits and all of her gear was enough to fill me with sadness, and yes, even guilt. Hannah sensed this as she squeezed my arm and asked me if I was okay. Nodding, I told her I would be. "Take whatever you need," I said to her, and when she started eyeing up the outfits, I told her no. "That's too much. Leave them."

A short time later, we left the storage unit with a duffel bag full of guns and several flash grenades which I put into the trunk of the Dodge, having to slam the lid three times since the lock wasn't working properly.

"What about Haedemus?" Hannah asked. "Since we have no backup, maybe we could use him."

"It's a long way for him to gallop," I said as we got into the car.

"Maybe I can summon him."

"Well, you summoned him from Hell, so I don't see why not."

"I'll try when we get there."

"I'm sure he'll be thrilled."

∼

IT WAS A GOOD HOUR AND A HALF'S DRIVE TO THE LOCATION

of the old boarding school, which was nestled deep in the countryside, far from the city and any surrounding residential dwellings. The cult couldn't have picked a better spot in terms of privacy and isolation.

All the way out here, no one could hear the screams.

We were parked halfway down a grassy lane and about fifty yards up ahead was a set of wrought-iron gates that stood about ten feet high. Beyond the gates was a road that led to the old boarding school building. Under the light of the cold moon, the building looked ominous perched up there on a hill, the clock tower and spires stretching up into the dark sky like grasping fingers, the white paint on the building's plaster surface long since faded to a sickly yellow color. If it weren't for the few lights shining from inside, you would think the building had been abandoned and left to rot, just like the body of Clare Jenkins had been.

"How many do you think are in there?" Hannah asked as she stared through the window toward the old school building.

"I don't know," I said. "I guess we'll find out soon enough."

"So what's the plan?"

"We go in, save who we can and take down anyone who gets in our way."

"And the leader?"

"We kill her."

Hannah nodded. "Slowly?"

I threw her a look. "Keep your demon in check there, killer."

"I just mean she deserves it, considering what she's done here to all those girls."

"You wanting to get your hands bloody again?"

"I'm getting that either way."

"I suppose," I said. "There's something else you should know, by the way."

"What?"

"Blackstar is involved with this cult. Don't be surprised if they show up once we move in."

"Blackstar? The company you used to work for?"

"Yeah. They've already warned me off this place. I told them I'd stay away. They're gonna be pissed when they find out we're here."

"Will they try to kill us?"

"I'm not sure."

"Do you want to pull out?"

I turned my head to look at her. "No."

She smiled. "Let's do it then."

ABOUT TWENTY MINUTES LATER, HANNAH AND I WERE standing outside by the car. Above us, the sky had darkened considerably as thick clouds formed, covering the moon and bringing the threat of rain as the distant rumble of thunder could be heard. Hannah and I both held Heckler & Koch MP5K's, our pockets filled with extra mags. My trench pockets also held four flash grenades. Standing next to Hannah was Haedemus, having been successfully summoned.

"I can't tell you what this means to me," Haedemus said. "It means so much that you would summon me here to help out. If I had a beating heart, it would be bursting from my chest with gratitude right now."

"So basically," I said, checking my weapon. "You were bored shitless until we summoned you here."

"Yes, that's about right," Haedemus said.

"Maybe you should get a human body," Hannah said. "So you can engage with this world more."

Haedemus stared at her for a moment. "I'm not sure how I feel about that. I like my massive cock. Downgrading to something of Ethan's size would be a considerable shock to my system."

"I'm not sure I want you in a human body either," I said. "You're annoying enough as it is."

"Yeah, fuck you, Ethan. You weren't saying that when I saved your ass from that hybrid guy who jumped you on the way to the beach."

"I had it handled."

"He had you pinned to the ground, and you were wincing like a baby."

"You'll be wincing like a baby soon if you don't shut it," I said.

"See, he's defensive," he said to Hannah. "He knows I'm right."

"Alright, Haedemus, enough," Hannah said, just as I summoned the Hellbastards. The five of them appeared beside me, still looking stoned, gazing around them like they didn't know where they were, which I guess they didn't.

"Hello, boys," I said. "I hope you're up for some mayhem."

"Mayhem, boss?" Scroteface said in a flat voice, staring at me with glassy eyes.

"How much more did you holy terrors smoke?" I asked them.

"Few more joints, boss," Reggie said. "We're good, though."

"Yeah," I said. "You all look it too. Cracka's eyes are like two piss holes in the snow."

Haedemus guffawed. "Two piss holes in the snow. Good one, Ethan. You're funny...sometimes."

Ignoring Haedemus, I said to Scroteface, "Can you handle this or do I have to send you all back?"

Snot Skull, wearing a little girl's flowery dress and red lipstick for some reason, started dancing about like a boxer, throwing sloppy punches in the air like he was warming up for the battle to come. "We got this, boss. Don't worry."

"We have the power, boss," Cracka said, raising his fist without much enthusiasm.

I shook my head at the state of them all. "What kind of fucking team have I got around me? Five Hellbastards who barely know what day it is, a Hellicorn with a superiority complex and——" I stopped when I looked at Hannah.

"Yes?" Hannah said, smiling. "You were saying?"

"Rules of engagement," I said, changing the subject. "Let's go over them. Only engage if necessary. We're here to free the girls that have been kidnapped, and the boys if there are any. Everyone else is fair game. There'll probably be hybrids in there too. Watch out for them. They're strong."

"As you know already, Ethan," Haedemus said.

"Yeah," I said. "Feel free to kill them. We don't need their kind running around."

"What if Blackstar shows up?" Hannah said. "Do we engage?"

"Not unless you have to," I said. "Blackstar is not to be underestimated. Their operatives are well-trained and know their shit. They won't hesitate to kill you if they have to. All of you. They have weapons that can do serious damage."

"So do we, boss," Cracka said, holding his over-sized penis in one hand.

As Haedemus burst out laughing, I told Cracka to shut up and get it together. "Alright, you's fucking degenerates, I'm just wasting my fucking breath here, aren't I?"

"Yes, you are, Ethan," Haedemus said.

"Well," I said. "In that case, let's get on with it. Lock and load, motherfuckers."

"Lock and load!" Cracka cheered.

21

There seemed to be very little in the way of security around the old boarding school building. As we climbed over the wall surrounding the place—Haedemus leaping clean over it—I saw no cameras or even any guards out on patrol. It seemed like the cult thought themselves safe in their isolation, an assumption we would soon fuck up the ass good and proper.

"We stick together as much as possible," I said as we made our way up a grassy slope toward the front door of the building, just as the first drops of rain started to fall from the sky. "Our objective is to locate the cult leader first. Once we take care of her, the rest should be easy. Try not to hurt any of the cult members. Most of them are probably brainwashed. The hybrids you can kill."

I was expecting some resistance before we made it to the front door, but we encountered none. No one appeared to spot us from inside, and no hybrids came running to meet us.

At least they didn't until Haedemus let out a massive fart that cracked the air like thunder. I'd never heard a noise like it. "What the fuck?" I said, shocked at the ongoing sound coming out of the Hellicorn's ass.

"I'm sorry," Haedemus said as he bent over slightly. "I... ate...something that ...didn't agree with me."

"A fucking hot-air balloon?" I said.

The Hellbastards thought the whole thing was hilarious and were practically rolling on the grass as they laughed uncontrollably, the blast of stinking gas escaping from Haedemus' asshole filling the air with an infernal stink.

With all the noise, I wasn't surprised to see a curtain twitch inside the school building, and a few seconds later, the front door opened as half a dozen men came running out, all dressed in dark robes.

"Contact!" I shouted, and immediately opened fire on who I assumed were hybrids. My initial burst with the HK downed one hybrid straight away, but the others moved so fast it was impossible to get a bead on them.

In seconds, they were on us. Five hybrids, all looking the same with smooth, bald heads and similar faces. Two of them started attacking me, flanking me on each side, both of them delivering punches and kicks at the same time.

With the HK hanging across my chest, I did my best to block the onslaught of blows coming at me at shocking speed, until that is, one of the hybrids kicked my leg out and I hit the deck. But as I fell, my hand immediately went to my sidearm, which I pulled out at speed and pointed at the nearest hybrid, shooting him three times in the chest before the other hybrid kicked the gun out of my hand. Using the same leg, he lifted it and was about to stamp it down on my face before Cracka leapt at him, clinging to the hybrid's face like an alien Face-Hugger, scratching at the hybrid's eyes as the hybrid tried to pry the little demon off him.

To help matters along, I took hold of the HK from my prone position and fired a burst that peppered the hybrid's legs, immediately causing him to fall. Cracka held on tight, and when the hybrid hit the ground, Cracka went to work on the guy's face, scratching and clawing and biting until the hybrid eventually started to scream, his face a bloody mess, his eyeballs scooped from their sockets and dangling against his cheeks.

Cracka laughed. "He ain't pretty no more, boss," he said gleefully, echoing the line from *Raging Bull*, a movie we all watched together one night.

When I got up, I saw that Haedemus had impaled one of the other hybrids on his razor-sharp horn. The hybrid was doing his best to pull himself off the bony protrusion, but his hands were so slick with blood that he couldn't do it, much to Haedemus' amusement. "You look like a stupid fuck hanging there," Haedemus taunted. "Here, let me help you."

With a sharp flick of his massive head, Haedemus drove the sharp edge of his horn up through the hybrid's chest and then through his skull, splitting the hybrid almost in two before he finally slipped off the horn and onto the blood-drenched grass.

A few feet away, Snot Skull was busy vomiting acid over the face of one of the other hybrids, while Toast shot fire at the guy's balls. Scroteface had his hand in the hybrid's chest as he appeared to try to rip out the guy's heart.

Reggie, meanwhile, stood to the side smoking a joint as he watched on. When he saw me looking, he raised a hand in half salute and said, "Boss," like he was the supervisor on some factory floor inspecting the work of his men.

That only left one more hybrid, and Hannah was taking care of him. She seemed to have tapped into her demon self as she stood up the hill a little, using her telekinetic powers to hold the remaining hybrid high in the air in front of her. With her back to me—her Visage looming darkly behind her—she had her hands out in front of her as she appeared to be slowly moving them apart like she was trying to stretch some invisible force.

When the hybrid started screaming, and his body began to stretch horizontally, I realized what she was doing. She was trying to tear the hybrid apart, and a few seconds later, she succeeded. With a final agonized scream, the hybrid's body ripped in half in mid-air, showering blood everywhere. As the two halves of his body hit the grass with a wet slapping sound —steam rising from the innards—Hannah relaxed her hands and turned around, her face dripping with hybrid blood. In her eyes, I saw the presence of Xaglath, who appeared to smile knowingly at me. "I thought you said these hybrids were strong?" she said.

Unsure of whether I was talking to Hannah or Xaglath or a combination of both, I said, "Clearly not to you."

She smiled again as she licked the blood from her mouth. "Clearly not."

After that, we wasted no more time and made our way into the school building. Stepping into the entrance hall, I expected to be met by more hybrid soldiers, but the hall was empty. Wood panels and old pictures decked the walls, giving the impression that you were stepping back in time. You could almost imagine the snot-nosed kids and strict school teachers who once frequented these hallways.

"Oh, very posh," Haedemus said as he stomped across the wood floor. "I wonder if they keep ponies out the back."

I shook my head at him. "Why don't you go around and see? Take your time. We'll wait."

"I think I'll just hang around here," he said. "Since I can't open doors, and since I don't do stairs either."

"Yeah," I said. "Good idea."

As the Hellbastards hung with Haedemus in the entrance hallway, Hannah and I checked the ground floor, opening doors and looking inside various rooms, finding no one.

After covering most of the ground floor, we headed upstairs to the first floor and started checking rooms there as well, only most of them were secured with electronic locks. "The girls that Clare talked about must be inside these rooms," Hannah said. "Drugged up, no doubt."

"I think you might be right," I said. "We'll come back for them later. Let's find Gretchen Carmichael first. Once we take her out, we'll come back and free whoever needs freeing."

Above us, we could hear muted footsteps and voices coming from what must have been an attic room. "Maybe they're all hiding because they know we're here," Hannah said in a hushed voice.

"Maybe," I said as the Hellbastards fell in behind me.

We soon found the staircase leading up to the attic room. Halfway up, we were met by two hybrids, both of whom had long daggers in their hands. Reacting quickly, Hannah shot both her hands out and used her power to stop the hybrids in their tracks, lifting them both up in the air. As she did, I raised my HK and fired a burst into each of their chests. When Hannah let them go, they both fell on the stairs in a heap.

"That was easy," Hannah said smiling, enjoying herself.

I was about to agree when I heard the Hellbastards shouting behind us. When we turned, we saw two of the hybrids that had attacked us outside. One of them had bullet holes in his chest; the other had half his face missing thanks to Cracka.

"What the fuck?" I said, raising my gun. "Don't these fucks die?" I opened fire on the two of them, hitting them both, the bullets driving them back down the stairs, but not killing them.

"We got this, boss!" Scroteface shouted, back in the swing of things as he led his crew toward the damaged hybrids, who were getting up again, now joined by two more of their kind, including the one whose head was melted by Snot Skull's acid vomit. How the hell he was still standing, I'll never know. The Hellbastards attacked with their usual gusto, holding the hybrids off as Hannah and I fired a few more bursts at them.

"Upstairs," I told Hannah when we'd finished firing. "We need to get to Carmichael before she fucks off on us."

At the top of the stairs we came to a door, and when I

tried the handle, I realized it was locked. I was about to boot the door when Hannah stopped me. "I can do it," she said, her Visage almost enveloping her.

"Wait," I said and handed her one of the flash grenades, getting ready with one myself. From inside, we heard voices, though it was hard to tell what was going on. Hannah then slammed one hand against the door and used her power to break the heavy wooden door off its hinges, sending it flying into the room.

A second later, I tossed my flash grenade into the room to a chorus of screams. Once Hannah had thrown her grenade, we both flattened against the wall until we heard the loud bangs going off inside the room.

Shouldering my weapon, I went in first.

Inside the large room, a group of naked females were crouched over or lying on the floor, their hands clamped over their ears, disorientated from the flash-bang grenades. Over by a large window there was a bloodstained altar, the surface covered in gore. Behind the altar stood a woman wearing dark red robes. She had braided blond hair and wide blue eyes that stared right at me, no sense of fear in them.

"Nobody fucking move!" I shouted.

"You have no right breaking in here," the woman behind the altar said, who had to be Gretchen Carmichael. She was well-spoken, obviously well educated, and had the arrogance of someone who had never wanted for anything in her life.

Ignoring Carmichael for a moment, I stared around at the naked girls, most of whom seemed to be young, all in and around Clare Jenkins' age. There were over a dozen of them, each of them covered in blood like they had been rolling around in the stuff before we got here. I also noticed the look in their eyes—hatred and aggression. Some of them looked like they wanted to attack us.

"Don't!" I warned them, backing up a little.

Most of the girls were on their feet now, standing together

like a bunch of crazed killers. Then out of nowhere, one girl vomited, puking up what appeared to be pure blood and bits of flesh that slapped wetly onto the wood floor.

"Hold it in, girl!" Carmichael shouted. "What you hold in your belly is precious!"

I didn't have to ask what was going on here. We had just walked in on a Drencher Host Ritual, which Clare Jenkins had told us all about.

The girls were covered in blood because they had just eaten some poor guy on the altar.

But if that was the case, where was what remained of him; the so-called drencher, the demon that had taken over what was left of his body?

A few seconds later, I had my answer as something landed in front of me, having just dropped from the ceiling. Backing up slightly, I stared in disgust at the thing that had landed on the floor. It was the top half of a young man barely into his twenties, ribs exposed as his guts trailed the floor. The thing held itself up by its arms, and from its coal-black eyes, it was clear this monstrosity was a demon, having hijacked the body of the young man, or what was left of him.

As Carmichael and the girls watched on, the drencher advanced toward me, and as it did, I fired a burst at it. But the thing was fast and was able to jump to the side with surprising ease, considering it was maneuvering on just two arms. As I swung round to fire again, the drencher leaped at me, propelling itself off the floor so it flew toward me with wild eyes and a screeching open mouth.

Next thing I knew, its bloody arms were around my neck, and its head was leaning in as it tried to bite my face.

"Fuck!" I shouted as I held the thing by the neck, taken aback by how preternaturally strong it was. It was like trying to wrestle with a slippery ape, and before long, it was using one hand to punch me on the side of the head continually. One of its punches caught me clean on the chin, and a second later I saw stars as my vision began to black out and I toppled over with the drencher still clinging to me.

When my vision cleared, the drencher's head was above mine, bloody saliva drooling from its open mouth over my face as its black eyes peered down upon me.

Then it said in a raspy voice, "I...will...eat...you."

As it gnashed its teeth at me, I jerked my head away from it. So instead, the thing bit down on my chest, its teeth biting into my flesh as I roared in pain. The drencher then pulled its head up sharply and came away with a lump of my flesh in its mouth. Despite the pain, a rush of rage went through me as I gritted my teeth and jammed my thumb into one of the drencher's eye sockets, pushing forward as I sat up and finally shoved the creature away from me.

When I stood up, I saw Hannah standing a few feet away. Her eyes were almost full amber, and there was a cruel smile on her face.

Fucking Xaglath.

"A little help?" I said.

In no hurry, Xaglath turned to face the drencher as it was pulling out the eyeball I had crushed with my thumb. Using her demonic power, Xaglath telekinetically lifted the drencher off the floor and flung it at the wall. The drencher screeched as it bounced off the plaster, sounding like its neck had broken.

When it landed, its head was tilted at an odd angle as it stared at us. Perhaps seeing it was now at a disadvantage, it went bounding across the floor on its two arms and leaped up onto the altar. As a shocked Carmichael jumped aside, the drencher then leaped off the altar and crashed through the window, disappearing into the night.

At that point, the Hellbastards entered the room, their eyes ogling the naked flesh everywhere. "Jackpot, boys," Scroteface said, rubbing his hands together and inhaling deeply.

"Forget the fucking jackpot," I told him, "and get after that thing that just jumped out the window."

The Hellbastards looked annoyed that they had to leave the room with all its naked delights, but they did as they were told.

Although Cracka couldn't help himself on the way out and stopped to talk to the gaggle of naked girls, who collectively stepped back, appearing freaked out by the little demon. "Cracka be back soon," he said. "Keep those pussies warm!"

A few of the girls hissed at Cracka as he made his way to the altar. Once atop the altar, he turned and shouted, "Wocka wocka!" before leaping out the window after the others.

"You'll pay for this desecration," Carmichael said, now standing in front of the girls as if she was trying to protect her assets, which is what the girls were to her at the end of the day —hybrid-making machines.

Tossing away the HK, I took out my sidearm and pointed it at her. "You're about to pay now, bitch," I said.

In response to my threat, the thirteen naked girls all crowded around Carmichael, shielding her from me as they hissed and spat in my direction, making sure I couldn't get a shot.

"Stand aside, bitches," Xaglath then said, waving her arms as she used her powers to forcibly toss the girls to either side of the room, the girls screaming as they were lifted into the air and then flung away like so much trash.

"Don't hurt them!" I said to Xaglath. "They're innocents."

"No one is innocent," Xaglath said, now turning her attention to Carmichael, who for the first time now seemed afraid as Xaglath used her invisible force to lift her off the ground and hold her in the air as Carmichael kicked her feet in a struggle to get free.

Once more, I pointed my gun at her.

"You'll never get away with this!" she screamed. "You can't kill me! Do you even know who I am?"

"I know full well who you are," I said, walking closer to her. "You're a spoiled rich kid with a penchant for evil and too much time on her hands." I took another step closer. "And now you'll have all the time in the world once I squeeze this trigger."

As I was about to shoot, however, I heard a noise from behind me. Footsteps were coming up the stairs. As Carmichael smiled, I turned around to see men in familiar black tactical gear storm into the room, hi-tech weapons raised and pointed in my direction.

A second later, I wasn't surprised to see Eric Pike walk into the room, his face set in anger. "God damn you, Ethan," he said as he looked around the room at the naked girls lying everywhere, and then at Carmichael as she continued to be suspended in the air by Xaglath. "I thought we had a deal."

"*You* thought that," I said as I continued to point my gun at Carmichael. "Not me. Did you think I was going to let this bitch get away with everything, just so you could collect some new specimens for Knightsbridge?"

"Yeah, I did actually," Pike said. "I thought you'd wised up over the years. Looks like I was wrong. You're as much of a stubborn asshole as you always were."

"And you're fucking deluded if you think I'm letting this bitch go free," I said.

"You'd better," Pike said, looking at his team, all of whom had their weapons trained on me. "If you pull that trigger, it's over for you, Ethan." He took a step forward. "Why don't you just put the gun down and maybe I'll let you walk out of here alive. It's not too late to salvage this situation."

A tense silence descended upon the room. I looked over at Xaglath, whose face was worried enough for me to know that Hannah was in there somewhere, probably panicking that I would get shot if I didn't comply, though she made no move to release Carmichael from her invisible bonds. From there, my eyes drifted to the girls lying around the room, most of whom looked lost and afraid now.

What if Callie was one of them? I thought. *What if Daisy was one of them, her belly filled with human flesh and demon seed?*

There was no way I could allow this to happen to any more innocent girls, nor allow anyone else to end up in the river like Clare Jenkins did.

There was also no way I would allow Blackstar and its puppets to tell me what to do.

"Ethan," Pike said, his face changing now as he stepped forward again. "Think about this. Do you really want to sacrifice yourself to kill that stuck-up bitch? Come on, man. We both know there will always be more like her. You won't change anything if you squeeze that trigger. You'll just be dead along with her."

My gun arm never wavered as I stood to the side, looking from Pike to Carmichael.

"Fuck you, Eric," I said.

Then I squeezed the trigger and shot Gretchen Carmichael in the head.

22

After I squeezed the trigger on Carmichael, I closed my eyes for a second as I waited on a hail of bullets to hit me.

But none did.

"Fuck!" Pike shouted from behind me. "Ethan, you fucking asshole!"

I turned around to see that the guns were no longer trained on me. Pike muttered something into his radio and a moment later another team of operatives filed into the room. "Round up the girls," Pike ordered. "We'll take them with us."

Once Pike gave the order, the operatives gathered up the girls, zip-tying the girls' hands behind their backs before pushing them out of the room. Most of the girls looked frightened and confused by this point as they were led away, but a few still had smiles on their faces as if they had somehow won, now that their wombs were filled with demon seed.

"Where the hell are you taking them, Pike?" I said.

"Shut up, Ethan," Pike said, pointing his finger at me. "The only reason you're not full of bullet holes right now is because, for some unknown reason, Wendell said not to kill you. If it were up to me, I'd shoot you my damn self."

"I'm sure you would," I said, wondering why Wendell Knightsbridge should be so concerned with my personal safety.

Xaglath had lowered Carmichael's body onto the blood-stained altar by now. When I turned to look at her, I saw a concern on her face that could only come from Hannah.

"What now?" she asked me.

"I'll tell you what now," Pike said, answering for me as he stared at Hannah. "You will get the fuck out of here before my men kill you, you demon bitch. My business with Ethan isn't over."

"Isn't it?" I said, raising my eyebrows.

"Far from it," Pike said, glaring at me, then turned to his men. "Get her outta here."

As the operatives approached Hannah, she stood back with her hands out in front of her, ready to use her powers against them until I told her to stop. "Just go, Hannah," I said. "Get Haedemus and go. I'll catch up."

Slowly, she lowered her guard. "You're sure?"

"Yes."

Still looking uncertain, she left anyway, showing no fear for the trained operatives who pointed their guns at her still.

When Hannah had left the room, Pike turned to me. "Carmichael might've been an uppity bitch, but she was the only one who knew what the fuck she was doing here," he said. "Wendell's going to be pissed we can't make any more hybrids, at least not until we can find someone else to conduct the ritual."

"My heart bleeds," I said.

"Oh, you'll bleed, alright," Pike said, just as I noticed half a dozen of his men let go of their guns so they could pull out telescopic batons that I knew also delivered a shock of electricity with every blow given.

Nodding, I soon realized what was about to happen. "I thought Wendell said I wasn't to be touched?"

"He said not to kill you," Pike said. "He didn't say anything about not beating you to a bloody pulp."

"You always were a petty cunt, Pike."

"And you were always an insubordinate asshole." He threw a glance at his men. "Go get 'em boys, and make sure he learns his lesson."

To ensure I didn't fight back, two other operatives shot me in the chest with rubber bullets that hurt like fuck and dropped me to my knees, hardly able to breathe now.

A second later, the other operatives with the stun batons were on me, raining blows and shocks of electricity down on me, relentlessly beating me as I did my best to cover my head with my arms.

With my eyes closed, I took everything that they gave me. As blow after blow impacted my body, I thought of Callie, and her smiling face, which was the last thing I saw before I fell unconscious.

～

WHEN I OPENED MY EYES, I THOUGHT I HAD LANDED IN HELL. Above me was a carpet of dense, black smoke that smelled almost sulfurous. There was also heat. Intense heat that seared my face and dried my eyes out.

As my vision refocused itself, a horrific face came into view; a dark, elongated face with blazing red eyes.

A face I soon realized belonged to Haedemus.

"Wake up, Ethan," he said, the smell of rotten meat on his breath. "You're missing the fire show."

"What?" I mumbled as I sat up and stared straight ahead.

I was sitting outside on the grass, and ahead of me was the boarding school, now ablaze. Flames raged all over the building, reaching through the roof, turning the sky above an infernal orange. Windows also blew out from the intense heat, the glass shattering as the flames forced their way out.

"They set fire to the place before they left," Hannah said as she stood beside me, staring at the burning building, the flames dancing in her dark eyes.

"Oh Jesus," I said, not because of the fire, but because of the pain that was itself like fire burning at every part of my body. My head hurt like fuck as well, though it took less punishment than did the rest of me. My back felt like a truck had run over it a few times, and my legs I could hardly move they ached so much. "Motherfuckers."

"They killed the rest of the girls," Hannah said in a somewhat distant voice. "The ones who weren't pregnant yet. One man held a gun to your head and said he would kill you if I tried to stop them. They shot the girls and then set fire to the building."

"How many?" I asked.

"How many what?" she said.

"Girls."

"Does it matter? One is too many."

Hannah was back. The pain in her voice at the girls' deaths was obvious. "There's nothing you could've done, Hannah."

"I could've killed them, the men."

"You should have."

"Then they would've killed you."

"You should've let them. How is my life worth more than those girls?"

She stared down at me, a trace of anger on her face. Then she shook her head and walked away.

"Was it something I said?" I asked Haedemus.

"Who knows, Ethan?" Haedemus said. "You do have a way of pissing people off, though."

"If you mention the beach, I'll kill you."

"Well, I wasn't going to, but—"

"No," I said, forcing myself to stand up. "Just no, Haedemus."

"Not even if I tell you my surname?"

"You have a surname?"

"Yes, of sorts. My first Master gave it to me."

"I don't care what it is," I said, crying out as I tried to straighten up, thinking now that most of my ribs were fractured, if not broken altogether.

"I'll tell you anyway," he said, standing next to me so I could lean on him. "It's Sassoon. Haedemus Sassoon."

A laugh escaped me, which I immediately regretted. "That's…the most ridiculous name I've …ever heard." I tried to contain my amusement for my ribs' sake. "It makes you sound like…a hairstylist…for poodles."

"Fuck you, Ethan," Haedemus said as we walked along, me still leaning on him for support. "Your savage amusement has destroyed any sense of nobility I had over my name. Thanks a lot for reducing me to a hairstylist…for poodles."

"Don't worry," I said as I inched along. "You can always change your name."

"Of course," he said, halting. "I can, can't I?"

"I didn't mean right now. Just keep walking."

"What about Haedemus the Mighty? That has a nice ring to it, don't you think?"

"For sure. Haedemus the Chatterer might be more apt, though."

"Ethan," he said, stopping again. "You really do offend me sometimes."

I was too sore and too tired to argue with him, so I patted his side. "Look, I'm just fucking with you. You're a valued member of the team, Haedemus, alright?"

"I didn't know we had a team, but I'll take it," he said. "I mean, I'm never done saving your ass, am I?"

"Wait," I said, stopping again. "Where are the Hell-bastards?"

"I haven't seen them," Haedemus said.

Scroteface. Report. Where are you?

Still chasing down the drencher thing.

Haven't you caught it yet?

It's fast. We'll get it, though.

You'd better. Report back when you do.

Yes, boss.

"Let's go, Haedemus," I said as we started walking toward the gates again. "I need a stiff drink or ten."

"Yes, and I'm sure Mistress Hannah needs a stiff cock after all that excitement."

"You're vile."

"Yes," he said chuckling. "Haedemus the Vile. I like the sound of that."

HANNAH WAS MOSTLY SILENT ON THE WAY TO THE CITY. SHE was driving the Dodge, since I wasn't in much shape to do so. Now and again, I would glance at her to see that she was staring straight ahead, a deep scowl on her face. After a couple dozen miles, I finally asked her what was up. "There's no justice anywhere, is there?" she said.

"What do you mean?" I said.

"I mean we did not save those girls. We just got most of them killed."

"We tried. Don't beat yourself up about it."

"How can you be so casual about things?" She turned her head for a second to stare at me. "It's like you don't care."

"I do care," I said. "I've just been around the block a few times, enough to know that there is no justice in this world, not in the way you're thinking. Bad people get away with shit all the time. That's just the way it is. There's no sense in beating yourself up about it."

"What's the point of this job then? What's the point in being a cop if you can't get justice for people?"

"Being a cop is not about getting justice, Hannah," I said,

scowling at her naïvety. "It's about damage limitation, that's all."

"We didn't limit much damage back there, did we? We caused more."

I sighed, too tired and pissed off to think about it. "We stopped a cult from kidnapping any more innocent people, plus we took out their leader. Damage limitation."

She went silent again for a long while and continued driving. Then, just as I was nodding off with my head against the window, she said quietly, "Maybe you're right, Ethan. When God cast me and a hundred thirty-three million others of my kind into Hell, everyone thought it was justice being served, but now I see that it wasn't. It was just the Creator using damage limitation. For how could it be justice to cast down so many of your subjects for merely doing what their heart told them to do? There is no justice in such an act—"

She may have said more, but I didn't hear it. Thanks to the full bottle of Mud I hadn't long consumed, I was soon fast asleep.

I STAYED AT CAL'S PLACE AFTER HANNAH DROPPED ME AND THE Dodge off, sleeping for several hours in the trailer before waking up feeling worse than ever. Looking at myself in the mirror, I saw my whole body was just one giant bruise. My face wasn't so bad, a few cuts and bruises here and there, but Jesus the rest of me looked like I'd been in a bomb blast. There was also a hunk of flesh missing from my left pectoral muscle thanks to the demonic drencher.

I sought out Cal's assistance, as I always used to in the past when I got badly hurt. He took me down into the bunker and laid me on a table before applying a range of different treatments from his apothecary. The flesh wound on my chest he filled with a disgusting looking substance that was the color of vomit, a murky brown with a stench to match.

"Something I've been working on," he said with a smile. "I'll be interested to see the effects."

"You haven't tested it yet?"

"I'm testing it now."

"That's reassuring."

When he applied a bandage over the wound, he told me I was done and that I should rest up.

"Can't," I said, wincing as I got off the table. "I got something I have to do first."

"What's that?" Cal asked.

"I have a location for the werewolf who killed Angela and Callie."

"Where'd you get it?"

"A reputable source."

"And you're going right now?"

"I don't think this can wait."

Cal stepped toward me. "You're in no shape to be fighting any werewolf," he said. "You can barely stand."

Managing a smile, I said, "Who said anything about fighting?"

23

R oughly six hours later, I was in the living room of a log cabin, located in the Great Woods a further forty miles past Redditch Village. The cabin had been hard to find, hidden amongst the trees deep in the woods, but I located it thanks to the directions Pike had written out for me.

To be honest, I wasn't sure if Pike had sent me on a wild goose chase until I spotted from a distance the person who lived in the cabin. Staying downwind of the place, I observed the cabin owner through the scope of a rifle as he stood outside chopping wood with a large ax.

Derrick Savage was tall and athletically built, sinewy muscles bulging as he brought his ax down on the logs, splitting them in half with one chop. He looked to be in his early forties, though his long grayish-brown hair made him look older. His dark eyes never stopped watching, even as he split the logs. Sometimes he would stop and sniff the air as if trying to pick up on any scents that were out of place. Such as mine, which is why I was careful to stay downwind from him.

I knew as soon as I saw the guy he was the one who had killed Angela and Maddie. Not just killed them but slaughtered them. I watched his dark eyes, and they told me everything I needed to know about him. He was a stone-cold killer, and even without his Lycan abilities, he was not a man you wanted to fuck with.

At least not directly.

Which is why I brought along a tranquilizer gun, the darts loaded with enough homemade sedatives to bring down King Kong never mind a werewolf.

When I was ready, I chose my moment and squeezed off a shot; the dart hitting Savage on the back of the neck. Upon impact, Savage froze and then dropped his ax as he felt behind him and then pulled out the dart, bringing it around to look at it. Still observing through the scope, I saw the look of surprise and then panic on his face as the drug started to take effect. My finger was ready on the trigger just in case Savage needed another dose, but I knew he wouldn't. Not with the massive dose I had already given him.

Soon, Savage began to stagger as he struggled to maintain his balance. Through the scope, I watched his eyes roll up into their sockets, and then I watched him keel over like a fallen tree, his head narrowly missing the chopping block.

I continued to watch his unmoving body for a further five minutes to make sure he was out good and proper. When I was sure that he was, I moved quickly toward the cabin and dragged Savage inside the sparsely furnished living room. Leaving him on the floor, I found a chair in the small kitchen and brought it into the living room.

Setting the chair in the middle of the room, I lifted the unconscious Savage into the chair, positioning him so he didn't fall back down again.

Then out of a canvas bag I'd brought with me, I took out a pair of heavy leather gloves and put them on. Also in the bag was a roll of razor wire, which I then wrapped around Savage's prone body, starting at his waist and going to his upper chest, securing him to the chair at the same time. If he tried to escape when he woke up, the razor wire would cut him to pieces.

Of course, he could probably break through the wire if he transformed into his full wolf form. But just in case that happened, I had brought along one of Cal's machete type blades, made from solid silver and designed specially to cut through a werewolf's thick hide thanks to the blade's partially serrated edge.

Once I had Savage secured, there was little else to do but wait until he woke up. As I waited, I had a look around the small living room. There were a lot of photos hanging up on the walls, with some sitting on a bookshelf. Most of them depicted Savage in military fatigues posing along with various other soldiers. From what I could gather from the photos, Savage served with Delta Force before he became a mercenary for hire.

There were other photos. Group photos of various men and women who I assumed were part of the pack that Savage belonged to. Every werewolf had a pack, even ones who live alone in the woods.

Though not for much longer.

Soon enough, Savage would have nothing but cold, eternal darkness.

I would see to that.

~

I WAITED WITH THE UTMOST PATIENCE AND RESTRAINT ON Savage waking up, which he did about two hours after I had secured him to the chair with the razor wire.

Sitting in a chair directly across from him, I watched as he opened his eyes and then groggily shook his head. It was only when he tried to move did he cry out as the tightly wound razor wire cut into him, slicing through his shirt and then his flesh.

"Fuck—" he growled as he looked down at himself, then stupidly tried to push against the wire, which only made the attached razors dig deeper into him.

A second later, he realized there was someone sitting across from him, and he snapped his head up to look at me, his large, dark eyes glaring, his nose creased as his lips peeled back so he could growl at me.

"Who the fuck are you?" he demanded.

I stared at him for a moment longer before answering. "You don't recognize me?" I said in a level voice as I cocked my head to one side.

"Why the fuck should I?" He leaned forward as he said it, causing the razors to bite further into his flesh, turning his face into a mask of pain and frustration.

"Because you killed my fucking family, that's why," I said as I leaned toward him. "You slaughtered my wife and little girl a couple months back in Crown Point. You remember that?"

Savage said nothing as he stared at me. Then his eyes turned bright yellow, and he started to smile, showing the beginnings of his fangs.

Standing up, I showed him the blade I held in my hand. "Go ahead," I said. "I'll cut your fucking head off before your claws even come out."

Growling in frustration, Savage's muscles appeared to increase in size for a few seconds, before shrinking back down again. Blood from the multiple slits and punctures on his body dripped onto the floor. Rivulets of crimson fluid ran over his thick forearms and down over his fingers. Almost to taunt me, he strained against the razor wire so it cut deeper into him, his eyes on me the whole time, showing me he didn't care about the pain. He was used to healing fast, but he wouldn't get the chance to this time.

"What the fuck do you want?" he said through clenched teeth.

"I want to know who hired you to kill my family." I pressed the edge of my blade against his throat, forcing his head back as the silver burned into his skin, causing him to grimace against the pain. "Tell me, and I might kill you quick."

"Fuck you!" he spat. "I ain't telling you nothing!"

"Wrong answer."

Removing the blade from his throat, I jammed the point of it into his left front deltoid, the silver blade pushing into his flesh slowly and deliberately until it had penetrated three inches.

Savage screamed with pain as I held the blade in him. "I'll fucking kill you! I'll fucking rip you apart!"

"Answer my question. Who hired you?"

"Go fuck yourself."

I pulled the blade out of him, causing him to scream once more. Then, from out of my trench pocket, I took out a small .22 pistol, the magazine of which held bullets containing silver nitrate on the tip. Pointing the gun at his right kneecap, I asked, "Who hired you?"

"I said go fuck yourself."

I squeezed the trigger and put a bullet in his kneecap. The caliber was small enough not to penetrate right through his tough sinews, so the bullet stayed in him, embedded in his knee somewhere as it released silver nitrate into his system.

Savage bucked in the chair as if his innards were on fire.

"I hear it burns bad," I said. "Is that true? Let's see what another dose does to you."

I pointed the gun at his left thigh this time and shot him again; the bullet staying lodged in his leg like before. "How does that feel now?"

"I swear to fucking god," Savage snarled between screams. "I'll fucking kill you! I'll kill you!"

The more he writhed against the burning silver nitrate, the more he sliced himself open with the razor wire, twisting and turning so he was almost sawing at himself. It wasn't too long before a length of intestine slipped out through the wire.

"You better calm down there," I said. "Before you saw yourself in half."

Savage continued to struggle for another few seconds before he finally stopped, closing his eyes as he fought against the pain, just like he'd done hundreds of times before no doubt. The man was no stranger to pain. He knew how much he could take, and how fast he could heal, given the chance—a chance I had no intention of giving him.

"Look, man," he said. "I'm sorry about your wife and kid, alright? It was just a job. You understand, right?"

The balls on this guy, trying that tact with me. Did he think he would gain my understanding, one brother in arms to another?

"I'm going to ask you one more time," I said, trying my best not to swing the blade at his neck just to get it over with. "If you don't answer me this time, I will empty the rest of this gun into your chest, and we both know that's gonna hurt like fuck. Pain beyond pain, right? We also both know you'll survive it. Death won't be any escape for you. So—" I spoke the next sentence in a slow, deliberate voice. "Who hired you to kill my wife and daughter?"

Looking down at the state of himself, at the blood dripping off him, at his innards slipping out, Savage sighed and shook his head.

"Alright, man," he said, done with resisting now, perhaps thinking he needed to buy time so he could heal and think of a way out of the situation he was in, even though there was none for him. "Some woman contacted me on the dark web. I met her, she explained the job, and I did it. That's all."

"Bullshit, that's all," I snapped, my anger rising to the surface. "Who's the woman? I need a name."

"I don't do names, man," he said. "I meet them, get the

details of the job and then give them an account number. Once the money is in the account, I do the job. That's it."

"You're lying." I pressed the tip of the blade against his throat. "There's more to it than that. Tell me what it is."

"Alright, alright, just take that fucking blade away."

I took the blade away from his throat. "Speak."

"For my own security, and in case anything goes wrong, I film the meetings with a hidden camera."

I froze for a second. "You have the woman who hired you on video?"

"Yeah," he said. "Some Asian woman."

Once more, I froze, this time for much longer. "Asian woman?"

"Japanese I think, I'm not sure."

A horrible feeling found its way into my stomach, and for a moment, I thought I would be sick.

There's no way, I thought. *It can't be. I'm just jumping the gun. There's no way it could be her...*

"Where's the video?" I asked in a quiet voice.

"Are you gonna let me go?"

"Where's the fucking video?"

He stared back at me. "I should explain something to you first. Your scent is all over those woods out there, and my pack, they'll pick up on it when they come here looking for me. If they find me dead, you'll have a whole pack of angry as fuck werewolves after you, and believe me, this is one pack you won't want after you. They'll not just kill you; they'll kill everybody you know. But if you let me live—after I give you what you want—I can make sure no one comes after you. We can let this go." He paused to stare at me. "So if I give you what you want, will you let me live? You'll be saving yourself as well."

"Just tell me where to find the video," I said as if he'd said nothing at all.

"Jesus fuck." He shook his head, perhaps realizing his plea

to stay alive had fallen on deaf ears. "At least consider what I'm saying, man. If you kill me, my pack will kill you and a lot more people besides. Is that what you want?"

"The video. Where is it?"

Savage smiled slightly as he stared at me. "God damn, you don't even care, do you? I guess I did a number on you, huh? Only out for revenge now, is that it? Well, I'm telling you, you won't live long enough to finish it if you kill me. Just think about that."

"I will. Now for the last time, where's the video?"

"The bookcase," Savage said, looking resigned now. "On a flash drive inside one of the books."

Quickly, I went to the bookcase. "Which one?"

"*The Call of the Wild* by—"

"Jack London. I got it."

Taking out the old book, I opened it up to find most of the pages hollowed out, and inside the resulting square hole was a black flash drive. I didn't need to ask if he had a computer, for I already saw one earlier sitting on the kitchen table.

Without saying another word, I walked into the kitchen and opened up the laptop on the table, inserting the flash drive into one of the USB ports.

A moment later, I was looking at dated files. Scanning the list, I found a date that was just a few days before Angela and Callie were killed.

Almost holding my breath, I clicked on the folder to find a video file inside, which I immediately clicked to play, pausing it again a second later.

What if it's her? I thought, swallowing, at the same time thinking, *There's no way it could be Hannah. She would never do anything like that. She had no reason to.*

After taking a breath, I clicked play on the video again, my chest tight as I viewed the screen. The video showed the inside of a cafe in the city somewhere, maybe downtown, it was hard to tell. Savage was sitting at one of the tables, the camera hidden on his person somewhere.

Then someone approached him from behind. A voice said, "Are you Mr. White?"

And God help me, I recognized the voice, and my face twisted up with despair.

"That's right," Savage said. "Take a seat."

The person came around and sat down, her face now in full view of the camera. I clamped my hand to my mouth as tears sprung in my eyes.

No, no, no...

"Let's get this over with quick," Hannah said in the video. "I have to get back to work soon. Here's the address." She pushed a piece of paper across the table at Savage. "It's a woman and a little girl. Will that be a problem for you?"

"I don't normally do kids, lady," Savage said.

"Fine. I'll double your fee. How's that?"

Savage paused before sliding a piece of paper of his own across the table to Hannah. "There's my account details. Once the money's in, I'll do the job."

"Good. The money will be in by tonight."

"Then our business here is done," Savage said, getting up without saying another word and heading out of the cafe, at which point the video ended.

I sat at the table with my head in my hands for a long time after. Then I played the video again and froze it on Hannah's face, just to be sure. Her clothes were a little different from normal—she wore a dark hoodie and blue jeans—but it was definitely her. There was no mistaking that face.

Clenching my fists, I said, "Why, Hannah?" as if she was here to answer me.

"Hey man," Savage called from the living room. "You get what you need or what?"

Removing the flash drive from the computer, I put it into my pocket. Then I lifted the silver blade and carried it into the living room with me, my face a blank mask at this point as I struggled to control my roiling emotions underneath.

Gripping the blade tight in my right hand, I stood in front of Savage and stared at him.

"Think about what I said, man," he said as he began to squirm in his chair. "Don't do this. You'll be killing yourself."

"You're a parasite," I said in a flat voice. "You butchered the only two people in the world who meant anything to me."

Tears rolled down my cheeks as I felt my emotions rise to the surface—the anger, the betrayal. The hatred for the man in front of me.

"Please, man, don't—"

Raising the weapon, I swung it as hard as I could at his neck, the silver blade cutting right through, decapitating him. His head fell to the floor with a heavy thump and rolled over against the wall, coming to a standstill with his eyes still open in shock.

After staring at his headless corpse for a moment, I sat down in the chair opposite, allowing the bloodstained blade to hang loosely in my grip. With my other hand, I reached into my pocket and retrieved a crumpled pack of smokes, shaking one out into my mouth before using a zippo to light it up.

As I smoked, I stared blankly at the floor, still trying to fathom what I'd seen in the video.

Who I'd seen.

No matter how much I thought about it, I couldn't get it to make any sense.

Why? I kept thinking. *Why would she do it to me?*

To them?

With no answers forthcoming, I tossed away my cigarette butt and went outside, going around the back until I found a generator and then a jerrycan full of gas. I carried the can into the cabin and started splashing the gas around the place, pouring the rest over Savage's headless corpse.

When I was done, I dropped the can and went outside. By

the front door, I lit another cigarette, drawing on it to make sure it was lit before tossing the lit cigarette inside the cabin. The burning embers of the cigarette immediately ignited the volatile fluid splashed everywhere, and within seconds the whole cabin was ablaze.

With smoke and intense heat filling the woods around me, I walked away from the blazing cabin and started for home.

For there was someone else I had to see now.

24

I felt Hannah's betrayal more keenly than I'd felt anything in my life before, except for the devastation I felt when my angels were taken from me.

By Hannah, it now seemed.

But why?

That was the question I kept asking myself over and over as I drove back to the city. And it didn't matter how many times I asked myself the question, for no satisfactory answers were forthcoming. No matter which way I looked at it, I saw no reason why Hannah would do such an evil thing as have my wife and daughter killed.

I wondered for a while why she never just did the killing herself. Then I realized she hired someone so she could keep her distance and ensure she wasn't implicated.

Maybe it wasn't her, I thought as I entered the city. *Maybe it was Xaglath.*

Either way, she was going to pay for what she did.

Taking out my phone as a cold rage started to settle in me, I texted Hannah:

WHERE ARE YOU?

A moment later, she texted back:

MY APARTMENT

Tossing the phone on the front seat, I pressed down harder on the gas pedal.

WHEN I GOT TO HANNAH'S APARTMENT, I DIDN'T EVEN KNOCK. I was so full of anger that I kicked the door in and stomped inside to find her in the living room, and God help me, she was wearing the same clothes that she had worn to the meeting with Savage.

"Ethan, what the hell——"

Before she could even finish, I leaned down and grabbed her by the lapels, lifting her up in my rage and slamming her against the wall.

"Why?" I screamed at her. "Why'd you do it?"

Hannah's face was a mask of shock and confusion as she stared back at me.

"Do what?" she said. "Ethan what——"

Roaring, I spun around and threw her across the room, and she crashed against the far wall. Before she could even recover, I picked her up again, holding her up in front of me. "Why'd you do it?"

"I don't know what you're talking about!" she screamed back.

"Liar!"

I threw her across the room again.

This time, when she landed, she jumped immediately to her feet, her eyes now glowing amber. "What is wrong with you?" she asked as her Visage loomed threateningly behind her.

Taking out my gun, I pointed it at her.

"You killed them," I said, my voice cracking with emotion. "You fucking killed them."

"Killed who?"

"MY FUCKING FAMILY! YOU HAD MY WIFE AND DAUGHTER KILLED!" I rushed forward with the gun and pressed it against her forehead. "WHY? TELL ME WHY!"

She stared into my eyes before shaking her head. "Ethan, I don't know what you're talking about. I—"

"Stop it! Stop lying!" I reached into my pocket and showed her the flash drive. "You're on video arranging the whole fucking thing."

A deep frown crossed her face as she shook her head. "There's been some mistake. Ethan, you know I would never —" She stopped then as something seemed to occur to her. "It's me on the video?"

"Yes, it's fucking you," I snarled. "There's no mistaking you. You're even wearing the same clothes as you are now."

Her face dropped, and she started to edge away from me as I continued to point the gun at her. "I—I—"

"What?" I said. "You don't remember?"

"No, unless…unless it was—"

"Xaglath?"

"Yes," she breathed.

Stepping toward her with the gun, she backed up near the window, her face now bathed in red neon light from the sign outside.

"I thought I could trust you," I said in a near whisper. "I thought I—"

I didn't finish as I shook my head and tightened my grip on the gun.

"Ethan," Hannah pleaded. "Don't, please—"

"I'm sorry, Hannah," I said, my eyes full of tears as my face twisted up with uncontained emotion. "I have to."

"Ethan, no!"

I shot her once in the chest, and she staggered back toward the window.

Then I shot her again, squeezing the trigger four more

times in rapid succession until she crashed through the glass and fell out the window.

With the smell of gunpowder in the room, I stood staring at the broken window as the wind billowed the curtains.

With tears running down my face and my body wracked with pain, I lowered the gun and walked to the window, leaning out to look down at the street below, expecting to see Hannah's body lying there on the wet sidewalk.

But there was no sign of her.

She was gone, leaving only a puddle of blood behind her on the ground below.

Letting the gun slip from my hand, I sank to my knees as the wind and rain blew into my face.

Then I opened my mouth and roared into the night so loud that even God probably heard me.

"This isn't over, Hannah!" I bellowed out the broken window. "You hear me? This isn't over!"

"Oh, I think it is," said another voice from behind me.

Grabbing my gun, I spun around and pointed it at the person now standing in the room. It was a dark-suited Japanese man in his late fifties. Flanking him on either side were two other men in suits, both much younger as they stood pointing their pistols at me. In my confusion, it took me a moment to realize who the men were.

They were Yakuza.

"Mr. Drake," the older man said. "My name is Kazuo Yagami. I'd like to speak to you about my daughter, Hannah."

Hardly able to compute what was happening, I shook my head and said, "What about her?"

Yagami smiled coldly. "I want what she has, Mr. Drake. And you will help me get it."

～

DON'T FORGET! VIP'S get advance notice of all future releases and projects. AND A FREE NOVELLA! Click the image or join here:
www.npmartin.com

Ethan Drake returns in BOOK 3—DEATH DEALERS. Turn the page for an excerpt or GET THE BOOK ONLINE NOW.

TEASER: DEATH DEALERS (ETHAN DRAKE # 3)

I barely said a word until we got to the Yakuza headquarters in downtown Little Tokyo. Even then, when I was seated at an oversized oak desk facing Kazuo Yagami—the leader of the local Yakuza clan and Hannah's father—I still said very little.

What was there to say, anyway?

Hannah Walker, demon that she was, had killed my wife and daughter for no apparent reason. In doing so, she had stuck a knife in my heart that I wanted to pull out and use to cut her throat from ear to ear.

Hannah was a mad dog, I realized, and like all mad dogs, she would have to be put down.

But her father, it seemed, had other plans.

He sat across from me in a plush leather chair, framed by the huge window behind him that afforded a widescreen view of the city all the way across the river to Bedford.

This was the first time I'd ever met the man in person, and he came across much how I expected he would. Dressed in a light gray suit that probably cost more than I make in a month, he seemed to be every inch the cold and ruthless Yakuza boss that his reputation made him out to be. Hannah once described him to me as being disarmingly congenial, which was how he came across now. The shark-smile never left his face as he looked at me with unblinking slate-gray eyes that had probably seen as much death and violence as mine had. He seemed to sense this himself as he gave me a look that bordered on admiration while one of his underlings poured me another whiskey.

"Since you started working with my daughter, I've been watching you from afar, Mr. Drake," he said. "I know you are not a man to be trifled with, and I respect that."

As I lifted my refilled glass, I said, "You do know Hannah isn't your daughter anymore, right?"

"Of course I know." He took a slim cigar from a wooden box on his desk and put it between his lips. A second later, one of his young underlings produced a zippo and held it out so Yagami could light the cigar. When the cigar was lit, Yagami waved the underling away, the boy hitting me with a cold stare that I guess was supposed to intimidate me, which I found laughable since the boy looked barely old enough to shave. Points for trying though. "I've known for a while now. I also know it was she who killed my *Kumi-in* and impaled him on the statue in the square."

"So why haven't you gone after her yet?" I asked him as I took out a cigarette and lit it, glancing at the enormous aquarium to my left, which appeared to be full of piranha. The gravel at the bottom of the tank seemed littered with gleaming white bones, making me wonder if they were human, and who they once belonged to. It didn't surprise me that Yagami enjoyed feeding people to the fishes, or maybe just their hands. I've no doubt it was a great trick to strike fear into people.

"Because if I did, people would die," he said, holding his cigar up, the smoke intermingling with that from my cigarette. "Once I realized what she is and what she is capable of, I decided it would be best to exercise caution."

"And you'd be right. How did you find out she's a demon?"

"I make it my business to know my enemies, Mr. Drake. Hannah has wanted to kill me ever since—"

"You strangled her mother to death?"

Kazuo's face hardened as a tense atmosphere took over the room. Behind me, I sensed his men move slowly toward me. When Yagami gave them a barely perceptible flick of his eyes, his men stopped moving. I got the impression that under other circumstances, my head would be getting submerged into the fish tank so the piranhas could feast on my face. As it was, the Yakuza boss needed me for something, so he let my insolence slide. "In my world, Mr. Drake, loyalty is everything."

"I hope you don't expect it from me," I said. "We might have a problem if you do. In fact—" I shook my head as I sighed, having had enough of this conversation already. "I don't know what I'm even doing here. I owe you nothing, Mr. Yagami. If I hunt down Hannah, it's because she had my fucking wife and daughter killed, not because you want me to find her." Stabbing my cigarette out in the ashtray, I stood up. "Thanks for the drink. I have to be going now."

When I turned around, two of Yagami's men were standing right behind me, eye-fucking me as they flexed their fingers in preparation for a fight. Staring right back at them, I told them to get out of my way, but they stepped in closer.

"I suggest you sit back down, Mr. Drake," Yagami said.

"Or what?" I said over my shoulder, bringing my gaze back to rest on the two Yakuza soldiers in front of me, the youngest of whom looked like he was itching to have a go at me. And the mood I was in, I was itching for him to try.

"I was hoping to keep this encounter conversational," Yagami said.

"Yeah, well," I said, flexing my own fingers now. "We don't always get what we want, do we?"

A pregnant pause settled in the room, during which I noticed the younger Yakuza move his right foot back ever so slightly.

Fucking amateur, I thought.

The guy's shoulders began to turn as he prepared to attack, but I struck first by throwing a lighting-fast right cross, my reinforced knuckles chopping down on the younger guy's chin. The strike was textbook. In shock, the young Yakuza staggered slightly before he collapsed to the carpeted floor in a heap, out cold.

Immediately after, I turned my attention to the other *Kumi-in*, drawing my fist back to hit him. But before I got a chance to throw the punch, he unleashed a snap-kick and drove his boot into my groin, doubling me over for a second, but long enough for him to bring his other leg around in a wide arc, his shin connecting with my thigh, the force of the kick causing me to drop to one knee.

In his arrogance, he stood like he had won, thinking he had gotten the better of me. Until I punched him in the balls, and he cried out in pain. When I hit him again in the same place, his cry was even louder.

As Yagami shouted for me to stop, I ignored him and grabbed the *Kumi-in*, twisting his arm up his back with one hand, grabbing a handful of his hair with the other before pushing him across the floor to the piranha tank. He resisted, of course, but I was too strong for him and too pissed off to give in. Before he could even protest, I dunked his head into the tank and held it there as he started thrashing around, sending water flying everywhere.

"Stop!" Yagami shouted, but again I ignored him, continuing to hold the struggling *Kumi-in's* head underwater. A second later, the water turned crimson with blood as the piranha attacked his face. That's when I let him up, noticing the bite marks in his cheeks as I flung him away across the floor.

As soon as he landed, the *Kumi-in* took out his gun and pointed it at me in a rage. I've no doubt he would've fired if Yagami hadn't shouted something in Japanese, making the guy lower his gun as he continued to glare at me in his rage while blood dripped from his face.

I turned to stare at Yagami, who was glaring at me like he wanted to shoot me himself. "Thanks for the drink," I said.

"I did you a courtesy by bringing you here, Mr. Drake," Yagami said. "And you disrespect me like this?"

"I'm no one's lapdog. You have enough footsoldiers already, anyway." I glanced at the two injured *Kumi-in*. "For all the good they did you."

"If you walk out of here, you'll regret it, Mr. Drake."

"Oh yeah? And why's that? You gonna kill me, Yagami?"

"As easy as that would be—"

"Not that easy."

His face tightened. "As easy as that would be, I'm not going to. I wanted to give you the option of finding Hannah and bringing her to me. But since you seem bent on making things difficult, I will now make you watch as I tear this city apart looking for her. I'll kill anyone who gets in my way, including you, Mr. Drake."

"Why the hell do you even want her?" I asked him. "Do you think you'll be able to tame her, to use her? The very idea is preposterous. She'd kill all of you in a heartbeat, believe me."

"Demon or not, she's still my daughter," he said, sitting back down.

"I don't think she was ever your daughter, was she?"

"On the contrary, Mr. Drake, Hannah has always been dear to me."

I couldn't help but laugh. "Seriously?"

"Just because you don't understand how things are done in my world, doesn't mean I don't care for Hannah. I've always cared for her. I made her strong."

"She became a fucking drug addict thanks to the shit you put her through," I said. "How is that caring for her?"

"*You* clearly still care for her," he said, deflecting my question. "Despite what you think she's done."

My jaw tensed for a second before I turned away from him. "I'm going now. Please stay the fuck away from me."

"I won't allow you to kill her."

Stopping on the way to the door, I turned around. "Then you'll have to kill me now if that's the case."

After staring at me for a moment, Yagami pulled a gun from the drawer in his desk and pointed it at me as he came around and walked toward me. For a second, I thought he would squeeze the trigger. Instead, he lowered the gun as a smile appeared on his lined face. "I don't need to kill you, Mr. Drake," he said. "My daughter will do that for me once you leave her no choice."

Maybe he had a point, but I didn't care. "You're deluded if you think she'll come to you after everything."

Yagami maintained his smile. "I don't think I am. You see, Hannah has only ever wanted one thing, and that's connection. I dare say that hasn't changed now that a demon has taken over her body. From what I understand about demons, they take on the characteristics and personality of the person they possessed. Hannah no doubt found that connection with you, Mr. Drake. But that connection is gone now, and Hannah is out there, alone, emotionally distressed. Lost even. You know her better than anyone. Do you think she'll turn down the chance at connection and belonging that I intend to offer her? And if she does, I have one other option."

"And what's that?"

Yagami smiled. "You aren't the only one to be familiar with the dark arts, Mr. Drake."

"You've no idea of the kind of power you'd be trying to tame."

Yagami's smile widened. "But Mr. Drake," he said. "I have no intention of taming it."

"Then you're even stupider than I thought."

"Watch your mouth, pig," the guy I knocked out said, having just woken up on the floor behind Yagami.

Ignoring the guy on the floor, I said to Yagami, "It's like I said earlier—just stay out of my way."

"You know I can't do that, Mr. Drake," Yagami said. "I'm also not above killing a police officer if it comes to it. I've done it before."

"I'm sure you have."

Yagami turned and went back to his desk. "The next time our paths cross, Mr. Drake, don't count on things being as amiable as they are now. If you chose to have me as an opponent, you will find me to be ruthless…and merciless."

"Right back at you, Yagami," I said, just before I walked out the door.

~

After I walked from the Yakuza headquarters to Hannah's apartment building to collect my car, I paused outside for a minute and looked up at the broken window as the curtains billowed out of it. Then I looked down at the sidewalk beneath my feet and saw the blood that was already getting washed away by the rain.

Sighing, I went inside the building and made my way up to Hannah's apartment. I knew she wouldn't be there, but I took my gun out nonetheless as I walked inside and checked the living room. When I cleared all the other rooms, I put my gun away and sat down on the couch, resting my head back as I closed my eyes for a few minutes. In my mind, I kept seeing Hannah's face on the video, asking Savage if he had a problem with killing women and children.

I had never felt so betrayed in my life, even though I knew

it wasn't Hannah that caused all this, but Xaglath. It had to be. There was no way the Hannah I knew would do such a heinous act as have my wife and daughter assassinated. The only thing that made sense was that she'd had one of her blackouts, which she used to get quite a lot, during which Xaglath would take over. But even then, why would Xaglath do such a thing?

Because she's a demon, I thought. *And demons don't need a reason to do evil things. Evil is their very nature.*

Still...

Opening my eyes, my gaze fell on the coffee table, and I spotted a white envelope sitting there, realizing it had my name written on it. Frowning, I reached over and lifted the envelope, opening it to find a birthday card inside. I'd forgotten it was my birthday today. Hannah obviously hadn't.

The front of the card depicted a cartoon cop with the words, "Happy birthday to the World's Worst Police Officer," written on it.

Inside, Hannah had written, "Only kidding!" followed by:

Happy birthday, Partner. Hope you don't feel too old :)

She had signed her name underneath, followed by three x's.

Shaking my head, I threw the card back on the table. "Happy fucking birthday," I said bitterly.

Get your copy of DEATH DEALERS online now!

MAKE A DIFFERENCE

For an indie author like myself, reviews are the most powerful tool I have to bring attention to my books. I don't have the financial muscle of the big traditional publishers, but I can build a group of committed and loyal readers...readers just like you!

Honest reviews of my books help bring them to the attention of other readers.

If you've enjoyed this book, I would be very grateful if you could spend just five minutes leaving a review (which can be as short as you like) on my book's Amazon page by clicking below.

And if you're still not motivated to leave a review, please also bear in mind that this is how I feed my family. Without reviews, without sales, I don't get to support my wife and darling daughters.

So now that I've shamelessly tugged on your heart strings, here's the link to leave the review:

Review Blood Summoned

Thank you in advance.

TEASER: BLOOD MAGIC (WIZARD'S CREED # 1)

When the magic hit, I was knocked to the floor like I'd taken a hard-right hook to the jaw. The spell was so powerful, it blew through my every defense. For all my wards and the good they did me, I might as well have been a Sleepwalker with no protection at all.

The faint smell of decayed flesh mixed with sulfur hung thick in the air, a sure sign that dark magic had just been used, which in my experience, was never good. Coming across dark magic is a bit like turning up at a children's party to find Beelzebub in attendance, a shit-eating grin on his face as he tied balloon animals for the terrified kids. It's highly disturbing.

I sat dazed on the floor, blinking around me for a moment. My mind was fuzzy and partially frozen, as though I'd awakened from a nightmare. I was inside an abandoned office space, the expansive rectangular room lined with grimy, broken windows that let cold air in to draw me out of my daze. Darkness coated the room, the only real light coming from the moon outside as it beamed its pale, silvery light through the smashed skylights.

I struggled back to my feet and blindly reached for the

pistol inside my dark green trench coat, frowning when I realized the gun wasn't there. Then I remembered it had gone flying out of my hand when the spell had hit. Looking around, I soon located the pistol lying on the floor several feet away, and I lurched over and grabbed it, slightly more secure now that the gun's reassuring weight was back in my hand.

There were disturbing holes in my memory. I recalled confronting someone after tracking them here. But who? I couldn't get a clear image. The person was no more than a shadow figure in my mind. I had no clue as to why I was following this person unknown in the first place. Obviously, they had done something to get on my radar. The question was what, though?

The answer came a few seconds later when my eyes fell upon the dark shape in the middle of the room, and a deep sense of dread filled me; a dread that was both familiar and sickening at the same time, for I knew what I was about to find. Swallowing, I stared hard through the gloom at the human shape lying lifelessly on the debris-covered floor. Over the sharp scent of rats piss and pigeon shit, the heavy, festering stench of blood hit my nostrils without mercy.

When I crossed to the center of the room, my initial fears were confirmed when I saw that it was a dead body lying on the floor. A young woman with her throat slit. Glyphs were carved into the naked flesh of her spread-eagled body, with ropes leading from her wrists and ankles to rusty metal spikes hammered into the floor. I marveled at the force required to drive the nails into the concrete, knowing full well that a hammer had nothing to do with it.

Along the circumference of a magic circle painted around the victim was what looked like blood-drawn glyphs. The sheer detail of them unnerved me as I observed in them a certain quality that could only have come from a well-practiced hand.

I breathed out as I reluctantly took in the callous butchery on display. The dead woman looked to be in her early thirties, though it was difficult to tell because both her eyes were missing; cut out with the knife used to slice her throat, no doubt. I shook my head as I looked around in a vain effort to locate the dead woman's eyeballs.

The woman looked underweight for her size. She was around the same height as me at six feet, but there was very little meat on her bones, as if she was a stranger to regular meals. I also noted the needle marks on her feet, and the bruises around her thighs. This, coupled with how she had been dressed—in a leather mini skirt and short top, both items discarded on the floor nearby—made me almost certain the woman had been a prostitute. A convenient, easy victim for whoever had killed her.

If the symbols carved into her pale flesh were anything to go by, it would seem the woman had been ritually sacrificed. At a guess, I would have said she was an offering to one of the Dimension Lords, which the glyphs seemed to point to. The glyphs themselves weren't only complex, but also carved with surgical precision. The clarity of the symbols against the woman's pale flesh made it possible for me to make out certain ones that I recognized as being signifiers to alternate dimensions, though which dimension exactly, I couldn't be sure, at least not until I had studied the glyphs further. Glyphs such as the ones I was looking at were always uniquely different in some way. No two people drew glyphs the same, with each person etching their own personality into every one, which can often make it hard to work out their precise meanings. One thing I could be certain of was that the glyphs carved into the woman's body resonated only evil intent; an intent so strong, I felt it in my gut, gnawing at me like a parasite seeking access to my insides, as if drawn to my magic power. Not a pleasant feeling, but I was used to it, having been exposed to enough dark magic in my time.

After taking in the scene, I soon came to the conclusion

that the woman wasn't the killer's first victim; not by a long stretch, given the precision and clear competency of the work on display.

"Son of a bitch," I said, annoyed. I couldn't recall any details about the case I had so obviously been working on. It was no coincidence that I had ended up where I was, a place that happened to reek of dark magic, and which housed a murder that had occult written all over it. I'd been on the hunt, and I had gotten close to the killer, which was the likeliest reason for the dark magic booby trap I happened to carelessly spring like some bloody rookie.

Whoever the killer was, they wielded powerful magic. A spell that managed to wipe all my memories of the person in question wouldn't have been an easy one to create. And given the depth of power to their magic, it also felt to me like they had channeled it from some other source, most likely from whatever Dimension Lord they were sacrificing people to.

Whatever the case, the killer's spell had worked. Getting back the memories they had stolen from me wouldn't be easy, and that's if I could get them back at all, which I feared might just be the case.

After shaking my head at how messed up the situation was, I froze upon hearing a commanding voice booming in the room like thunder.

"Don't move, motherfucker!"

∾

Get your copy of BLOOD MAGIC online today!

∾

TEASER: SERPENT SON (GODS AND MONSTERS TRILOGY BOOK 1)

They knew I was back, for someone had been tailing me for the last half hour. As I walked along Lower Ormond Quay with the River Liffey flowing to the right of me, I pretended not to notice my stalker. I'd only just arrived back in Dublin after a stay in London, and I was in no mood for confrontation.

I was picking up on goblin vibes, but I couldn't be sure until I laid eyes on the cretin. The wiry little bastards were sneaky and good at blending in unseen.

As I moved down a deserted side street, hoping my pursuer would follow me, I weighed my options. There were several spells I could use: I could create a doorway in one of the walls next to me and disappear into the building; or I could turn myself into vapor and disappear; or I could even levitate up to the roof of one of the nearby buildings and escape.

Truthfully though, I didn't like using magic in broad daylight, even if there was no one around. Hell, I hardly used magic at all, despite being gifted with a connection to the Void —the source of all magic—just like every other Touched being in the world.

Despite my abilities, though, I was no wizard. I was just a musician who preferred to make magic through playing the guitar; real magic that touched the soul of the listener. Not the often destructive magic generated by the Void.

Still, Void magic could come in handy sometimes, like now as I spun around suddenly and said the word, *"Impedio!"* I felt the power of the Void flow through me as I spoke. But looking down the street, there appeared to be no one there.

Only I knew there was.

I hurried back down the street and then stopped by a dumpster on the side of the road. Crouching behind the dumpster was a small, wiry individual with dark hair and pinched features. He appeared frozen as he glared up at me, thanks to the spell I had used to stop him in his tracks, preventing him from even moving a muscle until I released him.

"Let me guess," I said. "Iolas got wind I was coming back, so he sent you to what...follow me? Maybe kill me, like he had my mother killed?"

Anger threatened to rise in me as blue magic sparked across my hand. Eight words, that's all it would take to kill the frozen goblin in front of me, to shut down his life support system and render him dead in an instant. It would've been so easy to do, but I wasn't a killer...at least not yet.

The goblin strained against the spell I still held him in, hardly able to move a muscle. To an ordinary eye, the goblin appeared mundane, just a small, rakish man in his thirties with thinning hair and dark eyes that appeared to be too big for his face. To my Touched eye, however, I could see the goblin creature for what he was underneath the glamor he used to conceal his true form, which to be honest, wasn't that far away from the mundane form he presented to the world. His eyes were bigger and darker, his mouth wider and full of thin pointed teeth that jutted out at all angles, barely concealed by lips like two strips of thick rubber. His skin was also paler, and his ears large and pointed.

"I don't know what you're talking about," the goblin said when I released him from the spell. He stood up straight, his head barely level with my chest. "I'm just out for a stroll on this fine summer evening, or at least I was before you accosted me like you did..."

I shook my head in disgust. What did I expect anyway, a full rundown of his orders from Iolas? Of course he was going to play dumb because he *was* dumb. He knew nothing, except that he had to follow me and report on my whereabouts. Iolas being the paranoid wanker that he was, would want eyes on me the whole time now that I was back in town. Or at least until he could decide what to do with me.

"All right, asshole," I said as magic crackled in my hand, making the cocky goblin rather nervous, his huge eyes constantly flitting from my face to the magic in my hand. "Before you fuck off out of it, make sure Iolas gets this message, will you? Tell that stuck up elf...tell him..."

The goblin frowned, his dark eyes staring into me. "Go on, tell Iolas what?" He was goading me, the sneaky little shit. "That you're coming for him? That you will kill him for supposedly snuffing out your witch-bitch mother—"

Rage erupted in me, and before the goblin could say another filthy word, I conjured my magic, thrusting my light-filled hand toward him while shouting the words, "*Ignem exquiris!*"

In an instant, a fireball about the size of a baseball exploded from my hand and hit the goblin square in the chest, the force of it slamming him back against the wall, the flames setting his clothes alight.

"*Dholec maach!*" the goblin screamed as he frantically slapped at his clothes to put the flames out.

"What were you saying again?" I cocked my head mockingly at him as if waiting for an answer.

"Dhon ogaach!" The goblin tore off his burning jacket and tossed it to the ground, then put out the remaining flames still licking at his linen shirt. The smell of burned fabric and roasted goblin skin now permeated the balmy air surrounding us.

"Yeah? You go fuck yourself as well after you've apologized for insulting my mother."

The goblin snarled at me as he stood quivering with rage and shock. "You won't last a day here, wizard! Iolas will have you fed to the vamps!"

I shot forward and grabbed the goblin by the throat, thrusting him against the wall. "First, I'm a musician, not a wizard, and secondly—" I had to turn my head away for a second, my nostrils assaulted by the atrocious stench of burnt goblin flesh. "Second, I'm not afraid of your elfin boss, or his vamp mates."

Struggling to speak with my hand still around his throat, the goblin said in a strangled voice, "Is that why...you ran away...like a...little bitch?"

I glared at the goblin for another second and then let him go, taking a step back as he slid down the wall. His black eyes were still full of defiance, and I almost admired his tenacity.

"I've listened to enough of your shit, goblin," I said, forcing my anger down. "Turn on your heels and get the hell out of here, before I incinerate you altogether." I held my hand up to show him the flames that danced in my palm, eliciting a fearful look from him. "Go!"

The goblin didn't need to be told twice. He pushed off the wall and scurried down the street, stopping after ten yards to turn around.

"You've signed your own death warrant coming back here, Chance," he shouted. "Iolas will have your head mounted above his fireplace!" His lips peeled back as he formed a rictus grin, then he turned around and ran, disappearing around the corner a moment later.

"Son of a bitch," I muttered as I stood shaking my head.

Maybe it was a mistake coming back here, I thought.

I should've stayed in London, played gigs every night, maybe headed to Europe or the States, Japan even. Instead, I came back to Ireland to tear open old wounds...and unavoidably, to make new ones.

Shaking my head once more at the way things were going already, I grabbed my guitar and luggage bag and headed toward where I used to live before my life was turned upside down two months ago.

As I walked up the Quay alongside the turgid river, I took a moment to take in my surroundings. It was a balmy summer evening, and the city appeared to be in a laid-back mood as people walked around in their flimsy summer clothes, enjoying the weather, knowing it could revert to dull and overcast at any time, as the Irish weather is apt to do. Despite my earlier reservations, it felt good to be back. While I enjoyed London (as much as I could while mourning the death of my mother), Dublin was my home and always had been. I felt a connection to the land here that I felt nowhere else, and I'd been to plenty of other places around the world.

Still, I hadn't expected Iolas to be on me so soon. He had all but banished me from the city when I accused him of orchestrating my mother's murder. He was no doubt pissed when he heard I was coming back.

Fuck him, I thought as I neared my destination. *If he thinks I will allow him to get away with murder, he's mistaken.*

Just ahead of me was *Chance's Bookstore*—the shop my mother opened over three decades ago, and which now belonged to me, along with the apartment above it. It was a medium-sized store with dark green wood paneling and a quaint feel to it. It was also one of the oldest remaining independent bookstores in the city, and the only one that dealt with rare occult books. Because of this, the store attracted a lot of Untouched with an interest in all things occult and magical. It also attracted its fair share of Touched, who knew the store as a place to go acquire hard to find books on magic or some aspect of the occult. My mother, before she was killed, had formed contacts all over the world, and there was hardly a book she wasn't able to get her hands on if someone requested it, for a price, of course.

As I stood a moment in front of the shop, my mind awash with painful memories, I glanced at my reflection in the window, seeing a disheveled imposter standing there in need of a shave and a haircut, and probably also a change of clothes, my favorite dark jeans and waistcoat having hardly been off me in two months.

Looking away from my reflection, I opened the door to the shop and stepped inside, locking it behind me again. The smell of old paper and leather surrounded me immediately, soliciting more painful memories as images of my mother flashed through my mind. After closing my eyes for a second, I moved into the shop, every square inch of the place deeply familiar to me, connected to memories that threatened to come at me all at once.

Until they were interrupted that is, by a mass of swirling darkness near the back of the shop, out of which an equally dark figure emerged, two slightly glowing eyes glaring at me.

Then, before I could muster any magic or even say a word of surprise, the darkness surrounding the figure lashed out, hitting me so hard across the face I thought my jaw had broken, and I went reeling back, cursing the gods for having it in for me today.

Welcome home, Corvin, I thought as I stood seeing stars. *Welcome bloody home...*

~

Get your copy of SERPENT SON online today!

BOOKS BY N. P. MARTIN

Ethan Drake Series

INFERNAL JUSTICE
BLOOD SUMMONED
DEATH DEALERS

Gods And Monsters Trilogy

SERPENT SON
DARK SON
RISING SON

Wizard's Creed Series

CRIMSON CROW
BLOOD MAGIC
BLOOD DEBT
BLOOD CULT
BLOOD DEMON

Nephilim Rising Series

BOOKS BY N. P. MARTIN

HUNTER'S LEGACY
DEMON'S LEGACY
HELL'S LEGACY
DEVIL'S LEGACY

ABOUT THE AUTHOR

I'm Neal Martin and I'm a lover of dark fantasy and horror. Writing stories about magic, the occult, monsters and kickass characters has always been my idea of a dream job, and these days, I get to live that dream. I have tried many things in my life (professional martial arts instructor, bouncer, plasterer, salesman…to name a few), but only the writing hat seems to fit. When I'm not writing, I'm spending time with my wife and daughters at our home in Northern Ireland.

Be sure to sign up to my mailing list:
readerlinks.com/l/663790/nl
And say hi on social media…